Dangerous by Moonlight

By the same author

Fiction

The Virgin Soldiers
Orange Wednesday
The Love Beach
Come to the War
His Lordship
Onward Virgin Soldiers
Arthur McCann and All His Women
The Man with the Power
Tropic of Ruislip
Stand Up Virgin Soldiers
Dangerous Davies
Bare Nell
Ormerod's Landing
That Old Gang of Mine
The Magic Army
The Dearest and the Best
The Adventures of Goodnight and Loving
Dangerous in Love
Orders for New York
The Loves and Journeys of Revolving Jones
Arrivals and Departures

Non-fiction

This Time Next Week
Some Lovely Islands
The Hidden Places of Britain
My World of Islands
In My Wildest Dreams

LESLIE THOMAS

Dangerous by Moonlight

A Dangerous Davies Novel

Methuen

First published in Great Britain in 1993
by Methuen London
an imprint of Reed Consumer Books Ltd
Michelin House, 81 Fulham Road, London SW3 6RB
and Auckland, Melbourne, Singapore and Toronto

Reprinted 1993 (three times)

A CIP catalogue record for this book
is available at the British Library
ISBN 0 413 66990 4

Typeset by ROM-Data, Falmouth, Cornwall
Printed in England by Clays Ltd, St Ives plc

For Jeffrey and Sue Chamberlain

The croquet matches in summer,
The handshake, the cough, the kiss,
There is always a wicked secret
A private reason for this.

W. H. AUDEN

One

Winter suited Willesden. Its trees were created to drip, its canal to wear a muffler of mist, its pavements and roofs to reflect the lights of winter streets and the cloudy winter moon; few daytime things decorated the north-west London sky more poetically than the steam clouds from the power station cooling towers flying like the hair of God. The simile was not of Davies' making – he was of simpler stuff – but from the imagination of Mod, his friend, the philosopher of the dole queue.

'Winter becomes Willesden,' he repeated in a literary whisper, surveying both from the public library window. 'In the way that mourning becomes Electra.' He turned his bulbous eyes on Davies. 'If you get my drift.'

'Of course,' replied Davies. 'Totally.' He glanced at the reading-room clock. 'Isn't it time you knocked off,' he suggested.

'You wouldn't be the detective you are if you did not possess such powers of observation,' nodded Mod deeply.

'The little hand's on five and the big hand's nearly on twelve,' added Davies.

Ponderously Mod began to fold his books. 'Opening time,' he agreed sagely. 'What deduction!' He rubbed his eyes. It had been a long day in the reading room. He made a ritual of the closing of covers and Davies sat down, damp in his mackintosh, and waited while he completed it.

'What's been the problem today?' he inquired indicating the volumes.

'Well you might ask,' returned Mod. He carefully marked half a dozen pages with bookmarks given to him at the recent Christmas, a present from the policeman's dog, Kitty. 'These have proved very useful,' he said waving one quietly.

'They should last you the year,' pointed out Davies. It was the first week of January.

'I doubt it,' said Mod shrugging his big, untidy shoulders. He was wearing a red woollen jumper. It was now years since his jacket could be buttoned. 'They wear out, you know. Bookmarks. The rate I work.' He piled the cumbersome books and then appeared to measure the distance between his table and the Returns desk, the uprights of which framed the sulkily waiting face of the young woman assistant. Davies took the hint and picked up three of the books, leaving another three to Mod, who appeared a touch offended that he had not taken the whole pile.

'These weigh a ton,' said the detective.

'Wisdom does,' observed Mod. He coughed plaintively but Davies refused to pick up further books. 'Some wisdom is heavier than others, Greek wisdom particularly,' he added. 'I've been studying Homer. For the hundredth time of course, but one always finds yet another meaning, yet another nuance. Latin is an honour, and Greek is a treat, as Churchill once said.' He blinked: 'Possibly more than once.'

Davies grimaced. 'You've more or less got a job for life then?' They had arrived at Returns. Davies smiled at the girl assistant who scowled first at him, then at Mod and then at the clock. The philosopher appeared not to notice. He made towards his overcoat hung on the curly Victorian hatstand that was the library's prize possession. 'They don't make them like this now,' said Mod struggling into the patched garment.

'The hatstand?'

'The coat,' Mod corrected, pointing to it. 'You couldn't *buy* a coat now that would last you twenty years. And it wasn't new when I obtained it.'

'The owner so recently dead,' remembered Davies. They

headed for the door. The London rain was like a gauze over the main exit.

'And consequently with no further use for it,' provided Mod. He looked thoughtful. 'I wonder if they have overcoats in the Hereafter.'

'They wouldn't need them in Hell,' ruminated Davies. 'I suppose it's my turn to buy the beer again.'

'I'm afraid so, Dangerous. But tomorrow is glorious giro day. Tomorrow I push the boat out.'

They paused at the library door, like men unwilling to break their cover, but then, collars up, heads down, headed out into the damp and gritty evening street. Yellow-windowed buses sizzled by, cars with peering drivers, headed for firesides, wives and televisions; damp grit smeared the pavements and they could feel it in their soles. People hurried stoically by, West Indians, Africans, Indians, who had adopted Willesden's rain as they had adopted the place itself. Paler faces floated past, huddled under hats and anoraks. Three Irishmen approached arguing violently, hesitated and genially greeted Davies, before continuing both their journey and their dispute. The lit sign of the Babe In Arms appeared through the gloom. Davies quickened his step and Mod grunted like an old dog scenting home.

They stumbled gratefully down the two steps that were inconveniently placed directly inside the public bar door. People regularly fell both in and out. The Irish barman, called Pat Mulcahy, looked up with no surprise. The place was otherwise empty.

'First in,' said Davies rubbing the rain off his hands.

'Ah, are you not a policeman, Dangerous?' said the bartender shaking his head admiringly. 'You see things the rest of us would not notice.'

'I'll like to notice your grasp on the beer handle,' suggested Davies. He left Mod puffing in a chair, still bundled in his sogged overcoat. 'Mod's had a hard day,' he nodded. 'Two of the usual.'

'Never mind now,' said the Irishman soothingly. He leaned and called to Mod. 'Is it not giro day tomorrow? It is for me.'

He pulled the pints while Davies pondered the ramifications of the remark. 'You just do this for a hobby, do you, Pat?' he asked.

The Irishman remained untroubled. 'I'm only learning. A late entrant to the Youth Opportunities Scheme, sir.'

'Are you old enough for me to buy you a drink?' asked Davies.

'I am, sir, just.' Davies bought him one and carried the two pints of bitter back to the table. Mod was making the effort to get out of his coat. His arm was stuck and he began to flail about. Davies had to assist him. They sat down and sniffed at the beers before, after deliberation, lifting them to their lips in unison.

'I think,' said Mod quietly, 'that the persistent rain has penetrated the roof of this pub and is dripping into the beer. You ought to investigate.'

'Serious crime is not for me,' Davies replied truthfully. 'I'd have to get the big boys in.'

'What has been occupying you today?' inquired Mod. His interest was only mild, his eyes studied the dartboard as if it were the Rosetta Stone.

'Theft of newspapers from Pemberthy's, newsagent and confectioner, Ricketts Lane, NW10,' muttered Davies. 'It appears that over the course of the past few weeks, certainly since Christmas, up to a dozen newspapers a day have been disappearing from outside Percy Pemberthy's shop. They're delivered in the early hours and left outside his door. Somebody helps themselves.'

'The work of an organised gang, you think?'

'Could be,' said Davies. 'But I'll get them, don't worry.'

'Dangerous Davies strikes again,' nodded Mod. 'There's quite a lot of crime in the library, you know.'

'There is?' Davies looked interested. 'Somebody pinch that sullen girl's bum?'

'Nothing like that. She might even welcome a little attention. No, books stolen, books *vandalised.* Do you realise that in this area is someone who defaces books by cutting out the sexual contents with scissors? Now, I don't hold with obscenity or pornography, as you well know, Dangerous, but this is censorship. Censorship allied to vandalism. The Nazis all over again.'

'Might be worth looking into,' Davies sniffed. 'Once I've nicked the newspaper thieves.'

Mod was regarding his almost empty glass mournfully as though wondering where the beer had gone. Davies detected the look. 'One more and then we'll have to go,' he said. 'I'm going to the European Friendship Dinner and Dance tonight.'

'In Brussels?' inquired Mod dully. A smile ruffled his face as he handed over his stained glass. 'Look at the design the froth's made,' he pointed out appreciatively. 'As though an engraver had etched clouds on the sides. Just beautiful.'

'Cricklewood,' said Davies going towards the bar.

'What about Cricklewood?'

'That's where the European Friendship Dinner and Dance is. Not Brussels. It's friendship and co-operation between European nations. Krauts, Frogs, Wops, the lot.'

'One of Jemma's endeavours,' guessed Mod. 'That lady has certainly done her bit to pull the world together. But, I ask myself, is it enough?'

'*This* will have to be,' said Davies setting down the pints. 'We'll have to go. I must look nice for the dance.'

Davies' two most prized possessions, his dog and his car, were accommodated in a garage in a yard at the rear of the boarding house where he and Mod lived, Bali Hi, near the Jubilee Clock in Willesden. At the time the clock was put there, to celebrate Queen Victoria's sixty years in 1897, the yard had been occupied by stables and the dray horses of a local brewery. There still remained a touch, a smell even, of the hops and horse dung.

There were even the bones of a gas lamp in one corner, long unused, although once a man had tried to hang himself from there, saved by Davies going to feed his dog at the accustomed six o'clock. The man had not been suspended long and recovered completely when taken down and helped into the public bar of the Babe In Arms. He said later he had much to thank Dangerous Davies for, a sentiment echoed by a few in that gritty outer region of London. Everyone knew the detective by his nickname – the police, the criminal fraternity, those with a foot in both camps, and the stoical people who lived their lives among the old, ordinary streets and the new bleak estates and blocks of flats. His sub-title had, long before, become the Last Detective because, as everyone acknowledged, including Davies himself, he was only dispatched on an assignment if there was no one else to send or if there was such an element of danger that other officers were unwilling.

In the drizzling dusk Davies took the substantial evening meal to his dog Kitty, an animal of great size and unsteady temper. He had been described as a yak in a bad mood by a frightened sergeant who had experience with killer dogs. He always welcomed his food, however, his eyes lighting behind his shaggy fringe and his tongue hanging out like a great pink pennant. He gave a growl as his comfortable, warm and well-lit quarters alongside the ancient car were invaded by his owner and the shuffling Mod, but it was only a token.

The car, a Vauxhall Vanguard (once Davies had owned an ancient Lagonda), was rarely taken out into daylight now, although Kitty was walked regularly both by Davies and by a black boy called Valentine to whom the dog had taken a protective fancy. The lad was hardly taller than the animal but Kitty was placid and amenable in his company.

Davies gave the car a pat first and then diffidently put down the food dish (delicacies from the left-overs at the police station canteen, so famous for its cuisine that wrongdoers had been known to surrender there purposely to get a good meal, a favourite place for reporting from parole and surrendering to bail). He then added a pat for the dog.

'I have never understood,' muttered Mod who had watched the performance many times, 'why you pat the car first.'

'For good luck,' said Davies. He looked at the huge dog wolfing his dinner. 'Wouldn't you?'

'You'd better tell him about tonight while he's in a good mood,' suggested Mod.

'Not while he's eating.'

They stood at a decent distance while the animal cleaned the large bowl with his great tongue. 'Kitty,' said Davies carefully, 'I've got to go out tonight, so Mod will be taking you for your walk.'

The dog stared at them as though framing a reply. 'We're going to the pub, Kitty,' put in Mod. 'You like the pub.'

'What a treat,' encouraged Davies still staring at the dog which stared back. Kitty lay down and growled gently. 'He seems to be all right,' muttered Davies. 'Don't let him wreck the bar again.'

'They haven't got that cat now,' said Mod. 'It ran away after that.'

Each waved to the dog, who ignored them, and left the garage. 'I'm surprised Mulcahy lets him in there, though,' said Davies as they walked towards Bali Hi. 'There was a fair amount of damage.'

Mod was reassuring. 'Since they've been doing that bar food, it's much better,' he said as they trudged. 'Kitty gets plenty of titbits. And it's handy for the customers because they can wipe their fingers on him.'

'Put your beer on my tab tonight,' said Davies. 'That's beer, singular.' They paused before the stained-glass front door of the boarding house, each waiting for the other to produce a key. Eventually Davies found his lock-pick and opened the door into the dim hall. 'Don't go buying for all and sundry,' he added.

'I got carried away last time,' confessed Mod. 'Fulham winning like that.'

Mrs Fulljames, the landlady, always required that they washed their hands on entering the house.

'I'll have to nip up and get myself shining for the dance,' said Davies.

'I shall retire to my room,' said Mod. 'I can't stand the pre-dinner cocktail chatter in this house.'

Some of the guests at the Bali Hi boarding house had been in residence for years. There was Davies himself, Mod, and Minnie Banks, a famished-looking lady schoolteacher, who sometimes could be heard weeping alone in her room. There was also Doris, Davies' estranged wife. Although parted in every other sense they each defiantly refused to leave Mrs Fulljames' establishment, albeit occupying separate rooms. Their meetings were confined to the dinner-table.

This evening, Davies caused a stir by appearing in his elderly dinner-suit. There was a scraping of chairs as those at the table turned to look. Mrs Fulljames emerged from the steam of the kitchen to see what had happened. 'Well,' she said.

Davies straightened his saggy bow tie and shot his grubby cuffs as he sat at the table. He wished all the diners a polite good evening, especially some new residents, a Mr and Mrs Phelan from Ireland who were staying until Mr Phelan's mother either did one thing or the other in Central Middlesex Hospital.

Mrs Fulljames served the soup and while he waited for its surface to clear Davies turned a tight smile towards his estranged wife. Doris, likewise waiting for her soup to settle, sniffed: 'Doing a magic show tonight are we?'

'No. No. Completely wrong,' said Davies shaking his head as though the misconception was understandable. 'No, tonight I'm conducting the Berlin Philharmonic. Wagner and Beethoven.' He paused. 'Gladstone Park bandstand.'

'Such wit don't you think, Mr Phelan,' suggested Mrs Phelan looking directly at her husband.

'Such wit,' he agreed. 'Wit has come to be very dull in Ireland.'

'It has too,' she confirmed. She turned her attention to Mod as though he might know. 'The days of Oliver St John Gogarty are gone,' she said.

'Oh, they *are*,' agreed Mod glancing quickly around the table. 'Long gone.'

'You've got a lump of something on your lapel,' observed Doris nodding at Davies. 'Dried something.'

Davies lowered his eyes to the stain. He picked it off with his fingernail and sampled it. Disgust crossed Doris' face. 'Leek soup,' her husband concluded. He glanced towards Mod as if for support. 'St David's Day Dinner at the Gwalia Club?' he suggested.

'Leek soup it was,' agreed Mod admiringly. He shook his head towards Mr and Mrs Phelan. 'No wonder he's a detective.'

'St David's Day is in March,' said Doris.

'The first,' nodded Mod.

'Last year,' said Minnie Banks, always glad to join in the repartee, 'one of our infant class tried to eat a bowl of daffodils.'

They waited but she added nothing. 'It's been on there nearly a year,' said Doris with a shudder. 'That leek soup.'

'Ten months,' nodded Davies. Mrs Fulljames came from the kitchen and collected the dishes, examining each as if attempting to trace even a smear of anything left. 'What wonders have you performed tonight, Mrs Fulljames?' inquired Davies.

The table of faces looked up questioningly. Mod's cheeks beamed in the single light of the room. Mrs Fulljames, who habitually suspected a trap, examined each expression and then returned to Davies'. 'Lamb stew,' she announced. 'It's perfection.'

'And it *will* be,' said Mod informatively to Mr and Mrs Phelan.

Mrs Fulljames brought in two dishes of vegetables and a large earthen tureen of rumbling stew. From her place at the head of the table, which she now assumed, not having taken the soup, she doled it out onto the plates. The vegetables followed. They began to eat silently. Diffidently Minnie Banks fished a piece of paper from hers. It hung on her fork. Mod examined it. 'It's the sell-by date,' he guessed.

Mrs Fulljames looked abruptly anguished and made a move across the table. 'No, tell a lie,' amended Mod. 'It's the price.' He took Minnie's fork and handed it across to Davies. 'Don't you think so, Dangerous?'

'It can't be the sell-by date,' said Davies dubiously. Mrs Fulljames coloured as he spread the scrap of paper across the rim of his plate. 'Bargain meat ...' he read carefully. He looked up. 'Well there you are.'

'It's perfectly all right,' snapped Mrs Fulljames. 'If you don't like the food here, you know what to do. What you get is what you pay for.'

'Absolutely,' said Davies.

'Absolutely,' said Mod.

'So true,' murmured Minnie Banks. 'Very, very true indeed.'

'Of course,' said the Phelans in unison.

Obediently they all began to eat.

The following morning, after the European Friendship Dinner and Dance, Davies was lying sorely in his hospital bed, wondering what sort of fate brought him back there so frequently. Jemma had, of course, accompanied him in the ambulance, her luminous eyes loaded with pity and puzzlement. Mod arrived in the morning, nodding in recognition to nurses who had been there during Davies' previous confinements. He rubbed his chin, so stubbled that it sounded. 'You spend more time in here than most of the staff,' he observed to Davies.

'This', countered Davies, his jaw hurting, 'is no bloody time for wisdom.'

'You've got to stop doing it,' said Mod with grim emphasis. 'One day you're going to get yourself killed. Somebody will end up in prison.'

He opened his scraggy overcoat, revealing a scarred and bulging waistcoat, held by three buttons, and sat at the side of the bed. His eyes went briefly sideways towards the bedside locker.

'No grapes yet,' muttered Davies. 'I haven't been in long enough.'

'I was not seeking grapes,' put in Mod mildly. 'I was trying to ascertain the time by your watch.'

'They won't be open for another hour.'

'You'll be requiring something to read.'

Davies squinted towards him. 'Thanks. When I can manage to focus on anything. Something classical.'

'The Decline and Fall of Dangerous Davies,' Mod said thoughtfully. 'Jemma told me how it happened. Only *you* could be beaten up at a Friendship Dinner. A *European* Friendship Dinner. What hope has the Prime Minister got, I ask myself?'

'This Kraut called Jemma a Schwarzer.'

'It never was a pretty language. So you struck him.'

'He was striking *me* at the time,' corrected Davies.

'Very hard too, by the look of it,' said Mod scrutinising the damaged face and the pneumatic lip. 'You ought to take some leave, Dangerous. Go to the seaside.'

Davies grimaced. 'It's January.'

Mod turned his bulbous eyes towards the grey window. 'Spot on, as usual,' he observed. 'Why not go somewhere distant, exotic? The East, the Caribees, Mozambique?' Doubt again clouded his expression as he surveyed his friend's injuries. 'Providing, of course, the medical facilities were adequate. On the other hand, I believe that Bournemouth can be most recuperative. Robert Louis Stevenson went there.'

'Did he get better?'

'No. He went to the Pacific and died. You'll be familiar with his famous "Requiem".'

'I'd have to take the dog,' said Davies.

'Ah,' responded Mod. 'You'd consider it, then. Bournemouth.'

'Was Kitty all right last night?' asked Davies anxiously. 'He didn't wreck the pub did he?'

Mod became evasive. 'Not the pub,' he answered carefully. 'No, the pub was more or less intact. But there *was* some minor bother when that silly old woman, Mad Maggy they call her, you know the one with thin ginger hair ...'

'I know her,' frowned Davies with a creeping unease. 'And what was the ...'

'Minor bother,' completed Mod. 'Well she had a big hairy handbag and Kitty must have thought it was a cat. It looked like a cat ...'

'Yes, Mod,' said Davies sadly. 'Go on.'

'Well, you know what your dog thinks about cats. There was a disturbance, a fracas. Kitty went for the handbag and Mad Maggy tried to fight him off. Maggy says the dog got a mouthful of her hair, and she hasn't got much. Certainly Kitty was sick. Maggy says you'll be hearing from her solicitor.'

'Her old man got legal aid,' complained Davies. 'Now *she's* got a solicitor.'

'Or so she says. You may hear nothing more of it. But she'll consider that you owe her a favour. Perhaps next time her husband is in trouble ...'

'Knock for knock,' nodded Davies. 'She'll try and get her old man put away for longer.'

'*That's* more like it,' approved Mod his chins folding in a grin. 'Joking again. You're feeling better.' He leaned confidingly. 'I had a word with the surgeon,' he whispered, then nodded: 'Your usual one. He says that the injuries are not serious. Not by your standards. You could be out of here in a few days.'

'Thanks.' Davies sighed. 'Well, it will give me something I can look forward to ... Bournemouth.'

'That's the spirit,' enthused Mod. While Davies watched with a sort of dull surprise, his friend half turned, woke up the torpid patient in the next bed, and asked if he might borrow his *Daily Mail*. The man groaned and pushed his hand towards the newspaper. Mod thanked him but the head was already below the bedclothes again. Mod took the paper and opened it. 'Let's see,' he said squinting. He searched for and found his grubby glasses, putting them on with difficulty as though unsure of the location of his nose. 'That's better ... Here we are ... Weather at the resorts ... Bournemouth ... sleet ... temperature twenty-nine.' He looked up reassuringly. 'That's not too bad,' he ventured. 'It's almost above freezing.'

'I can hardly wait,' said Davies grimly.

Davies watched Jemma come into the ward and look around for him. How beautiful she was, brown and beautiful with her long body, her fine face and deep eyes and the gap in the middle of her teeth. But it was her walk that caught the eye, an unselfconscious, upright, but languid stroll. She glanced from side to side. Sick and prostrate men began to sit up.

She stopped at the bottom of Davies' bed and regarded him seriously. 'All this for me,' she said shaking her head and smiling at him. 'How do you feel, Dangerous?'

'Better now,' he said painfully. 'A bit better.'

She sat on the side of the bed, found an unbruised portion of his cheek and kissed him on it. His lips were too tender. A silence had dropped over the ward and other patients were straining to get a view of her. A man fell with a cry from his bed and a bedpan went clanging.

'They say you're not too serious,' she said patting him comfortingly.

'No, it feels better than usual,' he admitted. 'A couple of days and I'll be out on the streets again. Tempting providence.'

She regarded him reprovingly. 'You've *got* to have some sick leave,' she said.

'Bournemouth,' he nodded. 'Mod said I'm going to Bournemouth. It's said to be nice down there in January. I suppose you put that idea into his head.'

'We did discuss it,' Jemma agreed. 'I'll come with you.'

He attempted a smile and said: 'That should warm it up.'

She laughed lightly and gave him a gentle push on the chest. He winced. She said: 'I could do with a break myself.'

'Social Services busy is it?' he asked. 'The troubles of the world tend to multiply after Christmas.'

'Like the end of a truce,' she shrugged. 'You know young Valentine. His parents – both of them – have separately pissed off. Couldn't stand each other any more so they left *him.* Ten years old. I may bring him to Bournemouth. He's never seen the sea.' She glanced at him sadly. 'Dangerous, I'm sorry about last night. You didn't have to protect my honour. I've been called worse things than a Schwarzer.'

'Not in my hearing you haven't.'

Jemma sighed. 'It was such a pity. A European Friendship Dinner-Dance and it ends in a punch-up.'

'It was when they'd drunk a lot and started singing,' he remembered. 'There's nothing more likely to raise the ugly face of nationalism than singing.'

She nodded wryly. 'It was that Australian who started it.'

'Australian? What's an Australian got to do with European Friendship?'

'He got in somehow. Attracted by the drink, I suppose. Everyone thought he said he was *Austrian.* It was only when he started making trouble …'

'I saw him. He was bawling over that poor little bloke from Luxembourg. "Clip Go The shears", that's what he was singing. I ought to have realised.'

Jemma regarded her hand sadly. She still wore her wedding ring, bright on her slender finger. 'Everything got out of control,' she admitted. 'And after all that organising. And all for friendship.'

'Friendship's not an easy thing to organise,' Davies observed thoughtfully. 'Was there a lot of damage?'

'Only to people. There's two Frenchmen in Willesden General. One was hit in the Adam's apple with his own bow tie. One of those elastic jobs. There's a Dutchman down the corridor from here.'

'What about the German I clobbered?'

'Well you didn't. You'd had a few yourself by then, Dangerous. You missed him and hit the Dutchman. The one down the corridor.'

He looked regretful: 'You can't plan these things.'

'I don't think he'll recognise you. Everyone was at it. It never ceases to amaze me how men will attack other men at the first opportunity. At least women only bitch behind each others' backs. Fortunately, there was not a lot of damage to the place though. It belongs to the Maccabi Jewish Club and it's built to withstand attack. They've been rather expecting an assault from the National Front.'

'There's no peace,' sighed Davies. He regarded her glumly. 'Kitty had old Mad Maggy's hair last night. In the Babe. Pulled out a lump of it apparently.'

Jemma pursed her lips. 'I was trying to keep that from you,' she confessed. 'Until you felt better. I suppose Mod told you.'

'He would, wouldn't he,' said Davies.

'Well, let's look on the bright side. Just think. We're going to Bournemouth.'

As she spoke a fistful of rain splattered against the hospital window.

Two

Between Basingstoke and Winchester there was some damp but encouraging sunshine. The train ran by sparkling green fields and ploughed acres of curved, chocolate earth. Above the low Hampshire hills and wiry trees the sky was blue, pale and cold.

Davies surveyed it hopefully and mentioned that it might turn out all right. Jemma touched his dog's forehead and the animal groaned with pleasure. Valentine looked from the window and asked: 'Why don't they fill all this empty stuff with houses an' that?'

'I expect they will,' Davies assured him. 'Once the country's on its feet again.'

'When's that then?'

Davies shrugged. 'I don't know. I'm only a detective. I'm baffled.'

Jemma smiled her singular smile at him, the teeth set in the brown face and the gap in the centre of the teeth where the gaze went every time, no matter how long you knew her. He could tell she was grateful that they could bring Valentine. She had feared that his father might snatch him back or, worse, his mother. They would do it to spite each other.

'He'll have to come into my room, Dangerous,' she had said apologetically. 'I don't want him out of my sight. All this is a bit unofficial.'

'I thought it might be,' said Davies who sometimes wondered why a social worker had to take work home.

'You'll have Kitty for company.'

'I know, I know,' he said grimly. 'There's always that to it.' He regarded his great dog who growled malevolently. 'A holiday at the seaside might repair our relationship. Walks along the beach, me throwing stones.'

There had been no question of taking the car. Davies doubted if it would make the hundred and some miles anyway, and he feared the ravages of salt winds and exposed coastal weather on metalwork that scarcely left the garage in the yard these days.

Kitty sat with unusual aplomb, apparently enjoying the movement of the train and the delicate scent of Jemma. He growled warningly at the man who came to look at their tickets.

Mod, full of regret, had been left behind. He voiced his belief that somewhere, lodged in the back of his mind, was a government provision to reward the chronically unemployed with short holidays at the public expense but, fumble through the regulations though he did, he could not discover the statute.

'I could do with a break too,' he had announced morosely. 'Sometimes the library gets me down. The standard of reader in this area is not lofty. A woman came in yesterday and asked for *The Seven Pillars of Willesden.*'

Davies was privately not too sorry for Mod's absence. He needed respite from both Willesden and wisdom. His friend had already given him an extended lecture on Robert Louis Stevenson's sojourn in Bournemouth. 'There he wrote *Kidnapped* and *The Strange Case of Dr Jekyll and Mr Hyde,*' he announced, having just looked it up. 'It was the latter work which brought him fame. It was quoted from the pulpits of England, you know.'

Davies said he did not. They had been in the Babe In Arms and Mod piled on fact upon fact about Stevenson's life. Davies always knew when he had been swotting it up because he tended to repeat verbatim the phrases of the crib. He had reached in the caverns of his overcoat and produced a small, shabby book. 'This is on loan,' Mod had whispered.

'Although the library is not aware of it. A potted life of R.L.S.' He said it as though he had known the writer personally.

Sitting in the train Davies thought of Mod and Robert Louis Stevenson. They stopped at Winchester and Jemma quietly, her face close to him, sang the song 'Winchester Cathedral' to Valentine when he asked about the city. At Southampton the boy looked from the window and reported: 'There's a lot of posh people getting off 'ere. They got blokes to wheel their suitcases.'

Jemma and Davies joined him at the window, their three faces framed. Well-coated and hatted people were progressing from the first-class section of the train. Brightly capped porters conveyed piles of good luggage along the platform. The black boy thrust his head out and inquired: 'Where you lot goin' then?'

A man with his head projecting from a thick scarf turned. His grey moustache waggled as he spoke. 'On a cruise, son,' he said. 'West Indies.'

'I been in the West Indies,' said Valentine truthfully. 'My dad says I was born there.'

'I expect you have,' said the man, who had paused while the rest of the party moved on. 'Where are you going now?'

'Bournemuff.'

'You'll like it,' the man answered. 'I wish I were going there. Some places are such a long way when you get older.'

The train pulled away and soon ran beside choppy, dark sea-water; a scuffed ship was lying by a Southampton wharf. The sun had gone, the sky was low and melted into the sea. They went through the grey-green of the New Forest where they saw wild horses, on to Christchurch and then the train echoed into the tall-roofed station at Bournemouth.

Jemma helped Valentine down to the platform. Kitty, unprotestingly on a lead, wagged his rump furiously. His breath came out in short clouds. As Davies gained the platform one of the locks of his elderly suitcase burst. He embraced it frantically like someone trying to restrain a suicide.

'One thing you'll need to do while you've got time here, Dangerous,' advised Jemma, 'is to get yourself another case.'

Afterwards she thought how prophetic her words had been.

In Bournemouth the wintry sun was out again. The taxi drove along the sea front where they saw the waves were shining, toppling on the empty beach white as feathers. Valentine asked if they were real.

'This time of the year we get a lot of mornings like this,' the taxi driver claimed. It was odd how people only a short distance from London spoke as though they lived in a foreign land. The driver had agreed to take the dog only after giving him a long stare. Kitty acknowledged the situation and appeared to grin ingratiatingly. 'Trouble is the weather changes its mind about two in the afternoon.' The driver nodded forward through his windscreen. 'You can see it coming from the west. From the Old Harry Rocks.'

'Where are the boats?' asked Valentine. Nothing was floating on the sea. All their eyes swept the bay. The driver appeared a little discomfited. 'There's not all that many boats these days,' he admitted. 'In the summer they run a steamer trip over to the Isle of Wight, but, there's not a lot doing boatwise just now.'

They reached the Sea Breeze Hotel and while Jemma and the boy surveyed its bay windows Davies paid the driver. 'Fancy him noticing that,' mentioned the driver nodding at Valentine. Davies felt pleased. Then the man said: 'But I suppose some of them are quite intelligent.'

'Kids, you mean,' said Davies. The man looked embarrassed and said: 'Yes, kids.' Davies smiled at him and gave him a small tip, then turned to regard the Sea Breeze Hotel.

The windows and the glass of the revolving door mirrored the January sunshine. 'He'll never get through that,' said Davies nodding first at the dog and then at the door. A face appeared inside the glass. Valentine had already gone through it and was on his second circuit causing his face to appear curiously oblique. 'I'll ask,' said Jemma. She went through the door and caught the boy as he was about to take another turn. Davies waited with his dog. A man and a woman wearing identical grey expressions and cardigans took turns to come through the door. They stood inspecting Davies and Kitty.

'I thought it was a small dog,' said the woman tartly. She adjusted her ornamental spectacles. 'It's a big dog for a small dog,' the man said.

Kitty was doing his act of staring beseechingly into people's faces. The man's cardigan was saggy around his middle and Davies feared that the dog might be measuring it up for an attack.

'I'll pay the full big-dog rate,' he promised.

The woman sniffed up and down the road as if hoping some alternative business might present itself. None did and Davies could see that she had grudgingly made up her mind. 'Open it up,' she ordered the man. Muttering, the man began to pull bolts to fold one section of the revolving door. 'Gives the hotel a touch of class this door,' he mentioned. Kitty put his nose close to the lowered head. Davies eased him back. Jemma and Valentine were inside, the boy watching the conversion of the door.

'Of course, we don't discriminate at all about our guests,' sniffed the woman. 'As long as everyone behaves. But dogs, that *is* different.' She looked at Kitty again. 'I hope he's sanitary.'

'Pisses everywhere,' mentioned Davies. He had already made up his mind. Now he surveyed the hotel and the shocked faces of the couple. 'But I don't think this establishment will be good enough for him.'

Jemma had taken the cue and led Valentine out by the hand. Davies picked up the cases and they went down the road leaving the couple speechless in the doorway. When Davies eventually turned the woman was shaking her fist in their direction but her words were wafted by the wind. 'Old cow,' he said.

'Where we going?' asked Valentine. 'I didn't do nuffin.'

Jemma patted his hand and Davies said: 'No you didn't, son.'

'Don't you just hate them,' muttered Jemma. He could see how angry she was.

Davies was wearing a sly smile, however. He said: 'In the next issue of *Dogs Weekly* there's going to be an advert welcoming all dog owners to the Sea Breeze Hotel, Bournemouth. The bigger, the smellier, the more incontinent, the better. And the *second* dog is free.'

Jemma began to laugh. He set the cases on the pavement.

'What are we going to do now?' asked Jemma. He was conscious of her, the boy and the dog all regarding him trustingly.

'We're going in ... there,' he decided, pointing to the other side of the road where a large, old hotel stood blocking the low sunlight. 'That looks the sort of place where they don't discriminate against dogs.'

Jemma smiled at him and squeezed his arm. 'It's going to cost more,' she warned.

'Only the best is good enough for my dog,' muttered Davies. He patted Kitty's head and the animal growled threateningly. 'He knows,' he said.

They crossed the road. There was a wide band of sunshine between the buildings along the sea front and all three blinked and felt its slight welcome warmth.

At the Promenade Hotel there was no revolving door. They walked into a lobby where there were comfortably worn chairs, a shabby indoor palm and a polished reception desk. An old lady sat reading the *Daily Telegraph* and she looked up and smiled. A plump, pleasant-faced girl sitting behind the desk, her appearance slightly awry, smiled too.

'Have you got any rooms?' asked Davies.

'Rooms?' replied the girl. She blinked vaguely. 'Rooms? We've got so many rooms we're thinking of having a sale.'

'What a nice dog, Mr Davies,' said the old lady with the *Telegraph*.

‘Thank you,’ said Davies on behalf of Kitty. The lady lowered her newspaper to her lap and now smiled sweetly at the whole group.

‘Mrs Dulciman likes dogs,’ said the receptionist. ‘You used to have one didn’t you, Mrs Dulciman.’

‘A while ago,’ confirmed the lady. ‘Broadbent, a basset-hound. Before my husband went.’

Davies, faced with a fragment of information like that, was tempted to inquire where Mr Dulciman had gone. He desisted and signed the register.

‘Two rooms is it?’ asked the receptionist in her turn studying the group and attempting to ascertain who was with whom.

‘Two, that’s it,’ confirmed Davies. ‘I have to guard the dog.’

‘It’s off-season rates,’ she said pushing her wayward hair back from her round face. ‘Being January.’ She moved a little closer. ‘Thirty pounds a day for each room,’ she confided. ‘No extra for the dog. How long will it be for?’

Jemma said: ‘I have to go back to London on Monday with this young man. Mr Davies will be staying for a week. He needs the rest.’

‘I know how you feel,’ said the girl to Davies. ‘I’ll show you the rooms.’ She took two keys from a rack, walked around the counter and then returned to get the right keys. ‘I’ve been here long enough,’ she tutted. ‘You’d think I’d know, wouldn’t you.’ She led the way towards a curling staircase. Smiling, Valentine ran his hand along the polished banister as they went up.

‘They’re nice, these rooms,’ said the receptionist. ‘Sea view. Not that it’s much this time of the year.’

They walked into the first room and Jemma laughed and said: ‘Just beautiful. So light.’ Her hands opened towards the windows, big and bayed and full of the sky and the sea streaked with steely sun. The boy went to the sill, stared out and said: ‘Cor.’

‘The other room’s more or less the same,’ said the girl.

'Bathrooms *en suite.* They're booked all through the summer.'

She showed them how the kettle worked for the tea maker and took their orders for morning newspapers. 'I'm Mildred,' she said, adding 'unfortunately.'

'Nice girl,' said Jemma when she had closed the door. 'But unhappy.'

'The other one knew your name,' said Valentine to Davies.

'The old lady in the lobby,' confirmed Jemma. 'She called you Mr Davies.'

Davies said: 'She heard the receptionist after I'd signed the register.'

'No, it was before that,' said Jemma. 'When we came in and she mentioned the dog. "What a nice dog, Mr Davies," she said.'

Valentine went to the bursting suitcase which Davies had brought into the room. He held out the label and said: 'It's on this. Big letters. See, it says: "Davies".'

'That's from when I went on the police trip to Boulogne,' said Davies. 'Everything had to be labelled in case of stuff getting nicked. Not just by the police but generally.'

Jemma touched the boy's head. 'That was very observant, Valentine,' she said. 'You should be a policeman, like Dangerous.'

The boy surveyed Davies' still-bruised face and said: 'No thanks.'

Although the winter afternoon light would go early (by four o'clock the sky was striped like a red banner across the western sea), there was still a little time for them to go onto the beach.

Valentine needed a bucket and spade and they went with Kitty on his lead along the shops trying to buy them and receiving strange looks. Eventually a set, preserved in plastic, was procured from a storeroom, the shopkeeper bringing the package out, blinking, as though he himself had been kept in the dark since the previous late September.

'Always buy at this time of the year,' said Davies with the air of a man who dealt in things. He went on: 'You never know about inflation, do you? A bucket and spade could be double by July.' He sniffed around. 'I might even buy a rubber dinghy.'

The shopkeeper's eyes came out of their creases and he humphed with laughter as if it were the best quip he had heard all January. His wife, who had been concealed behind a counter barricaded with confectionery, appeared with the guilt of someone who has been in hiding, and offered them chocolates from a dark, half-empty box. 'It's all there is to do around here in the winter,' she said. 'Scoff chockies. These are nice. Black Magic.'

She looked directly into Jemma's face and then into the boy's, and appeared embarrassed. 'They're nice,' she repeated.

Jemma smiled and took one. Valentine, encouraged to do so, took two. Davies said that he did not want to spoil his afternoon tea. Kitty thrust his nose towards the box and the woman gave him one also.

They left the shop, the boy swinging the coloured bucket by its squeaky handle and tapping its side with the spade. They were wrapped against the chill. 'Played cricket in worse weather than this,' boasted Davies sniffing the promenade air. The beach was flat, yellow, vacant, but for a shadowy man walking a shadowy dog; the waves rolled low, the sky breaking into shreds of blue and casting pale, pretty sunshine.

'Since when did you play cricket?' asked Jemma taking the boy's free hand.

'Me? Cricket?' sniffed Davies. 'I was the David Gower of X Division in the old days. All grace and touch.'

She laughed at him and hugged his bulky waist. 'I bet it *was* the old days too.' Kitty was standing looking at the beach in amazement. He barked and pulled the lead.

They walked, then, all together, ran along the sand and brittle shingle, wind softly buffeting their faces. The boy swung the bucket and waved the spade. 'Whee!' he shouted as he ran. 'Whee!'

Davies pulled up breathless. 'All this fresh air,' he complained. The others ran on. He let the dog go after them and called: 'It can damage your health, you know!'

He watched them go, full of running, their exclamations coming back to him over the salt air. He stood and examined the wrinkled sea. He could not remember when he had last been on the sands.

A single gull, not far from the shore, cried as if it had witnessed something alarming. There was not a ship in sight from one horizon to the other. To the west the strange figures of the Old Harry Rocks stood like scenery at the side of a stage. He heard the distant shouts as Jemma and the boy turned back. He would have liked to marry her if he had not already got a wife back at Bali Hi, Willesden. He could get a divorce, of course, but the legal requirement of living apart might be difficult to authenticate because neither he nor Doris had ever moved out of Mrs Fulljames' house; each defied the other to do so. He paid her rent and living expenses. What a way to live a pair of lives. In any case he doubted whether Jemma would marry him. She also had a husband somewhere, back in the French Caribbean. He wondered what the boy Valentine could hope for in the future. Probably not a lot. It would be a shame if today were a high spot in his life.

As they neared him along the beach their two dark faces were shadowed in the fading light. The dog hared around in circles. Valentine had something in his bucket.

'Dangerous, he found a starfish!' said Jemma breathlessly. 'Look, it's perfect.'

'Got all its legs,' confirmed the boy. 'There's no gaps.'

'There's not a lot in life like that – no gaps,' observed Davies. His rough grin appeared as he transferred his face to the boy. 'Want to make some sandpies before it's dark?'

Valentine rubbed his nose on the sleeve of his anorak. 'What about a sandcastle?'

'He's deprived,' Jemma smiled at Davies. 'He's never had a sandcastle.'

'Oh, all right,' said Davies. 'Pies are neater, that's all.' He knelt down on the dry, chill sand. 'It's only going to be a small one.'

'That'll do,' the boy said spreading his arms. 'We'll build a big bugger tomorrow.'

'A big sandcastle,' corrected Jemma, prim but emphatic.

'That's what I said,' said the boy. He knelt on the sand beside Davies and Jemma, curiously brushing the knees of her jeans first, did likewise. Kitty sniffed, pushed at them, then began digging a hole of his own. Davies had never seen his dog so happy. They worked industriously. Davies took the coloured bucket from Valentine and filled it with sand from the waterline. 'It won't stick if it's not damp,' he explained. He turned the bucket upwards and the sandpie sat perfectly formed, a portal of the castle. Davies smiled and said: 'Blimey, I can still do it.'

Valentine watched in admiration. 'Let me 'ave a go now,' he asked. He took the bucket to the shore and filled it with sand, keeping one cautious eye on the small, advancing waves. He returned laughing and Davies showed him how to turn the bucket face down, how to pat the sides with the spade and carefully lift it off to reveal the perfect pie.

'Cor,' said Valentine straightening up, delight filling his face. 'That's bloody good, that is.'

'It's very good,' Jemma again corrected mildly. She grinned towards the squatting Davies. 'You're quite a dab hand at this, Dangerous,' she said.

'I practise down at O'Gorman's builders yard at Neasden, mucking about in their sandpile.' Again Valentine ran down to the shoreline.

'Once,' said Davies, 'when I was doing surveillance in O'Gorman's – somebody nicking lead – I *did* amuse myself by trying to build a sandcastle.' He eyed the boy still filling his bucket and said to Jemma: 'It'll be out of the question tonight, I suppose.'

'It's difficult,' she agreed softly. 'Me with Valentine and you with your dog.' She glanced towards Kitty lying exhausted on the shingle. She made the shape of a kiss to Davies. 'But you never know.'

The sky was getting dark and they were getting cold. The small castle was finished. 'Could do with a cup of tea,' suggested Davies rubbing his hands.

Valentine glanced up. 'And chocolate biscuits?' he suggested.

Jemma nodded. 'And I want some cake,' she said.

'We can come back tomorrow,' said the boy surveying the sandcastle. 'Carry on then.'

'It won't be here,' Davies told him.

The boy was aghast. 'Why not? Who's going to nick it?'

'The sea,' said Davies nodding at the metallic water. 'The tide comes in and washes everything away.' He straightened up and glanced at Jemma. 'We'll have to start over again.'

A crimson bar of sunset was lying across the sea, now almost black. The gull was still calling. 'What's he making all that racket for?' asked Valentine. They each took a hand and walked along the beach with him towards the end of the daylight. 'Can't he find his way? Is he lost?'

'He wants tea and chocolate biscuits, I expect,' said Davies.

'And cake,' said Jemma.

That evening they went to a fish and chip shop that had a big back room with tables, and then returned to the hotel and watched the television in the residents' lounge. They were the only occupants except for an old, open-mouthed man who slept throughout. Before he went to bed Valentine gave Davies a friendly slap on the leg and said: 'Thanks for the sandcastle.'

'Enjoyed it,' answered Davies truthfully. He followed them upstairs and went to his own room. Kitty awoke with his customary growl but allowed Davies to take him out onto the promenade. The wind blew into the faces of the man and the dog. There was a trace of moon through rushing clouds and the sea sounded strongly. The dog examined the unfamiliar night as if it might contain a trap but then walked amiably. Another dog and another walker approached. It was the receptionist going back towards the the hotel. 'Duty patrol,' she said. Her face was round and pale.

The dog sniffed casually at Kitty who sniffed back but neither discovered any interest. Kitty began to pull at the lead. 'I'll walk on,' said the young woman. 'They're different star signs.'

Davies laughed and took Kitty into the wind a further three hundred yards before turning. He saw the receptionist going into the hotel. He wondered what sort of life she had.

Some men were laughing in the bar and the dog half lifted its ears. 'Come on,' said Davies tugging at the lead. 'You're not joining in. I've got a biscuit for you in the room.'

Kitty allowed himself to be encouraged upstairs. Davies settled him in his basket, and then attempted to move the basket from blocking the bathroom door but the dog objected with a growl. Davies made a mental note to visit the landing toilet before going to bed. The dog curled into a huge, hairy roll and Davies said good night as he let himself out of the room leaving the bedside light on.

Jemma came down to the bar. They went to a table near the window. Mildred, the receptionist, was serving behind the bar. The laughing men had gone. The room was almost as deserted as the street outside. 'You had to leave the light on for your dog?' said Jemma.

'In case he wakes up and doesn't know where he is,' explained Davies a little shamefaced. 'Dogs can be disorientated, you know. And I don't want him howling like the Hound of the Baskervilles.'

He gave her a glance. 'What are we going to do?' he inquired. 'If anything.'

Jemma touched his hand. 'Once Valentine's asleep I'll try and creep in to you,' she promised, grinning. 'Quite romantic, isn't it. Back stairs stuff.'

She finished her drink. 'I'll go now,' she said. 'Stay awake, won't you.'

'All night long,' he promised.

Before she went she kissed him on the cheek. Davies finished his pint and went to the bar for another. 'They keep you busy,' he said to Mildred.

'Don't tell me. In a hotel like this you have to do everything. The barmaid has to go home at ten.' She looked towards the door. 'She's beautiful, your lady,' she said almost wistfully and handing the drink to him. 'I wish I was beautiful like that. Where's she from?'

'She's French West Indian,' said Davies.

'I wish I was.'

A small, silvery head appeared at the door. The voice was firm. 'Good night, Mildred.'

'Good night, Mrs Dulciman,' the receptionist called back. 'Sweet dreams.'

'Good night, Mr Davies,' added the old lady. Surprised, Davies answered: 'Yes ... oh, good night.'

'Mrs Dulciman,' said Mildred when she had gone, but still in a whisper. 'Lovely little lady. Lived in this hotel years.' She leaned closer across the bar, her rotund bosom resting on it. 'Lost her husband five years ago.'

She whispered again. 'When I say "lost" that's what I mean. "Lost". He vanished. They found a body in the sea, but they were never sure.'

'She keeps late hours,' observed Davies looking at the clock over the bar.

'Playing bridge,' said Mildred. 'There's lots of widows around here. It's funny how they outlast their husbands. They have a club even. Bournemouth and Boscombe Widows' Luncheon Club,' she recited. 'Every month. They have a lovely time.'

'But she's not sure she's a widow,' pointed out Davies.

Mildred looked as though she had never thought of that. 'Well, she's as good as,' she said. 'Nobody's going to find Mr Dulciman now.'

Three

After he had been in bed for an hour, Davies was still awake and alone except for his dog breathing tremulously from his basket, and blocking the bathroom door. Turning restlessly towards the window he saw that an almost ethereal light was spreading across the curtains; the moon was out there. He eased himself from the bed. The room was chill; the hotel heating went off at midnight. He ineffectually pulled the collar of his pyjamas up around his neck and went to the window. With a theatrical gesture he pulled back the curtains and blinked with pleasure at the extent of the moon. It was in the three-quarter phase, clear of clouds now, floating alone in the sky, and flooding the sea with silver. So clear was it that he could even make out the blunted creases of the waves and their whiteness as they fell against the beach. He could almost feel the moonlight on his face. Half turning he glanced at the far wall, lit now like a cinema screen, beyond which he could imagine Jemma quietly breathing through her sleep.

While he was out of bed he thought he might as well go to the lavatory but before he could turn he saw a movement on the beach. At first he was not sure, thinking it could be a trick of the patterned light and the changing waves. But pressing his nose close to the cold pane he saw that it was not. Someone was walking along by the water, slowly and alone. He glanced at his watch. It was one o'clock. He hoped that they were well wrapped up, whoever they were and whatever their motive at that strange hour of a January night.

The shadow disappeared into deeper shadows and, after

trying to detect it for a while, he continued with his intended visit to the lavatory. Moving on tiptoe despite the silent bareness of his feet, he approached the door guarded by his dog. The animal had not moved his position since Davies had gone to bed and had smiled fondly towards him before switching off the lamp at the bedside. Now, however, he lifted a baleful eye, the glance of an inconvenienced tiger, so dark and yellow.

His naked foot raised almost over the dog and the basket, Davies halted. 'It's all right, Kitty, old mate,' he tried. 'It's me. Your master. You remember your master.' The dog showed no signs of doing so. His donkey-sized nose lifted and he grunted, the grunt deepening to a growl. 'Oh, come on,' said Davies pleading for sportsmanship. 'I've *got* to go, so that's that.'

Kitty did not think that was that. His whole shaggy face emerged from the warm blanket of his own body and, both eyes now open, he emitted an uncompromising warning. Davies withdrew the poised and exposed foot and retreated to the bed. Kitty with a satisfied mumble returned to embracing himself and began to breathe vastly and regularly. Davies waited then tried again. Sidling towards the dog and the door he lifted his foot a tentative six inches. From the depths of the hairy mass another growl emerged. With a dancer's continuing movement Davies swung his foot to the side and in the same balletic twist went towards the door of the bedroom. Turning he muttered something towards the dog but not loud enough to wake him. He went out into the corridor. It was warmer out there and there was a small subdued lamp burning on a table, its light showing the way to the stairs.

He knew where the lavatory was because he had been there on the way to bed and he made to go in that direction but then, after pausing, he knocked on Jemma's adjoining door. It was a brush of the fingers, so light he hardly heard it himself but the door was opened softly, swiftly, and her dark face appeared with a pale finger to her lips. 'Can I use your bathroom?' whispered Davies. 'I can't get near mine.'

Jemma, still with her finger against her lips, but a half-smile each side of the finger, slid out into the corridor. She was wearing a slender silk robe. Without saying anything she led the way towards his room and Davies, in his workmanlike pyjamas, mauve and cream stripes, followed her, his heart rising.

Once inside his room she started to laugh. 'Poor Dangerous,' she said. 'Can't get near his own loo.'

Kitty, at once hearing her voice, looked up with something near a smile of pleasure. The huge dog trundled from his basket and stood wagging his long ragged tail like a banner. 'Good Kitty,' murmured Jemma while Davies looked at both animal and woman with admiration and envy. 'Back to bed now,' she suggested ruffling Kitty's forehead. He obeyed gratefully. She turned to Davies: 'You also.'

Obediently he climbed into his bed. The curtains remained open and the unchecked moonlight fell into the room. 'Romantic,' Jemma smiled. 'But a bit blatant, don't you think.'

'Nothing worse than blatancy,' he agreed. Watching her standing so beautifully he would have agreed to anything. He opened the bedclothes for her. She, however, went to the window and with a brief kiss blown at the moon pulled across the curtains, transforming herself into a silhouette.

'Can you see?' Davies inquired anxiously from the bed. 'I'm over here.'

'I know where you are, Dangerous. I'm coming in.'

She slid off the robe and it fell silently around her feet. She was wearing a light nightdress of the same silk, the straps luminous across her brown shoulders. She climbed easily into the bed and sat across his stomach. Then she leaned forward and kissed his worn face. 'I'll have to go back,' she said. 'Afterwards.'

'As long as it's not before,' he said. 'Is Valentine fasto?'

'Deeply fasto,' she told him. 'It's air and sandcastles.'

'I've got to build another in the morning,' he said. 'I've been planning it. It's going to have a ...' Ignoring him she pulled the counterpane up around her shoulders like a cloak.

'I hope you're going to take those pyjamas off,' she said. 'I never realised you could buy cardboard pyjamas.'

'Take them off?' he grumbled. 'I'll get cold.'

'Not with me, you won't.' She regarded him wryly. 'But it's all right. Keep them on. It's homely.'

'Will you undo my trouser cord?' he asked. 'You're sitting on it.'

She laughed lightly but he could see her face was now becoming set as it always became at these times. She sat above him like an Egyptian cat. 'I'll handle the cord,' she whispered. She undid the bow and the knot, pulled the thick trousers around his hips and said: 'There it is.'

'I thought it was,' he whispered back.

She remained above him while they made love, sometimes sitting on him, sometimes leaning right over him like a hard, slim rider on a horse. When they came to the end, she moved as close and clutching as she could before raising herself upright with a cry and then falling on top of him again. They lay in friendship and quietness against each other. Then Jemma said: 'I think it's time for some moon.' Carefully she eased herself from him and in two steps went to the window. The dog glanced up briefly but saw who it was and returned reassured to sleep. Jemma threw open the curtains. 'Enter *la lune,*' she smiled. The silver light obediently filled the room. He could clearly see her smile now and her fine eyes in the dark face.

'Don't clear off yet,' he said from the bed.

'I wasn't intending to,' she said. She climbed in beside him. His big arms and her slender arms entangled around their bodies. They kissed fondly. Then she leaned up and studied his face in the bed. 'Dangerous by Moonlight,' she whispered. 'How wonderful.'

At four thirty in the morning it began to howl and rain. Davies and the dog turned simultaneously in their sleep, each emitting a selfish, satisfied groan.

Wind was still hammering at the windows when the panes were eventually filled with leaden daylight. Over breakfast they watched rain streaming on the glass and the waves churning on the shore.

'No need to damp the sand today,' said Valentine looking at Davies.

Jemma and Davies exchanged glances. 'You tell him,' suggested Davies.

Jemma grimaced but said confidingly to the boy: 'I don't think it's going to be a morning for sandcastles.'

Valentine paused half-way down a sausage. 'Swimming then?' he suggested. His eyes came up hopefully to look at each in turn. 'We could go swimming.'

Davies returned his doubtful eyes to the window. The rain was lashing so furiously that the breakers were reduced to dull white smudges. A seagull tried to keep its balance in the wind. 'We mustn't get out of our depth,' he said.

To his consternation Jemma said: 'Why not?'

'I didn't bring my bathers,' said Davies hurriedly.

'I did,' said Valentine.

'So did I,' put in Jemma. 'I told you to bring them, Dangerous.'

'But ... it's January ...'

'There's a swimming baths,' she told him. 'Olympic-sized.'

Davies surveyed her glumly. 'Oh good,' he said. 'I'm glad it's Olympic. It takes me twenty lengths just to get into my stride. But I still haven't got any trunks.'

The waitress was bringing a second pot of tea. 'Bertie will help,' she said to Davies. 'If you want swimming trunks, he'll find you some. He's the porter. People leave them in the summer.'

They found Bertie in an octagonal glass cubicle in the lobby which had been unoccupied when they had first arrived, a wispy man with creased eyes peering through the glass like an ugly and unsold puppy in a pet-shop window.

'Swimming gear,' he said heavily. 'We *do* have some

available.' He gazed with a fragment of forlorn hope at Jemma but being a hall porter and a realist, he transferred his look to Davies. 'It's for you, is it, sir?'

'Nothing fancy,' said Davies. 'None of these Speedos or anything. Just something plain.'

Bertie sniffed. He had a tuft of fair hair on his otherwise thinly thatched head and the light of the lobby shone through it like a light bulb. 'Something plain is all you'll get, sir, I'm afraid. The stuff people forget is not so much forgotten as abandoned. They don't think it's worth taking home.' He sized up Davies once more. 'Just come down to the basement.'

They walked towards a polished wooden door at the distant end of the lobby. Davies heard Valentine ask Jemma if she thought he would be all right down there. He followed Bertie down some rough stairs. 'It's not very nice underneath,' the porter called over his shoulder. 'The gloss, such as it is in this place, is above stairs.'

They arrived in a long, grim corridor with lagged pipes running its length. One pipe was hung with garments, like stiff pieces of drying fish. Bertie took one of them and shook it. There was a discernible crack as he did so and dust came out in clouds. 'The place where old swimming costumes come to die,' he confided. He held up the grey and sagging garment. 'How about that?'

Davies reached out and put his finger through a hole in the material. Bertie nodded stoically and replaced the trunks on the pipe. 'A bit brittle some of them,' he said. He brightened a little and reached for another pair of bathers. 'How about a nice stripe?' he said.

He handed the trunks to Davies. The stripes were wide and red, white and blue. 'Very patriotic,' he observed. 'These will do.' He held them across his middle. 'And they'll fit.'

Bertie looked genuinely pleased. They began climbing the stairs again. 'The lady and the lad are all fixed are they?' he said.

'They are. They knew about the swimming baths. I didn't. What's it like, Bertie?'

'The swimming baths. Oh, I've not been there, sir. I'm not what you would call aquatic. Horses are more my line.'

'You ride, do you.'

'No sir. I bet.'

The municipal swimming pool was like a great greenhouse except that it had none of a greenhouse's silence. It was filled with shouts that bounced in the steamy air. The water was green and warm. Outside the rain persisted.

In the dressing-room Davies timidly drew on the red, white and blue striped trunks, gazing down at them with a dropping heart. They gave him the appearance of an old-fashioned pantalooned acrobat. He could not remember when he had last taken off his clothes to appear in public; several years at least, the Lido at Ruislip he eventually recalled, during an investigation into an indecent exposure. Certainly the sun had not beamed upon his body for a long time; it was putty pale to the neck. He peered down at his navel as if it might be blinking.

Someone with a sadistic sense of humour had placed a full-length mirror in the dressing-room and he surveyed his exposed appearance with the doubt, less the laughter, of someone confronting a distorting looking glass on the pier. He was glad that his bruises were subsiding.

'Here goes,' he muttered giving the trunks a hopeful hitch. Nervously he sidled into the swimming-pool area. To his relief there was no crowd waiting to howl derision; everyone was occupied with the excitement and activity of the huge bath. Valentine was already in the water. His dark head bobbed up like a fisherman's float almost at Davies' feet. 'You don't arf look white, Dangerous,' he shouted.

'Never take my vest off if I can help it, son,' Davies replied evenly. He saw Jemma then, swimming gracefully towards them. She held onto the side and smiled up at him. 'Come on in,' she said.

'I know, I know,' he grumbled, 'the water's lovely.' He examined it like someone trying to detect loveliness. 'I will in time. It's not something I like to do in a hurry. Even Channel swimmers need preparation.'

Athletically she slid from the bath, her lean black figure slotted into a dark blue one-piece swimsuit. Like a gymnast she curled herself around, using her hands as pivots and sat poised on the side, still looking up at him. He was surveying the busy bath. People of all ages were ploughing up and down, children were shouting, and, at the centre of it all, a big man trawled through the water like a tugboat.

Valentine shouted: 'It's warm as anything, Dangerous.'

Jemma rolled her eyes gently. 'Come on, in you get,' she encouraged.

'Oh God,' muttered Davies. He eased himself down onto the side of the bath and then with a soft push from Jemma, tipped himself into the water. He came up spluttering. His arms swished sideways.

'You can swim, can't you?' asked Jemma suddenly anxious.

Valentine shouted: 'I'll save you, Dangerous!'

With as much grace as possible, Davies caught hold of the rail. 'Swim? of course I can swim. All police officers can swim. We have to rescue people from canals and whatnot. It's just that I'm not used to the water, that's all. I don't ... I don't like the way it engulfs you. Let me do it in my own good time.'

Ponderously splashing and spluttering, he set off swimming along the edge of the bath, each crawl stroke awkwardly studied. He changed to a heavy breaststroke up and down the pool and then pulled in to the side like a vessel coming gratefully to a quay.

'You reckoned you was going to do twenty lengths,' pointed out Valentine treading water. Jemma was floating easily beside him. The big man who had been trudging up the centre of the bath came to the side also.

'I *said* twenty lengths,' Davies told the boy in the water. 'But I didn't say all at once, did I.'

'All the same, they are,' agreed the big man who had now moored himself alongside the pool. 'Think we can do anything they can.' He studied Davies for some time. 'And you're a bit younger than me.'

He was elderly but powerful. Even his bald head looked powerful. His heavyweight shoulders, emerging from the water, were those of a wrestler, pale and muscled. He blinked the water from the wrinkles of his eyes and with a great exhibition heave, he levered himself from the water. Davies saw that his left leg had been amputated at the knee.

The man saw him looking. 'War wound?' asked Davies a little embarrassed.

'Horse and cart,' replied the man in a way which indicated he had given the response often. 'Ran over it when I was a kid. Five.'

He lowered the truncated leg into the water so that its endlessness was hidden. 'That was bad luck,' said Davies.

'S'pose it was,' replied the man. 'Don't actually remember much about it. Only the horse making a terrible row. My mother said it made more fuss than I did.' He gazed down at the leg in the water. 'Pity, I wanted to be a policeman.'

'I'm a copper,' admitted Davies. 'London.'

'Never been there,' said the man. 'Too far for me, London.'

With a surprisingly gentle entry he went into the water again. Davies watched him swim powerfully but, it seemed, thoughtfully and then he turned and with a green bow wave came towards the side again. 'I know everything there is to know about this town,' he said. He blinked the water from his eyes. 'That's if you need to know anything.'

Davies shook his head. 'No, no. Off duty, I am. On leave. I'm just down here to get my health and strength back.'

As if reassured the man once more levered himself out of the bath and sat on the side, the water running from his huge shoulders. Jemma and Valentine were beckoning from the far side of the pool. Two elderly women suddenly, and with synchronised whoops, launched themselves from one end.

'They're not supposed to do that,' muttered the man. 'No diving or jumping allowed.'

'At their age I would have thought they're taking a bit of a risk,' said Davies.

'When you're old you take risks,' shrugged the big man. 'It don't seem to matter so much.'

They had Sunday lunch in the hotel at a table in the window overlooking the desolate January beach. Valentine kept glancing from his roast potatoes in that direction but even he could see it was unlikely that any sandcastles would be constructed that afternoon. Jemma was taking him back to London in the evening. 'Are you sure you'll be all right, Dangerous?' she asked. Her anxiety was sincere, her eyes grave.

'I'll be careful of the women and the roads,' he promised.

She laughed. 'You'll get bored,' she forecast. 'You'll be back by Wednesday, Tuesday even. You'll miss Mod and the Babe In Arms.'

'I have a planned programme,' he replied confidently. 'A regime to get me fit and well. And it doesn't include swimming.'

'Swimming's good,' said the boy. He made the motions of the crawl.

'All right for some,' admitted Davies. 'But my schedule is long bracing walks on the beach with Kitty. A few pints at lunchtime in the Moonlighters Club, a siesta, a little reading in the lounge, bath, drink, dinner and bed.'

Jemma regarded him quizzically. 'Well, that's fine for the first day. What's the Moonlighters Club?'

'Where Bournemouth's élite meet, the beer is apparently drinkable and the prices reasonable. My friend Phineas – him with the missing leg – told me about it. He knows everything about this place.' A parsnip on his fork, he half turned towards the glass dining-room door. Mrs Dulciman was leading in a straggle of middle-aged and elderly women, all chattery and well dressed. A waft of perfume moved with them as they came into the room. 'What a niff,' complained Valentine.

'Bournemouth and Boscombe Widows' Luncheon Club,' intoned Davies. 'They come here every month.'

Jemma glanced at him again. 'My, my, you do get to know things, Dangerous.'

'Copper's instinct,' he said, raising his glass of red wine.

'A widows' luncheon club,' repeated Jemma. 'What do they do? Apart from talk about being widows.'

'Live in the past,' he suggested. 'Chat about old times, old husbands and that sort of thing.'

The ladies were sprightly and of varying shapes, sizes and hair colours, laughing and arranging their pearls and their coiffures as they found their seats and sat around a big oval table. Mrs Dulciman placed herself at the head, near the door, and remained standing while the others fidgeted with their chairs. There were twenty women around the table, Davies counted them. He thought that the youngest was about fifty. Mrs Dulciman lightly tapped her fork on the tablecloth and said quietly: 'Ladies, Absent Friends.'

Oblivious of the people at the other tables, the women bowed their heads for one minute. When they raised them again there were some apparent furtive dabs at eyes with lace handkerchiefs, but the wine waiter busily appeared and private grief was suspended.

'You don't have to travel far to find a strange country,' observed Davies as he walked with Jemma along the promenade. The afternoon sun was in the middle of a fleeting and wan appearance. Valentine had opted to stay in the hotel with Kitty and watch football on television.

Jemma pushed her slim arm into his overcoated elbow and said: 'That's a very profound statement, Dangerous.'

'Which one was that?'

'About the strange country.'

'Given the opportunity I can be quite literary,' he replied airily. 'And this is a literary town, you know. Shelley, Robert Louis Stevenson, all that crowd. Probably regulars at the Moonlighters Club.'

Her heels sounded on the paving of the promenade. There was a shuttered fortune-teller's booth and a closed shed that in summer sold ice-cream. People, taking advantage of the patently brief sunshine, were walking, some with their dogs, and a few glanced at the slim black girl and the heavy white man. 'You've been reading the guide book,' said Jemma.

'Robert Louis Stevenson,' he corrected. 'Nicked by Mod from the library.'

'Wasn't it odd, the widows meeting for lunch like that,' she continued. 'They couldn't wait to pass the photographs around, could they. Grandchildren, nieces and nephews, I expect. They love all that.'

'Deceased husbands too,' Davies told her.

'You think so?'

'Oh yes. There were a few ghosts doing the rounds at that table. "That's my Harry and that's Marmaduke just before he went. And remember this day down at the Yacht Club." '

'Sad really,' she said. 'That's the trouble with happy marriages, somebody's got to go and somebody's got to be left behind in the end. A penalty for doing something well.'

The sun vanished as though it had somewhere better to go. They turned away from the breeze and began to walk back in the direction of the hotel. 'Most of the widows did not seem too mournful,' he pointed out. 'There was a good deal of giggling and hands over the mouth stuff, and one or two guilty blushes.'

'Always the detective,' she smiled. 'You love digging around in the past, don't you. Turning over old ashes. You've always been at your best doing that sort of thing.' She glanced at the elderly walkers now progressing in the other direction. 'And there's plenty of past around here.'

'It's full up with it,' he agreed. 'There's whole layers of the past in a town like this. I bet we've walked by a few mysteries, one or two nasty secrets, in the last fifteen minutes. Who can go through a lifetime and hand on heart swear they have never wanted to commit a murder, tried to commit one or actually did.'

She studied the passers-by with new interest. 'And everyone looks so sedate and decent,' she said.

Davies sniffed as though testing the air and the atmosphere at the same time. 'One of the books Robert Louis Stevenson wrote in Bournemouth was *Doctor Jekyll and Mr Hyde*,' he observed.

As they waited for the InterCity from Poole, Davies told Valentine about the railway engines that used to be. The boy refused to believe they ran on *coal*. Then he said: 'What I want to know is why that old dear 'ad a white stick.'

'Which old dear was that?' inquired Davies, tentatively. Jemma glanced at each in turn.

'The one in the 'otel. She 'ad a stick when she was sitting down in the dinner room but when we got there first, to the 'otel, she was reading the paper.'

'That's right,' confirmed Jemma. 'She was. But I didn't see her with a white stick.' She returned to Davies with a touch of amusement. 'Did you?' Davies shook his head.

'It was leaning against 'er chair. An' when she got up she took it out wiv her.'

The snub yellow nose of the train eased into the platform, the sound of its entry drowning the station announcement proclaiming it. 'You ought to be a copper,' Davies said to the boy once more. Again Valentine replied that he would rather not.

They shook hands gravely and the boy said: 'Fanks for the castles and everything.'

Davies said: 'I'll have to build them on my own now.' As he said it he realised it was true. He was going to be by himself again. He kissed Jemma and she whispered: 'Try and last beyond Wednesday.'

'I'll be brave,' he said.

The train went, vanishing metallically into the darkness of late afternoon. Davies found himself trudging as he went from the station. It was not far and he decided to walk, collar up and face down against the thin rain. Washy lights were showing in the various hotels along the way and he looked up and saw a window with smudges of people gathered in what he thought must be a cocktail bar. He trudged on.

These days he was not often lonely. But now, suddenly, he had neither Jemma nor Valentine, nor Mod, only his dog. Loneliness was the lot of policemen. They were like sailors in a way, often unaccompanied, in the dark, hardly knowing where they were going.

He had always realised that his own solitariness had made Doris, his wife, lonely too. Even when they were living together, as distinct from living in the same boarding house as they did now, a separateness had happened, a division, a mutual barrier. Poor Doris, he thought. She was young once. So was he.

He tried to console himself with the thought that he still had his dog, moody though he was. He reached the hotel and brought Kitty down from the room for an evening walk. The rain had thickened and he was glad to find a pub where there were no other dogs. He bought a pint and wondered how long he could stand being on holiday.

He was much cheered by the morning. A bland and blameless sky, the sea made almost blue with clean neat waves coming up the beach, and the sun giving Bournemouth, he thought, a little of the grand aspect of Nice, where he had never been. He had a cheerfully large breakfast, read the *Daily Mail* and the *Daily Express*, folded them beneath his arm and went down to the shore with Kitty.

Even his dog seemed to benefit from the bright morning. He ambled along, sniffing at the wet patterns left by the tide, smelling deeply into the plastic neck of a washed-ashore detergent bottle and jumping optimistically at the most adjacent of the swooping gulls.

Davies breathed deeply as he strode, his eyes watered and

he began to feel warm in his overcoat. An elderly woman in a track suit, done up like a pink bundle, approached from the promenade. She was swinging a tennis racquet. As he watched, and the dog sat down and watched also, she took something from a paper bag and bringing the racquet back in a serving action, propelled it into the air. The gulls squawked and fought over the projectile. Davies looked at Kitty and the dog returned the puzzled glance.

'It's a new way of feeding the birds,' Davies told him.

The woman saw his attention. She took another piece of bread from her bag and whanged it into the air among the wheeling gulls. 'It combines sport and humanity!' the woman shouted. She struck a third crust and then putting the racquet below her arm, strode past him down the beach, the harassing gulls following her.

Davies led his dog up the promenade. The benches were well populated with people, mostly elderly, enjoying the pale sun and sniffing the ozone. He wished some of them good morning and agreed that it was a fine day to be alive. 'Every day is,' one elderly man called after him. He took the dog back to the hotel. Kitty appeared exhausted by the open-air activity and sank gratefully with not even a growl into his basket. Davies went to an Indian newsagents and bought a *Sporting Life* for he thought he might occupy some of his time by selecting possible winners. He also purchased three picture postcards and wrote messages to Jemma, Valentine and Mod while he had a cup of coffee in a snack bar.

Standing in the queue at the post office he realised that three places ahead was the short sturdy form of Mrs Dulciman. She had a ring of fur around her neck and a jaunty little hat with a feather. A young man left the counter and the post office girl called after him. 'Your change! You've left your change!'

The youth did not hear her but in a moment Mrs Dulciman was pursuing him and having caught him outside the door, brought him back to claim what was his. He thanked her shyly. Not bad, very swift off the mark, Davies thought, especially for an old lady holding a white stick.

Four

There was a horse called Winter Season running that day. Bertie, the porter, was in his glass enclosure when Davies returned to the hotel, his newspaper open at the racing page. He wore an expression of wrinkled doubt.

'Fancy Winter Season?' asked Davies. 'Good name.'

'Might, sir. But might not,' replied Bertie. He opened the curious little window in the cubicle and pushed his head through like someone with a secret. 'Never go by the names myself. Playing into their hands, I say.'

'What do you reckon then?' asked Davies. He squinted through the glass at Bertie's paper spread on the polished shelf. The porter sniffed. 'Winter Season's as good as anything,' he agreed. 'It's soggy underfoot and they say in here ...' He nodded towards the newspaper. 'They say he likes that. Five to one's not too bad.' He looked up, his forehead expanding benignly. 'Do you want me to put it on for you, sir. I have arrangements.'

Davies felt in his back pocket. 'Thanks. Will you. Fiver each way.' He glanced up to see how the amount registered. Bertie reacted with a considered nod. 'That's about what it's worth,' he said. 'Come and watch if you like. It will be on the television. I'll be watching.'

Davies said he would. It was still only eleven so he went to the room and brought Kitty down on his lead. The dog had taken to the life of the hotel. He came down the stairs swinging his great tail and sniffing at the dining-room door from which a remnant of the smells of breakfast still drifted.

'Looks as if *he* could run in the two-thirty,' suggested Bertie sizing up the animal.

'He's big enough,' conceded Davies. 'But lazy.' Kitty looked around with what appeared as a smile.

'Why's he called Kitty?' inquired Bertie leaning through his window. 'A he?'

'A mistake,' shrugged Davies. 'I was never able to get near enough to find out.'

Persuading the dog away from the dining-room door, he took him through the back entrance of the hotel and onto the beach. It was a flat day, dove-coloured sky and sea. The beach stretched wet and almost vacant but the lady he had seen propelling bread to the birds with a tennis racquet was doing it again. Kitty jumped hopefully towards the whirling gulls. The woman had exchanged her pink track suit for one of turquoise. He greeted her affably and admired her accuracy with the bread. 'An ace service every time,' he smiled.

'That was *once*,' she replied blithely. She paused in mid-serve and looked reminiscent. 'A long time ago.' She projected another crust into the sky and the crying gulls. 'But then, most things were.'

The gulls screamed greedily. 'You never see a happy gull,' she said philosophically.

She lowered the racquet. 'You should drop in at the Moonlighters Club,' she said as if she had come to a decision. 'It all happens there, you know.'

'So I've been told,' he agreed. 'I'll make sure I do.'

Kitty was tugging at the lead and he was forced to follow him. 'Let the dog off,' the turquoise woman called after him. 'It's not really allowed but you can't go through life just doing what's allowed!'

'No,' he agreed half-heartedly. 'No, I suppose you can't.'

He saw Mildred, the receptionist, coming from the hotel bouncing studiedly over the sand. 'Let him off,' she agreed. 'They can't hang you for it.'

She did it for him, bending and unclipping the dog's lead.

Kitty gave her a swift grateful glance and took off, running wildly along the fringe of the water, head down, bounding and yelping, until he was a dun dot in the distance.

'Sod it,' said Mildred dully. 'That's typical, that is.'

It was pointless chasing the dog. Glancing towards the promenade for anything in the shape of authority, Davies lowered his head and began to walk after the animal. Mildred stepped beside him.

'I always like it down here,' she said.

'Bournemouth?'

'The beach. Just being on it.'

'Do you come down here at night?'

Mildred looked startled. 'How do you know?'

'I saw you. I think it was. The other night. Early hours really. There was a moon.'

'Oh, yes. Well sometimes I don't sleep and I only have a small room. It seems to close itself around me, trying to grab me. I have to get out somewhere.' Hardly pausing, she said: 'Mrs Dulciman wants to see you some time. She'll be in this evening. She says she wants to ask you something.'

Phineas, the big one-legged man that Davies had met at the swimming bath, was wedged against the club bar.

'The club's called the Moonlighters because that's what the smugglers around here were called in the olden days,' he said. He swept his hand across the breadth of the window, the iron-grey sea running across it like a curtain. 'All this coast, infested. What they call The Chines, you know, the gulleys running down from the cliffs to the beach.'

He lifted his tankard and Davies did also, minutely timed like two large puppets on the same string. 'All them, The Chines, was contraband paths,' continued Phineas with a smuggler's wink. 'There wasn't really any Bournemouth then. They only built Bournemouth because they thought it would make dying people healthy. They still do.'

He drank deeply. In one movement he could, Davies saw, impressively dispose of almost half the pint tankard's content. 'Moonlighters,' he repeated profoundly.

Davies looked around the big, shabby room. There were tables and round chairs, polished by years of backs, there were some desultory flowers on a table in the corner, a television set staring blankly from an alcove, and black-and-white photographs on the walls near the door. A silent man and a watchful woman sat in one corner each with a tiny unsipped glass of sherry. Davies looked out of the damp window to the grey background of the English Channel. Conversation had ceased. A moan of wind came from beyond the window. 'Bournemouth lost on Saturday again,' mentioned the barman reappearing.

'I could play better. With one leg,' said Phineas.

'Who are they in the photographs?' inquired Davies attempting to add to the conversation.

'Members,' croaked the man of the sherry drinkers.

'Most of them dead,' put in the woman.

Phineas followed Davies to the door and balancing his stump on a chair of convenient height, pointed to individual photographs with his stick. 'They don't go in for colour pictures a lot,' he said. 'Not here.'

'Black and white shows people's characters,' suggested Davies, still attempting to contribute.

The sherry drinker said: 'Hah.'

'Life's black and white,' philosophised his companion loudly.

Davies scanned the photographs, pretending detailed interest. There were groups of mostly elderly people smiling raggedly, some standing artificially upright, others not bothering, men shaking hands, women kissing. There was a party outing with the coach in the background, and a croquet competition where the wind appeared to be about to blow away the participants, and several formal dinners and dances. 'Who's that?' he asked, pointing to a straight-backed man dancing with a lady in a long frail dress, leaning back as though she was about to fall.

'Vernon Dulciman,' said Phineas.

Davies felt his heart move. He had the uncomfortable feeling that a mystery was trying to find him. It had happened before. It was like a medium attracting a restless and undesirable spirit. 'Good dancer, Vernon,' continued Phineas. 'But there, he was in submarines during the war.'

'Oh,' blinked Davies.

'Made him neat. Said he used to practise dancing on the submarine.'

'Everything he did was neat. He was a neat man,' put in the woman sherry drinker.

'Neatest thing he ever did was to vanish,' said her companion.

Bertie had just turned on the racing when Davies knocked on his door at the hotel. The room was like a storehouse, boxes and containers stacked around the walls, behind the baggy settee and armchair, and with suitcases lined up as though in some lost-property office.

'Most of it's mine,' explained the porter apologetically. 'As I've moved around. Never been one for throwing things away, me, so I've carted it with me wherever I've been working. Some of that stuff I haven't opened for years. I reckon I'm here for keeps now, though, it's been ten years, so I don't expect that junk will be moving again.'

He frowned towards the television screen. 'Sit down, sir,' he invited. He was in the big chair himself so Davies sat on the settee feeling it groan and give under his weight. Bertie opened a box of matches and took out a spent match which he pushed into one of a series of small holes in the tuning panel of the television. The picture flickered and contracted before filling the screen adequately. Horses were being led into an enclosure. 'Match of the day, I call this,' said Bertie ponderously displaying the matchstick. 'But it does the business.' He peered closely at the image. 'Now which is Winter Season?' Without taking his eyes away he said: 'I put your fiver each way on. I did the same for me. Maybe you're lucky.'

'Not generally,' admitted Davies.

'Maybe today,' said Bertie. 'Would you like a drink? Anything. Beer, vodka, creme de menthe. I've got it all here.'

Davies said he would have a whisky if there was one. Bertie got up and went to a cabinet which lit up garishly as he raised the lid to display ranks of coloured bottles.

'Any preference?' he asked.

'Any one.'

'What about a nice malt. Got several malts.' The porter glanced over his shoulder. 'Working like I do has got its perks,' he added.

Davies had a malt whisky and they settled to watch the screen. 'He looks all right, Winter Season,' mentioned Bertie. 'All four legs working.'

They watched in comfortable silence. Davies was aware of occasional traffic outside the semi-window, half below ground. He realised it was getting dark. The room was close and homely. Being a porter was not a bad life.

'The job's got its ups and downs,' said Bertie as if reading the thought. 'This is the cushy time of the year. Summer's murder. Rowdy kids all around the place. Now, when you've only got a few people ... residents ...'

'Like Mrs Dulciman.'

'Nice old lady. She'll probably stay until she dies. Now *he's* gone.'

'Where's he gone?' asked Davies deliberately.

Bertie looked away from the screen even though the horses were under starter's orders. 'Who knows?' he said. 'Gone somewhere. Five years ago.' His attention returned to the screen. 'They're off,' he said without excitement. They watched. At the third fence Winter Season fell. 'He's come a cropper,' said Bertie mildly. 'Like Mr Dulciman.'

*

Apart from the direct physical assaults that had long been part of his work experience, Davies enjoyed good health. The onset of any ailment, the Willesden willies, a canal cold, toothache, even a hangover headache, he would tackle with a couple of double scotches, one swiftly following the other, and followed by another as a safety measure, at the bar of the Babe In Arms. His body had grown to understand this simple cure and to react dutifully to it.

But, late that drizzling night, as he was tugging Kitty along the promenade for the dog's outing before bedtime, he felt the touch of something new. Kitty was not keen to promenade in the wet and was irritable. As they stumbled through the chill, thin rain with the midnight breakers dim and thundering, Davies was aware of a constriction in his throat.

His face was beaming hot despite the sheen of damp and there was sweat underneath his vest. His eyes rolled as though seeking help along the empty sea front. Yellow street lamps fused into omelettes. He was ill.

Having taken the dog to their room and seen him subside grumpily but gratefully into his basket, removed now from the bathroom door, he went unsteadily down to the bar.

'You're ill,' announced the woman tending it. 'I can see you're ill.'

'I don't feel so good,' Davies agreed miserably. He ordered a double scotch.

'Your eyes give you away,' she said.

He sat aching on the bar stool. She approved of the whisky. 'Although brandy's better. The rougher the better too. Burns through your system and drags everything out. Drags it. Germs, phlegm, everything.'

There was no one else remaining. Rain slid down the windows like tears. 'I thought Bournemouth was supposed to be healthy,' he suggested weakly.

'Oh, it is,' she said hurriedly. 'Supposed to be. It's the trees, the pines, giving off vapours. But looking at you I'd say it was too late for that.'

Davies groaned. 'So it's no good me going out and sniffing at a pine.'

'Better go to bed and stay under the blankets,' she advised. 'I'm closing up anyway. Unless you want another.'

Davies said he did. He drank it straight down and went to bed. His whole body seemed to be groaning. He had never realised that being ill was like this. 'Oh God,' he mumbled. 'I do feel poorly.'

All through the night great doors and windows seemed to be opening and closing. Spasms of hot air were at once followed by icy blasts that whistled through his pipes and shook his bones. His throat felt cracked. The sheets were soaked with sweat. 'Kitty, Kitty,' he croaked. 'Oh, Kitty.'

The dog snored on. He would have been no help anyway. He was no St Bernard. Davies shivered so much the bed vibrated. Then he fell into a sticky sleep from which he awoke as a grim bar of grey light was appearing over the curtain rods. His mouth was arid, his throat raw. For a while he thought he had wet the bed. He felt so low and lonely. Where was Jemma? Where was Mod? Where was anybody?

Mildred came in at nine o'clock, briefly knocking and pushing a cup of tea before her through the opening. 'I hear you're not ...' she started. She saw his state and said: 'Oh, you're not are you,' her voice dropping. He held out his pale, damp hand from the bedclothes for the tea. She helped him to put it to his parched lips. 'I'll get the doctor,' she said. She went to the door and then turned and studied him. 'Yes, I'll get him,' she repeated and went out hurriedly.

Davies went into a ragged sleep and the next time he woke the door was opened by Mildred with the doctor, a gingery man, following her. 'Never had malaria, have you?' he asked conversationally as he opened his bag. He shook his thermometer and put it into Davies' mouth. Davies hummed and shook his head to indicate that he had never had malaria. The doctor took the thermometer out and peered at it. His ginger eyebrows went up. Mildred was hovering near the door.

The doctor looked at his throat. 'Nasty,' he said. 'Like Aladdin's cave. Your tonsils are rotten, you know.'

'All of me feels rotten,' suggested Davies.

The doctor laughed. 'You'll be all right in a few days, a week at the most. I'll give you some antibiotics and then you'll have to sweat it out. Pity you never had those tonsils removed when you were a child.'

'My mother was always busy,' croaked Davies.

Jemma came down on the following day, bringing with her a photograph taken of the regulars in the Babe In Arms holding up their pints and wishing him a swift recovery. She surveyed him anxiously but tried to smile. 'By God, Dangerous, you can't look after yourself can you,' she said. She kissed him on his cheek, where he pointed, as though he had been injured again.

She checked the bottles and jars at his bedside and stayed an hour trying to soothe him and telling him news from Willesden. It was mostly a monologue with Davies merely croaking and nodding. She then went down to fetch a tray of tea but after that she had to leave. She had abandoned a meeting to come and see him and he understood that most of her life was taken up trying to help people who were less fortunate than he was, although at that moment he might have argued the point.

'What about Kitty?' she asked.

'Take him home, please,' he wheezed leaving a space between each word. The dog sat up expectantly. 'The doctor's afraid he might catch this.' Jemma laughed and gave him a gentle push. But her eyes dimmed with concern again. 'I don't know what we're going to do about you, Dangerous,' she said huskily. His plight was bringing out the social worker in her. 'I'd marry you if I could.'

'You may need to bury me,' he said miserably. He lay back on the pillow and regarded her with a bleak expression.

She bent and kissed him again, this time on his damp forehead. 'Still,' she added with an attempt at cheerfulness.

'This is the first time I've known you to be ill.' She paused: 'As distinct from injured.'

Kitty was eager to leave. Davies saw them go out of the door and it was closed on them. He lay back mournfully, watching the swiftly fading light of the afternoon. At that time of the year the day could not wait to go. He could see through the window the dark line of the sea, growing thinner by the minute. There was nothing on it; not a ship, not a light.

Mildred brought him two poached eggs on toast. 'They look like your eyes,' she said studying his eyes. He could only eat one, and the toast grated like wood in his sore throat. She ate the second egg having thought to bring a fork.

'I've had an unfortunate life,' she said as though she had been waiting to tell him about it and this was the perfect opportunity. Her skirted hips overhung the sides of the bedside chair. 'Look at my name for a start. There's not many girls of twenty-five called Mildred.'

Davies attempted to look surprised. He raised his eyebrows and shook his head.

'It's dead true,' she asserted. 'Mildred ... it sounds like someone who's afraid of working in a cloth factory, doesn't it. Mill-dread. My mum called me that after some auntie of my dad's. She was always trying to please him. Up until she pushed him down the stairs. But they didn't know what they were doing to me. Sod Auntie Mildred. I've tried calling myself other names ... Tammy, Nicky ... but somehow I get found out and it's back to bloody Mildred.'

It was a one-sided conversation but he was grateful that she had come. He patted her hand in appreciation. She left but came back immediately with the evening paper. 'The *Echo* might cheer you up,' she said. 'The new unemployment figures are just out. And there's been a nasty accident ... and Bournemouth lost.' He managed to say: 'I heard.' As she was leaving she turned at the door and half whispered: 'Mrs Dulciman still wants to see you. Just as soon as you're a bit better.'

*

It was two further days before his malaise began to leave him. His throat eased, his temperature quietened and his eyes dried. He spent much of the time propped up on the pillows wagering against himself on the appearance of a boat on the sea. One appeared on the second afternoon and he viewed it as a sickly castaway might do.

Bertie came up to see him and brought the racing paper to see if he fancied anything. He picked a seven-to-one runner at Kempton Park, a horse called Dry Throat, but it lost by a neck. Mildred brought him some poached haddock and ate most of it herself while telling him of her life's bad luck from the day of her birth in Newcastle when, due to a road mishap, the ambulance taking her mother to hospital had been halted for an hour on the bridge across the River Tyne. 'That's where I was born, up on that bridge, neither one side nor the other. In fact, in limbo,' she related. 'That's why I eat too much.' She regarded him as though she did not expect to be believed: 'It's compensation.'

On the third morning Mildred came into the room and asked if Mrs Dulciman could come and see him now. Davies, reading an analysis of local jobless, and having read an even deeper analysis of Bournemouth's problems in front of goal, was glad to accede. The old lady came into the room daintily, with a sedate smile and a bright eye. She was wearing a dark-blue dress with lace at the collar and cuffs. She did not have a white stick.

'So glad you're better, Dangerous,' she said. She regarded him anxiously as she pulled up the bedside chair. 'You don't mind me using your eponym, I hope.'

'No, please be seated,' he said.

'Everyone else, at least those who know you, calls you Dangerous, I imagine. I heard the little black boy call you that.'

'Generally that's how I am known,' he agreed.

'And why is that?' Her eyes fixed him, wanting to know. 'You don't look very dangerous.'

He laughed, still roughly. 'And I don't feel it, Mrs Dulciman, believe me,' he replied. 'They just call me that. It started a long time ago.'

'You are a policeman, I believe.'

'Yes. In London. I'm a detective constable.' Her face was pink with wisps of grey hair around her forehead. 'That's how I got the nickname. They knew I was harmless, the coppers and the criminals, so that's what they nicknamed me. Dangerous. They used to send me on jobs that nobody else wanted to do. They still do.'

The old lady looked thoughtful. She framed the question carefully. 'Why *do* people commit crimes, do you think?'

Davies swallowed and held his tender throat. 'Well, let me see.' He regarded her carefully. 'Some do it because they are driven to it, some because it looks easy, some can't help it.' He paused. 'And there are those ... who do it because they're evil.'

'Yes. That's quite a comprehensive list. Do you think you would be able to solve a crime for me?'

'Me?' He clutched his throat at her suddenness. It hurt. 'But ...'

'I would pay you a fee. Five thousand pounds,' she said firmly. 'Half now and half when you've cleared it up.'

'But, Mrs Dulciman, I'm a full-time officer, I couldn't take on anything like that. I'm out of my patch, my area ... the local police wouldn't ...'

She laughed quite heartily. 'Oh, *they've* tried. Well, they said they'd tried. It's my husband. He vanished five years ago.'

Davies nodded. 'Yes, I heard,' he said. 'And please don't misunderstand, Mrs Dulciman. I'm very flattered and it's a generous offer, but I'm not able to do anything like that. I'm not *allowed*. You should get a private detective if you're serious about it.'

'Serious,' she echoed. 'Oh, *I'm* serious enough. It's other people. I had a private detective. A weedy-looking man who was always combing his bald head and had a perpetual cough, lying on wet grass I imagine, keeping observation and suchlike. But he was utterly useless. All right for spying on adulterers and that type of person, but quite hopeless otherwise.'

She regarded him sagely from behind her shining glasses. 'Revenge,' she said mildly. 'You didn't mention revenge.'

Davies blinked then realised. 'Oh, yes. In the reasons for crime. No, you're right, I completely overlooked revenge. That's one of them, of course. Crimes against the person generally.' He smiled. 'You don't often get somebody stealing a bike for revenge.'

'It would be to ride or to sell,' she nodded seriously.

'Why now, do you want to find out for sure what happened to Mr Dulciman?' he inquired. 'It's been five years.'

'I need to.' She did not ask him how he knew. Instead she responded briskly: 'When he first vanished naturally the police made inquiries. Some shoes were found and some remains washed up from the sea but the findings were inconclusive. They might have been Vernon's but then they might not. I certainly couldn't recognise them. Then I asked this Pengelly man, this private detective.' She sniffed. 'He says he's Cornish. Can you imagine a Cornish private detective?'

'I've never thought about it,' admitted Davies.

'They are good at concealing things, the Cornish, that's why they made good smugglers, but I don't know about finding out. Anyway this one was no good at all. I paid him off and he went back to spying on people breaking their marriage vows.'

'So why now? After five years have gone by.'

She gave a small sigh. 'Well, it's been on my mind. And then you arrived. I thought the moment I heard you were a detective that you might be the person to find out. You give me a feeling of confidence.'

He blinked at the compliment, then said: 'Do you miss your husband, Mrs Dulciman?'

'Miss him? Good gracious no! I couldn't stand him. He was a dreadful man. Appalling.'

'But you still want to know where he went. What happened to him. If he is alive or dead.'

'I would certainly like to find out. He left a substantial amount of debts and, I subsequently discovered, a substantial amount of money. I had to pay off the debts, naturally. But I cannot lay my hands on the money. Most of it anyway. I have to wait seven years until a court will declare that he is presumed dead.' She waited, then said: 'I may not live that long myself.'

'I see.'

'Besides which I would genuinely like to know *who* did for him, if he was done for. I don't like unsolved mysteries, as popular as they are on television and in books, and I don't want to lie on my deathbed still trying to work this one out.'

He laughed and patted her hand. There were light-blue veins protruding from the skin. There was a knock and Mildred came in with a tray of tea. 'Thought you'd like some,' she mumbled. 'It's quite mild out now Mrs Dulciman.'

'Yes, Mildred,' returned the old lady smiling gently. 'For the month of the year.'

Mrs Dulciman told her to leave the tray and the old lady studiedly poured the tea. They drank quietly saying nothing now. It was darkening outside the window. But it was quiet. 'I'll have to give it some thought, Mrs Dulciman,' said Davies looking at her over the rim of his cup. A tear of tea ran down the side and he caught it on the saucer he held beneath. She handed him the plate of biscuits and putting the saucer on the bedclothes in front of him he took one.

'Half the fee would be payable on agreement,' she repeated. 'Half on completion. When will you let me know your decision?'

'I'll be leaving at the end of the week,' he said. 'Could I let you know then? The difficulties are as I said – I'm breaking the rules. A serving policeman can't just go off on his own and take up a private case. Also I will be in London and I would need to get down here to Bournemouth a lot.' He grinned at her. 'It might have to wait until my summer hols.'

She smiled almost fondly before sharply breaking a biscuit in two. 'There are weekends,' she pointed out. 'Or days off. I presume even with the present lawlessness in the country policemen do get some free time. It would just be like doing a spare-time job. What do they call it, Mr Davies?'

'Moonlighting, Mrs Dulciman. It's called Moonlighting.'

Five

Jemma drove along the New Forest road, the dual carriage-way that cut in half the ancient hunting chase of William the Conqueror. It was a sparkling day but the sun was already low and shining between naked branches. A herd of deer grazed. The motorway was straight ahead.

'So you refused. You told her you could not do it,' she said.

'I had to,' said Davies from the depths of his overcoat. 'How can I do something like that on the quiet? I'd be drummed out. And I couldn't spend enough time on it, not to justify the money. I'd be short-changing the old lady.'

'It's a lot of money, Dangerous, five thousand,' she pointed out. 'Think of what you could do with that.'

Davies sniffed. He still felt low. His face was pale with deep, dark lines. 'I could buy a new dog, I suppose,' he said. 'I'm glad Kitty has been behaving.'

'Well, he has with *me,*' said Jemma cautiously. 'I took him for a walk through the cemetery, twice, and he's as good as gold.'

'When he likes you, he likes you,' nodded Davies his face framed in the cleft of the overcoat, his voice muffled. An unhappy thought struck him. 'Has Mod had any trouble with him?'

She appeared to be deeply concentrating on the road, straight, four-laned and with only scattered traffic. 'The motorway's not far,' she muttered.

'Tell me,' said Davies grimly. His weary eyes turned sideways towards her.

'Tell you?' she asked ingenuously. She smiled towards a group of shaggy New Forest ponies. 'Look at that. So pretty.'

'Tell me about Kitty and what he did with Mod,' he insisted in a low voice. 'Don't tell me the bugger wrecked the pub again. I warned Mod ...'

'No, no,' said Jemma inclining her head like someone struggling to find something good to say. 'No, the pub was intact, just fine. In fact everybody said what a good dog Kitty was. They thought his stay in Bornemouth had done him good.'

'What then?'

'It was that man with the hot-dog stall,' she said with a slow despair. 'The one near the Jubilee Clock.'

'Oh God. I knew it was only a matter of time. That dog's had his eye on him. What happened?'

'The man's going to sue you,' said Jemma grimly. She kept her eyes on the route. 'I've always thought he was dodgy anyway. The stench from those onions and the Environment Depart ...'

'*How* much damage?'

She sighed. 'The stall and the man were both wrecked,' she said getting it off her chest.

'Jesus. Kitty didn't bite him?'

'No. Kitty's mouth was full of sausage meat. But the whole stall collapsed. The man was a nervous ninny. He's going to sue for loss of earnings, mental anguish, the lot.'

Davies moaned. 'Hot-dog man's mental anguish,' he recited slowly. 'I can see the headlines now. What am I going to do?'

'Five thousand quid might come in handy. You may need to buy him off or settle out of court.'

Davies sighed. 'Five thousand,' he repeated. 'It might just be an old lady rambling on.'

'Mrs Dulciman doesn't strike me as the rambling-on type,' observed Jemma firmly. 'Did you ask her about her white stick?'

'No. I didn't like to. She was carrying it in the post office when I was sending off the postcards ...'

'Oh yes, we got our cards. Thanks. Mine was a view of Westminster Abbey.'

'Oh. It must have got in there by mistake. Sorry. But Mrs Dulciman was in the queue and some chap didn't pick up his change and she was off after him like a shot.'

'With her white stick.'

'Yes.'

'Does she really think somebody did for him?'

'Her very words. She wants to get it cleared up because there's money hanging on it and she needs it. He has to be presumed dead.'

They reached the beginning of the motorway and turned towards London. 'Why do you think she needs the money? If she's offering to pay you five grand, half up front, then she can't be all that short.'

'She's the sort of lady who has her reasons.'

The eastward course of the motorway altered towards London. They were driving into January cloud. The countryside gave way to industrial estates.

'How exactly did Mr Dulciman go?'

'Vernon Dulciman,' said Davies. His head had descended into his overcoat again. 'I didn't want to go into too many details. Not if I'm not going to take it on.'

'I still think you should. What sort of person was he?'

'He learned to dance in a submarine,' replied Davies.

Her profession had afforded her a shield against surprise. 'Resourceful eh. Was he popular?'

'With some ladies apparently, although not with Mrs Dulciman.'

'I see. How did you learn all this?'

'By accident, mostly. Before she ever asked me to look at the matter. In the Moonlighters Club.'

'Ah, what's that like?'

'On the quiet side,' he said. 'You can hear people sipping their sherry. But there's undercurrents.'

'And Mr Dulciman was a member.'

'Has his pictures plastered all over the wall. Mr Dulciman dancing, Mr Dulciman winning the croquet competition, Mr Dulciman on the club outing.'

'With Mrs Dulciman?'

'Sometimes. Almost out of sight.'

'Why would she be so keen?'

He shrugged. 'I don't think I'd better talk any more, Jemma,' he said. 'The throat. Sing to me if you like.' His head had almost vanished into his collar. But he said: 'She thinks she's going to die soon. She just wants to know.'

For several years Davies and his wife Doris had slept within six inches of each other, competing in midnight snoring contests, but as estranged as any couple would ever be. Their rooms were divided by a flimsy wall, their beds either side of it. When either awoke in the dark hours they could hear the other stirring and wheezing.

Davies felt guilty about his wife and, as he returned to Bali Hi, Willesden, the self-reproach returned. He was unable to explain why neither he nor Doris did not move out: the policeman had no alibi. Each still regarded the tall, dull, red-brick, Victorian house as home. Neither would have admitted it but there remained a certain odd security in the fact that they were both there. If they did not belong to each other, they belonged to Bali Hi.

'We thought you'd come back all brown and bristling,' said Mrs Fulljames as she introduced the shepherd's pie that evening. 'Nice shepherd's pie,' she said.

'In January,' said Davies, 'there are limited opportunities for bronzing in Bournemouth. In fact I spent most of the time in bed with ...' he glanced slyly at Doris at the other end and the far side of the table, '... tonsillitis.'

Doris sniffed heavily enough to divert the steam rising from the potatoes that roofed the shepherd's pie. 'You should have had them out years ago.'

'Probably so, Mrs Davies,' he returned evenly. 'But in a busy life what time ...'

'You've been in hospital often enough,' put in Mrs Fulljames as she sat down at the head of the table.

Doris nodded forcefully. 'You should have got them to do something with them while you were there.'

Mod coughed and Minnie glanced at him gratefully. As a single lady she did not like domestic arguments. 'Children these days', she said in her timid voice, 'don't seem to have their tonsils out. We rarely get absentees from school for that reason.' She paused. 'One of the few reasons actually.'

'Have you still got your tonsils, Mod?' asked Davies in a chatty way.

'I don't know,' replied Mod. 'I don't remember ...' He began to open his mouth towards Minnie. 'Here, have a look ...' he began.

'Mr Lewis! Really!' admonished Mrs Fulljames. 'Not when you are eating shepherd's pie.'

'Oh sorry,' mumbled Mod. He made a little, seated bow towards Minnie. 'Forgot.'

'We have a gardener,' announced Mrs Fulljames hurriedly. 'Only part-time but since none of the men in this house ever bothers to do a bit of weeding, I think he will be an asset.'

'He'll be a superman, more like it,' put in Mod. He looked embarrassed again. 'I mean ... there's a lot of garden out there.'

'Half an acre, almost,' Mrs Fulljames answered with prim pride. 'Although I don't imagine you have ever ventured to the far end, Mr Lewis.'

Mod nodded over his food. 'The weather never seems to be good enough.'

Davies said: 'He's having a burn-up. I saw the smoke from the fire when I went down to the yard.'

'This little chap likes making fires,' continued Mrs Fulljames. 'It's the big attraction of gardening for him, I suspect.' She smirked. 'He works for various houses along here. That Mrs Firkin, at Valdemosa, you know. Apparently he went into her front hall and took out the day's papers to light a fire.' She giggled a little. 'Nobody had even read them.'

'What's his name, the gardener?' asked Davies suspiciously. 'Does he know that bonfires are municipally frowned on?'

'Oh. He's just a lad. Calls himself Elvis.'

'Smurfitt,' recited Davies. 'Prime suspect in the big newsagent theft case, at Pemberthy's newsagents. He was using them for fuel. Never proved.'

'Oh, he's known to the police!'

'More to the fire brigade. You'll need to watch him. Make sure he keeps his fires outdoors.'

'It doesn't need a gardener,' said Mod as they trudged towards the Babe In Arms. 'It needs a goat.'

'Elvis will put it to the torch,' forecast Davies, his head bent against the drizzle. 'To coin a phrase he's a couple of matches short of a box. Things tend to ignite when he's in the vicinity. He was the prime suspect when the bog in Gladstone Park burned down.'

'It's hard to start a blaze in a public convenience.'

'A challenge, I expect.'

They turned the corner at the top of the road. The illuminated sign of the Babe In Arms, showing an orphan in an almshouse, beamed like a beacon. 'Didn't think much of her shepherd's pie,' sighed Mod.

'It was a small shepherd,' agreed Davies.

They reached the public house and opened the figured-glass door which, it was said, had never been broken. They stepped down into the bar. It was warm and rosy, an illustration, if any were needed, that the London pub fulfilled a function, sheltering its regulars from fog, frost and families; a safe place where a man could choose his company.

'Heard you was dead, Dangerous,' said Mulcahy the barman. 'We was going to have a collection.'

'You can still have it,' suggested Davies. He ordered two

pints and bought the barman a drink for his kindness and concern. He and Mod retreated to their corner table.

'What am I going to do about the dog?' sighed Davies.

'Sausage meat flying everywhere,' remembered Mod moodily. 'The man wants five hundred pounds.'

A Scotsman who claimed once to have been a medical orderly came to the table and, without asking, took Davies' pulse, his own hand shaking as he did so. 'It's irregular, Dangerous,' he said.

'I don't wonder with him taking it,' said Davies when the man had faltered back to the distant end of the bar.

'A shame to be taken ill at the seaside,' mentioned Mod drinking deep into his tankard.

'A temperature of about a hundred and ten,' said Davies quite proudly. 'I was the warmest place on the south coast, believe me.' He glanced up at Mod. 'And I turned up a bit of a mystery.'

Mod looked displeased. 'Oh, not another of your hobby cases,' he sighed. 'God help us, you go off on sick leave, you get sick when you're on sick leave, and you turn up a whodunit.'

'There it was, lying in wait for me.'

'But *Bournemouth.* It's bad enough around this manor when you've sniffed out some old, unsolved business that nobody else wants to know about, but Bournemouth's miles ...'

'There's a five-thousand-quid fee.'

'When do we start?'

Davies said: 'We're not.'

'Not for five grand? What's the case?'

'A man went missing, vanished five years ago. He may be dead.'

Mod examined the remaining beer thinly swishing in the bottom of his glass. 'I could help!' he said. 'You know I'm good at routine inquiries.'

Davies ruminated. 'Anyway, I don't think so. It looks like a long job and it's too far away.'

Moodily Mod drained his glass and said: 'I'll get them' collecting Davies' tankard by the handle.

'I knew I'd timed it right,' approved Davies. 'Coming back on Friday.'

The door opened and a man engulfed by a damp anorak and hood came in. 'Ah, Dangerous,' he said with relief. 'Caught you.' He nodded around the bar. 'Thought you'd be at home.'

'Hello Bunny. You in disguise?' The man pulled down his anorak showering water. 'Have a drink.'

'On duty, mate, so I'll just have a small scotch.'

'Mod,' Davies called towards the bar. 'Single scotch for Bunny.'

'Oh, I'll get it,' said Bunny. 'Your mate's unemployed isn't he.'

'His lifelong occupation,' nodded Davies.

Bunny went towards the bar and Mod's frown softened to a smile as he said he would pay for the round. Mod returned to the table. 'What a civilised copper,' he beamed. 'And what a sense of timing.'

Bunny returned to the table. Davies formally introduced them. Bunny smiled. 'Seen you around,' he said. 'Didn't you used to work up at Cricklewood?'

'Long ago,' admitted Mod trying to look downcast. 'In the days of jobs.'

Davies turned to the policeman. 'What's your problem, Bunny?'

'Well, I know you're not on duty until Monday, Dangerous, but I thought I'd try to catch you.' He looked concerned. 'Are you better, by the way?' He pulled his head back and studied Davies. 'You look all right.'

'Sea air,' explained Davies. 'What's going on?'

Burrows appeared pleased. 'I'm going on a promotion course, Dangerous. Monday. The boss said I had to leave a case with you. Burglary. I put the file on your desk.'

'Where's the job?'

'Power Station Lane.'

'Much taken?'

Burrows grimaced. 'Everything that could be shifted. They even nicked the food from the fridge. Half a pound of cheese ...'

'Could be mice.'

They laughed and Davies bought a round. A discontented fat man came in and leaned his stomach against the bar. Mod whispered to Davies: 'The bloke from the hot-dog stand.'

The man walked heavily towards them: 'Your dog's wrecked my life,' he said. 'He's vicious.'

'Clumsy,' corrected Davies. 'Wrecked your life? That's a bit strong.'

'Well, all right, my catering business.'

'Your hot-dog stand.'

'Yes.'

'How much?'

'Five hundred quid.'

Davies reached for his back pocket: 'Fifty for cash?'

'All right,' said the man. He took it. He decided not to stay for a drink.

Davies said: 'We could go down to the station now, Bunny, if you like.' He turned to Mod: 'If Jemma turns up will you entertain her?'

'With refreshments and wisdom,' offered Mod.

Davies and Burrows went into the drizzle. 'Funny business,' said Burrows from below his anorak hood. 'Everything went. Except the furniture. Even the ruddy newspapers. The *Sun* and *The Times*. Nicked.'

'Could have been that kid Elvis, you know the one,' suggested Davies.

'Why him?'

'He's been half-inching newspapers to start bonfires.' He sniffed against the rain. 'But I can't see him stealing cheese. It's not his sort of crime, Bunny.'

Apart from a swaying drunk singing tenderly and hugging

himself and an old muttering woman, the lobby of the police station was empty. The desk sergeant waved to them.

Davies wished the old lady a good evening. She ceased muttering. 'Hello, Mr Dangerous,' she said looking pleased. 'Will you help to find my cat?'

'Lost it again, have you?' he said.

'Stolen more like it. They take him off to mate him because he's a thoroughbred. When he comes back he looks so shagged out.'

'It's got to stop,' agreed Davies.

'The sergeant said he's going to phone up,' she answered mysteriously. 'But I think I'll go home and see if he's turned up. 'Night, Mr Dangerous.'

Half the known world was quietly batty, thought Davies, not for the first time. He went into the CID office and taking a stray dustpan and brush from his chair, he sat down. Burrows pulled a chair up and they went through the file.

'There's blood on the floor,' observed Davies looking down. 'Either somebody's been stabbed or it's PC Westerman having a nosebleed.'

'He's probably put the cell keys down his back again,' said Burrows.

Two men in suits came through the far door. 'Harvey and Johnson working overtime,' suggested Davies in a low voice.

'Murder inquiry. That Willis girl. They've found her.'

'Hello, Davies. Finished malingering?' asked Detective Superintendent Harvey. He was not a nice man.

'Finished on Monday next, sir. Officially.'

Harvey grunted and the pair went into the glass-fronted office at the far end of the room. 'They've found her?' Davies asked Burrows.

'What's left of her. Buried on Wormwood Scrubs.'

'Somebody who knew the area then.'

Burrows frowned as if he wished he had thought of that. 'Quarter of a mile from the prison,' he said.

'They have exercise runs around the Scrubs,' said Davies. 'Locations like that are liable to stick in a con's memory ...'

'You ought to mention that to Harvey.'

'I never like to,' shrugged Davies. 'He always says he's already thought of it.'

He picked up the file and they went out into the Saturday night again. The lights from the three public houses in the main street glowed like enticements. There was nothing else in the street but wet pavements, shut shops, a few wandering cars, and people shuffling in oddments under the yellow street lights. Burrows was going home. 'Must get my packing done. First thing Monday, I'm off.'

'Good luck, Bunny,' said Davies. He watched the anorak hurry through the rain and turned to face the wet street. They had even closed the bingo hall. The recession, they said. He shook his head. A country must be in a bad way when they closed its bingo halls.

By midnight he was feeling more contented; he was lying in both Jemma's bed and her arms and she was singing to him by the light of the bedside lamp. He opened his eyes. 'What was that?'

'A cradle song,' she told him.

'I don't know where you get them.'

'Mendelssohn,' she said.

He turned on his back and murmured: 'Good sing-song in the pub tonight wasn't it. Don't get many like that these days.' He regarded her carefully. 'I've never before associated you with "I've got a lovely bunch of coconuts".'

She laughed and kissed him. 'I nearly missed it.'

'What did you have to do?'

'I was getting little Valentine settled. I hope. He's gone to his auntie. I'm just praying his crappy mother and crappier father keep out of the way, that's all.'

Her frown melted in the lamplight. 'The choir have got

a musical evening. Not the usual serious stuff ... not *Elijah* or anything ... all sorts. You should come, Dangerous. Valentine is going to sing with me. We're doing "I can feel it all over".'

'They've found the body of that girl, Julie Willis. Remember?' said Davies.

'I heard. Poor kid. Soliciting in Edgware Road, wasn't she.'

'Found her buried on Wormwood Scrubs. What they call a shallow grave.'

She said seriously: 'You could have your own murder case, Dangerous.'

'You've been talking to Mod,' he sighed. 'All he wants is a few days at the seaside. A change of scene and brewery.'

'And I think he's right.'

Davies groaned. 'I *can't*, love. I can't keep going down to Bournemouth and back like a yo-yo. And if the Met found out I'd be thrown out on my ear. After years of endeavour.'

'You'll have to go and find out who stole the cheese then,' she sulked. He eased himself up and kissed her deeply. Her breasts shone in front of him and he touched them with his nose.

'Oh Dangerous,' she sighed. 'What am I going to do with you?'

He grinned quietly at her. 'Do you want me to give you a list?' he said.

In Power Station Lane the cooling towers stood behind the low terraced houses like monstrous chessmen. The towers had always held a fascination for Davies. They reared against the flat industrial sky, their white smoke blowing and drifting, mixing with every sort of Willesden weather. He now smiled at them in respectful recognition.

Mr and Mrs Horace Perryman, who had been robbed of everything that moved, lived in a middle-terrace house called

Safari Villa. It was built of grey-yellow brick with the lantern jaw of a bay window occupying most of the small garden area facing the street.

'Come on in,' said its owner. 'Not that you're going to do any good.'

He was pale and waddling, his stomach stretching the braces he wore to the shape of twin bows, his bedroom slippers flattened; there was stubble on his chin and a wet film on his eye. 'Look at bloody that,' he said as they entered the denuded room.

Mrs Perryman, a person in an overall, was occupying an armchair staring at a blank wall. The impressions of the legs of the missing television set were still imprinted in the carpet. 'She can't believe it's gone,' said the man.

'Can't believe it,' his wife confirmed. She took Davies in with a swift, beady look, as if he might have done the job himself. 'I'd offer you a cup of something, but there's no cups,' she muttered. 'We're drinking from jam jars we are, until the insurance man's been.'

'A thorough job,' observed Davies inadequately as he looked around.

'Locusts,' said the man with a sort of sob. 'All they left is the stuff they couldn't move. They left our bed but they nicked the bedclothes.'

'We've been kipping in our overcoats,' complained the woman. 'Where's the other copper gone? We told him everything before.'

'Detective Constable Burrows?' said Davies. 'He's gone on a course.'

'Very nice,' sneered the woman. 'For him.'

'I hope I will replace him adequately,' muttered Davies.

'I've seen you,' put in the man jabbing his finger. 'Mooching about the streets. I never realised you was a copper.'

'In disguise, I expect,' said Davies. 'Now let's see. I've got this list of stuff that was taken.' He unfolded the piece of paper Burrows had left him and sniffed. 'Anything you would recognise for certain? I mean it might be difficult to recognise a piece of cheddar. Fancy nicking the cheese.'

'Desperate men,' said Mr Perryman.

'And there's your cup,' reminded his wife.

'A cup?' asked Davies arching his eyebrows.

The man regarded him without hope. 'A silver cup,' he said heavily. 'A trophy. I won it at Butlins ...'

Davies opened his notebook. 'So it's got your name on it.'

'No. But it's got Butlins' name on it, ain't it. I won it at Clacton a few years ago.'

'What was it for?'

The man looked as though he preferred not to tell. But his wife said: 'Tap.'

'Tap dancing,' confessed the man. He had gone pink under his stubble. 'I used to do it. And tell jokes.'

Davies quietly glanced at the bulging braces. 'Tap dancing and jokes.'

'Not at the same time,' pointed out the wife. Her tone changed. 'He'd do a bit of a tap then tell a joke, wouldn't you. He was very good.'

'Very good,' confirmed Mr Perryman. 'But the cup was quite small.'

'He came third,' said the woman. Her husband stretched his grimed finger and thumb apart. 'About that size.'

'Ah, that's something anyway,' Davies assured them. 'There can't be many of those.' He regarded each of them carefully. 'And you've no idea who might have cleared you out?'

'If I knew we'd have been around there,' said the man.

'Get the telly back,' put in his wife.

'Emptying the fridge,' said Davies shaking his head.

'Hungry,' said the woman.

'The back door was forced,' said Davies.

'In and out that way,' said Mr Perryman. 'There's an alleyway runs along the backs of the gardens, or what they like to call the gardens, rubbish dumps most of them since this lane went ethnic.'

'We're the only non-ethnics in this terrace,' said his wife.

'Next door?'

'One way Indians, the other Irish,' the man said. 'We count Irish as ethnic. O'Callaghan they're called.'

'The Indians are called Fatti,' said the woman looking at her husband's stomach.

For the rest of the week it rained; iron cold January rain, thick to thin and back to thick again. It seemed it rained all night and then all day. Gutters gurgled, the sky was like a sponge, the earth soggy.

Detective Constable Davies spent the entire time walking the streets, from door to door, showing photographs and reciting a description of Julie Willis, aged sixteen, asking over and over if anyone knew her, or had known her, if they had seen her and when. He was soaked.

An old lady believed he had come as a reply to a prayer. She took him in for a cup of tea, which he had to make because she was so arthritic, and then cried when he had to leave because she had seen nobody for days and nights. He went and bought some groceries for her and telephoned Jemma. But the old lady did not trouble the social services for long before she died.

Nobody said they had seen Julie Willis and nobody wanted to know about her. What was another wandering girl?

On Sunday Davies felt as if his tonsillitis was creeping back. But he still went to the car-boot sale. It could not rain any more; the sky seemed incapable of it; the sun blinked out over the sopping scene. The car-boot sale was near the Welsh Harp, which was as close to the country as Willesden ever got, a green sward around a big lake. The water reflected the washed-out sky.

Davies knew what he was looking for and it was not long before he saw it. 'That's a nice little silver cup,' he told a man standing by an open boot.

'Silver? Ah, you'd be right there,' said the vendor, a perky Irishman with a 1970 Ford. 'You're a man with an eye.'

'For some things,' mentioned Davies picking up the cup. Engraved on the side was: 'Butlins, Clacton, 1974.'

'Good year 1974,' he said.

The Irishman was getting worried. 'For silver was it?' he said eyeing Davies anxiously.

'For Butlins,' said Davies. 'What's your name?'

'Can you give me a reason?'

'The reason is I'm a police officer.'

'O'Callaghan.'

'Where do you live?'

'Power Station Lane. You'll be knowing where that is.'

'I know the house that was done over.' He lifted the cup. 'Where you got this.' The Irishman started to look sideways. 'Now I don't know about this,' he said.

'What did you do with the cheese?'

O'Callaghan looked at him helplessly: 'I ate the cheese,' he said.

Six

On Monday there was a letter for Davies when he got back to Bali Hi in the evening.

'Thought I'd better preserve it,' said Mod.

'What's that mean?' asked Davies taking the envelope. They were in the hall by the raincoats.

'That kid, the one with the sticky eyes, who's supposed to be taming the garden ... Elvis.'

'What about him?'

'He asked the postman if he could help with the delivery. Then he inquired if there were any old letters the postman didn't want.'

Davies looked aghast. 'So he could ...'

'Ignite them,' finished Mod dolefully.

Davies took the letter to his room. He sat on the bed. It was postmarked Bournemouth. Carefully he opened it.

'Dear Mr Dangerous Davies,' it said. He smiled and glanced at the signature. Louisa Dulciman. He read:

> *I am very sorry to pursue you like this after you had so firmly but charmingly declined my offer of an 'unofficial' assignment but there has been a very strange and slightly macabre development* – my husband's teeth have turned up!
>
> *I received a package in this morning's post and the set of false dentures were enclosed – with no note, no explanation. As I write this they are on the table by my bed. I would recognise that grating smile anywhere. Even artificial teeth have a certain life, a certain set angle if you like, and these teeth*

undoubtedly belonged to Vernon Dulciman. I only have to look at them to see the rest of his face form around them. It is most uncanny.

Whatever am I going to do, Mr Davies?

He put the letter down to his lap and stared at the bleak single window of his room. It faced onto the back garden and there was a glow of a bonfire in the evening darkness.

'That's creepy, teeth,' said Jemma that night in the Babe In Arms. She regarded Davies potently. '... Poor old dear. She must be scared out of her wits.'

'So much so,' pointed out Davies tapping the letter, 'that she's got these gnashers sitting at the side of her bed.'

Mod blew out his cheeks and then inhaled dramatically, a sign that his thoughts were deep. 'But it's all the more intriguing, isn't it, Dangerous?' he observed. 'Most, most mysterious.'

Davies turned his eyes from one to the other. Their faces were expectant. 'You two,' he complained. 'You're thinking of endless weekends in sunny Bournemouth, that's all.'

'The fee would ease a few problems,' sniffed Mod.

'Whose?'

Jemma shut her eyes as though to extinguish a thought. Her eyes were so powerful that when she closed them she looked like a different person. 'A poor, elderly lady, getting teeth through the post,' she sighed.

'Stop it, will you,' pleaded Davies. They were all distracted by the approach of a black girl who had come in from the rain, a thin child with eyes and forehead protruding from a coat covering her head. She was wearing a school blazer under her makeshift hood. 'Miss,' she said to Jemma. 'Miss, mum sent me.' She drew a breath and recited: 'Mr Cooldridge is trying to kill Mrs Cooldridge again. Can you come?'

'Paradise Walk,' said Jemma standing up. 'How hard is he trying?'

'Don't know, miss,' said the girl in her north-London voice. 'But 'e's giving it 'is best shot. It's because of Mrs Cooldridge been 'aving it away.'

'As distinct from at home,' muttered Davies. He rose. 'I'll come with you.'

Jemma unconvincingly held up her hand. 'No need. I can handle it.'

'I'll come,' he repeated. 'I've never seen a murder committed.' She glanced gratefully at him. 'Look after the drinks will you,' he said to Mod.

They went out into the drizzle, the young girl clicking along before them on her spindle legs. 'If he kills 'er can I 'ave a look?' she called over her shoulder.

'You can be first,' promised Davies.

Paradise Walk was not paradise, but it was only a walk. They went down a flight of stone steps. Sounds, violent sounds, were issuing through a thin front door. The windows of the tenements opposite were blobbed with silhouetted heads.

'Stay here,' said Davies to Jemma.

'Look, I know them ...'

'I don't think that's going to help.'

A voice from the windows opposite called: 'It's Dangerous! Good ol' Dangerous.'

With them all watching he knocked authoritatively on the door. Silence fell inside. Then came a woman's plaintive howl. The door flew open and the massive Mr Cooldridge was there.

'You!' he bellowed. Like a man with not a moment to lose, he punched wildly at Davies who managed to take most of the blow on his arm. But the force of the assault sent him staggering and, with a last-minute wobble, falling down the next flight of stony steps. He landed at the bottom almost rolled into a ball and groaned.

Jemma charged towards the door. 'Cooldridge, you idiot!' she bellowed. 'Assault on a police officer! You'll go down!'

'Officer?' inquired Cooldridge with surprised mildness. 'Which police officer?'

Ineffectually Jemma pounded the big man on the chest. She pointed down the steps. 'What the hell do you think that is?' Davies was trying to get to his feet.

'Oh sorry,' said Cooldridge genuinely. 'I didn't look. I thought it was that bastard Rufus Ruggley. He what's been romancing my wife.'

It was only an outpatient job this time. Merely examination, x-rays, and something to soothe the bruises. But Davies felt injured. 'I've been ill,' he complained to Jemma when they were waiting to see the doctor. 'I've been getting soaked all the week and that on top of tonsillitis, not to mention the going over I got at the European Friendship Dinner and Dance ...'

'When will it stop?' she asked.

'That's what I ask myself,' he said regarding her with hurt eyes. 'How could he think I was his wife's lover, for God's sake? Rufus is *black.*' He paused and added sorrowfully, 'I'm just black and blue.'

She tried not to smile. She patted him. 'It was so dark, that was the trouble,' she murmured soothingly. 'And he was so out of control he couldn't see properly. He knew Rufus was coming around to straighten things out. Instead he straightened you out. It was very sporting of you not to prefer charges, Dangerous.'

'To allow him to go back to his weeping, forgiving, repentant wife,' groaned Davies. 'I always seem to be piggy in the bloody middle.' He looked seriously at her. 'I feel terrible. I feel really terrible.'

'Have you got any leave owing?'

'Ten days from last year.'

'You'll have to take it,' she said decisively. 'We'll go off somewhere where you can rest.'

His eyes focused her with difficulty. 'Bournemuff?' he croaked.

'Is that Mrs Dulciman?'

'Mr Davies, it's you! I know your voice even now.'

'Oh, yes. Well ...'

'What have you decided, Mr Davies?'

He paused. He was committed now. 'I have some leave owing, so I thought I would ...'

'Take on my case!' She sounded thrilled. 'How wonderful! His teeth are snarling at me right now. Perhaps we will find out what happened to the rest of him.'

'Er ... yes. Well, we can try. One thing, though ...'

'What is that?'

'I appreciate your offer of an advance on the fee ...'

'Half. Is that satisfactory? Two thousand five hundred pounds.'

'Well, I'd rather not, Mrs Dulciman. I have no idea whether I will be able to find the answer to your husband's disappearance. It looks a very complicated case ... so I would be happier if the fee were paid *afterwards*.'

'But ...'

'I think it's the right thing to do,' he insisted. 'I don't even know how much time I can give to it.'

'But you'll be taking a risk,' she pointed out. 'You could be in trouble. Your career could be ruined.'

He laughed. 'No danger of that, Mrs Dulciman. But I will only take the case on that basis. When it's cleared up – if it's cleared up – I get paid.'

In the end Jemma could not go. One of her problem families had rioted. Her car was thus unavailable and so, with a surge of determination, Davies backed the old Vauxhall Vanguard out of the garage and summoned Derry, an oil-streaked young man, to come to the yard and start it. Derry had a guilty conscience. 'Any time, Mr Davies,' he said.

'This crate has to get to Bournemouth,' said Davies.

He might have said Valparaiso. 'That's a long way, Mr Davies,' sniffed Derry. 'In this.'

He muttered and tinkered below the bonnet. 'How many people?' he asked, his voice hollow in the cavity.

'Two men and a dog,' said Davies. Kitty began a low moaning from his bed in the garage. Davies called reassuringly. 'Yes, yes. You're coming. Don't worry.'

Derry eventually emerged and climbed into the threadbare driving seat. To his and Davies' astonishment, he started the engine. 'That's brilliant,' breathed Derry proudly. 'Getting life out of this heap.' He peered at the speedometer. 'It's done eighty thousand.'

'That's the second time around,' admitted Davies.

He gave Derry a fiver. As the boy left Mod arrived. 'We're going to tempt providence, are we?' he frowned.

'It's time she had a little run out,' shrugged Davies. 'We're off as soon as you've packed your silk pyjamas and handmade suits and shirts into your designer luggage.'

'That shouldn't take long,' said Mod. 'We could be in open country, driving south-west by lunchtime. I will navigate.'

'Bournemouth,' read Mod ponderously as they travelled. 'Hampshire. Fine beaches, good amenities. Winter Garden, only four hours from Waterloo, omnibuses to outlying areas. Hotels from three guineas a week.'

'When was that?' asked Davies. Kitty was snoring on the back seat.

'Nineteen thirty-two,' Mod responded turning to the fly-leaf of the guide book. 'It was the only one left. The up-to-date guides had all been stolen. People tend to plan their holidays at this time of the year.'

He folded the book seriously. 'Do you know what else has

been purloined from the library, Dangerous?' he said. 'The hat stand. That fine Victorian piece. The thief simply walked in and carried it off. Nobody saw it go.'

'I'm not surprised,' commented Davies. 'Everybody's snoozing.'

'Studying,' corrected Mod. He sniffed towards the windscreen and narrowed his eyes. 'Bournemouth straight ahead,' he intoned.

'It had better be,' responded Davies. 'We're on the motorway.'

Mod looked discomfited. 'Things change so much,' he grumbled. 'And one tends to become very parochial.'

'When one hasn't been out of Willesden for five years.' Davies was pleased with the car. It sang as though happy to be on the road again, oblivious as its driver to the tooting annoyance of overtaking trucks and coaches.

Basingstoke and Winchester went by. After the Southampton Docks exit the road became dual carriageway across open moorland, the brown and emerald of winter in the New Forest. They turned the car off at the Rufus Stone, where King Rufus was killed by an accidental arrow fired by one of his hunting party. Mod shook his head. 'I still can't accept it, Dangerous,' he said. It was a bright, nearly a spring, day with filtering sunlight through the oaks.

'What's that?' asked Davies who was walking Kitty among the trees.

'An accident,' sighed Mod. 'Why, I ask myself, was the culprit safe in France so swiftly?' He waved a finger. 'The King's death was common knowledge in certain religious quarters, the day *before* it happened.'

'Murder, you reckon,' said Davies as they climbed back into the car. The dog was surveying the trees.

'Most foul,' nodded Mod.

They set off on the journey once more. 'I trust I will be able to assist in the case of Mr Dulciman,' mentioned Mod. 'What a strange name for a start. Literally "a sweet fellow".' He glanced craftily towards Davies. 'What will we do with the fee, the advance?'

'There won't be any fee,' said Davies. 'Not until it's cleared up.'

'No fee?' echoed Mod aghast.

'I told Mrs Dulciman on the phone that I'd only undertake the job on that basis.'

'Expenses ... ?'

'Expenses only. She insisted on that. But no solve, no fee.'

Vernon Dulciman's dentures were placed, as she had described, on the bedside table. Davies found himself involuntarily returning the grimace.

'I have put them there only for your benefit, Mr Davies,' said Mrs Dulciman gently. 'I'm afraid I couldn't have him grinning at me all the time, waking up in the night and being faced with that. It was bad enough when the rest of him was present.'

'You didn't like him very much, Mrs Dulciman.'

'He was a horrible man,' she said without hesitation. A faint pink flush came to her face. 'I'm so glad you changed your mind, Mr Davies. Although I would still be happier if you would accept an advance on the fee now.'

Davies shook his head. She led him into the sitting-room. She had a small suite in the hotel, three rooms and a kitchen. The room overlooked the sea.

She motioned him to a rose-patterned armchair. 'It would be under false pretences,' Davies told her. 'I can't guarantee anything at all. All I can do is try.'

'Who is that large gentleman with you? I saw you both arrive with your dog.' She paused and her silvery head moved forward. 'Your dog is well, I trust?'

'Far too well at times,' Davies sighed. 'He's just wrecked a perfectly good hot-dog stand.'

'And the gentleman? Is he your minder? That's the term isn't it?'

'In this case it isn't,' smiled Davies. 'If anything, I mind him. That's Mod. Mr Modest Lewis. He tries to help.'

'Ah, your Doctor Watson.'

Davies agreed there were similarities. 'Can I see the packaging the teeth came in?' he asked. 'You did keep it?'

'Of course. It *is* a clue!'

She went to a bureau near the door and took out a folded piece of brown paper and a small bow of string. 'There,' she said. 'Exhibit Number One.'

'Sealing wax,' frowned Davies looking at the string. 'You don't see sealing wax much these days.'

'You might around here,' she said. 'In Bournemouth there is much living in the past, you know.'

He unfolded the brown paper on a Pembroke table, then glanced at her anxiously. 'Is this all right, using the table?'

'Of course. Tables are for use. This will still be in excellent condition long after I am gone.'

He returned to spreading the wrapping. 'Been used before,' he said. 'By the look of it. All these creases. Funny to use nice pink sealing wax and scruffy old paper.' He peered at the address.

'I've tried to recognise the handwriting,' she put in. 'It could be disguised of course.'

He grinned and pointed. 'And look at that. They were going to put a sender's name. Here they've written "sender" but then they realised it would not be a good idea. Force of habit, I suppose.'

'Or a further tease,' she suggested.

He nodded. 'Could be.' The string was just string as far as he could see. The name and address was in proper ink, no ball-point or felt pen. The writing was bold and curling. 'Mind if I keep these?' he inquired.

'Of course you may. Would you like the teeth as well?'

Davies glanced through the door into the bedroom where he could clearly see the dentures, clamped, gleaming white. 'Er ... no thanks.' He studied them from a distance. 'How can you be sure they are Mr Dulciman's?' he asked. 'One set of teeth looks more or less the same as another to me.'

She led him once more into the other room. 'I am absolutely certain,' she said firmly. She walked over and picked up the teeth without qualms. Davies felt a shudder. She set them down on the bedside table again, turned the small lamp on them and repeated: 'I know they are his.'

Picking them up she held them at the level of her nose. Fascinated, Davies watched her. 'There,' she said. 'He was three inches taller than I am. From this level it becomes even more clear to me. I can almost see the rest of his face forming, growing around them, and then the rest of his body.'

'Were you that close, very often?' asked Davies.

'Occasionally we confronted each other,' she said with a touch of sadness. 'It had not been an intimate situation for some years.'

'Well, Mrs Dulciman,' said Davies, 'I think that the first move will need to be a full statement, an explanation, of all the circumstances. Background. I will need that.'

'And when would you like to do that? It's one of my bridge nights tonight.'

'You're very keen.'

'Very. There are no half-ways with bridge. You can't take it or leave it. Would you like to come here tomorrow morning, after breakfast, and I'll tell you all I know about Vernon Dulciman and his disappearance. Bring Mr Lewis with you if you wish.'

'Good,' said Davies. 'He can write it down. He has a sort of shorthand he's concocted himself.'

'I shall look forward to it,' she said. 'Ten o'clock, say?'

He was about to leave when he decided to ask. 'Mrs Dulciman, did I see you with a white stick? In the post office last week?'

The pink touch appeared on her cheek again. 'You certainly did. You *are* a good detective, Mr Davies.'

'Thank you. Do you need a white stick? I mean …'

She laughed a silvery laugh. It was a glimpse of what she must have been like when she was young. 'Good gracious no. My friend Sybil Hargreaves, it's hers. She was just in front of me in the post office queue. And you were there too? I didn't see you. She's registered blind you know. I was only holding it for her while she fumbled with her purse.'

'It looked a bit odd,' he said smiling. 'When you charged off after that chap who had left his change. And you still had the white stick.'

Mrs Dulciman hooted. But not loudly. 'I remember! So I did. How odd that must have looked!' She became serious. 'And how very observant of you. I'm always having to pick up her stick for her. I think I carry it more than she does. She leaves it behind and when she needs it she can't find the thing.'

He laughed with her and went towards the door. They shook hands, her thin, veined, gentle hand in his, large and firm. 'I'm so glad you have taken on my little case, Mr Davies,' she said sincerely. 'I knew I was right to ask you and I'm even more sure I was right now.' She smiled. 'What a clever man you are.'

She was waiting for them on the following morning, the coffee made in a shapely pot, a wisp of steam from the spout caught like a cobweb by the sun streaming through the window from the direction of the sea. She was wearing a light-brown silk dress and a delicate gold necklace. Her eyes were bright behind her glasses from which hung a slim, shining cord. Davies was glad that Mod was wearing a tie, even though his shirt was crumpled. She greeted them genially.

'Majestic view,' enthused Mod, going to the window. He spread his arms. 'The great, long sweep of the sea.'

'It's wonderful having it close,' agreed Mrs Dulciman. 'Sometimes when the tide is in and the weather is stormy it seems to come right below the window. It is just like being on an ocean liner but without the ups and downs.'

She was interested in Mod's name: 'Mussorgsky's first name was Modest,' she observed. 'Were you named after him?'

'No, ma'am,' said Mod. 'After Tchaikovsky's brother.'

They sat down. 'How was the bridge?' inquired Davies politely. 'Did you win?'

'I'm afraid not. My partner's thoughts appear to have been somewhere else. That's Mrs Cloudsley-Clive. You may have seen her on the beach hitting bread to the gulls with a tennis racquet.'

Mod's eyebrows rose slightly. 'Yes, I know,' Davies said. 'We've conversed. Novel idea really.'

'She's full of them, Nola,' said Mrs Dulciman. 'When you get on in years people don't mind you being eccentric. In fact, they rather expect it. It's one of the small compensations for such things as liver spots.' She changed the subject quickly. 'How is Kitty this morning?'

'Active earlier,' Davies told her. 'Flat out now.'

'He's in my room and he snores like a grampus,' said Mod.

Mrs Dulciman put her cup on the low, glass table and said: 'Now, to business. The whole story.'

Mod took a rolled school exercise book from his pocket and peered doubtfully at the point of the pencil he produced next. He wet the back of his hand and tried it out. 'Indelible,' he smiled when he looked up.

'Some things are,' observed Mrs Dulciman. 'Now where shall we start?'

Davies said: 'We need to establish the basics, Mrs Dulciman. Your husband's full name was ... ?'

'Vernon Algernon Dulciman,' she recited.

'His age?'

'He was sixty-two when he ... when he disappeared. That was five years ago.' She glanced up. 'Shall I just go on?' she inquired. 'It will save you having to ask questions.'

'Please.'

'We were married twenty-four years ago, this year, 14 June. In London. Caxton Hall. It used to be very fashionable for weddings then.' She had been looking at the backs of her hands but now her eyes came up. 'Not in church because Vernon had been married before,' she smiled. 'He had a past.'

'What was his profession?'

'He had retired. He decided to finish when he was sixty. That's when we came down here. We were quite happy until then. It was this place that changed him. Something here.' She said it quietly and bitterly.

'And what ... was his profession?'

'Oh, yes, sorry. He was a photographer. Quite well known in London at that time. Society weddings and suchlike, social events, comings-out, Ascot. He was very busy during the season. Vernon Dulciman of Mayfair. Does that ring a bell?'

Davies shook his head and Mod looked intently at his exercise book. Slowly his face came up and he shook his head too.

'Quite well known,' she repeated. 'Not a celebrity in the way that these photographers are today. He believed that his place was behind the camera.'

'And you were quite happy together in those days.'

She looked thoughtfully sad. 'Yes, as I told you, it was only when we arrived here that things changed. In London we had a mews house in Kensington, and we had a comfortable life.'

'What prompted Mr Dulciman to retire? Sixty is not very old for a photographer is it.'

'Oh, various reasons. There were difficulties over the lease of the studio, the profession changed. There were all these young men starting up, whipper-snappers he called them, and he had some minor heart trouble. He decided he'd had enough.'

'But you did not buy a house down here or a flat? You lived in this hotel.'

'This was merely meant to be temporary. We were going to look around for somewhere but property at that time went sky-high. Prices were just silly. Our terms here were most reasonable, mine still are. And, when he changed so much, I suddenly could not see any way forward. It was very odd wondering if you had a future with someone to whom you had been married for years. Very strange indeed. It was still in the back of my mind to look around for somewhere, but that's where it stayed. And then ... poof ... he vanished.'

'Could you describe how he went ... as far as you know. Do you remember what happened on the last day he was seen?'

She made a small grimace. 'I recall it perfectly,' she said. 'There had been nothing very exceptional about the day. It was early autumn, September, and the weather was fine. I went to the cinema with a friend in the afternoon. Mrs Freda Gordon, she is one of the ladies in our club that meets here for lunch once a month.'

'The Bournemouth and Boscombe Widows' Luncheon Club,' said Davies.

Mrs Dulciman regarded him with appreciation. 'Exactly,' she smiled. 'Yes, the cinema. Vernon was out the whole day, he often was. He came back in the evening and we had a drink and a sandwich, that's all. Each of us liked to get through that part as quickly as possible. He always had lunch at the Moonlighters Club or somewhere and in the evening he would only have something light. And I have not had much of an appetite for some years. So the arrangement suited me. We had a snack and watched the television news. Then he went out ... out through that door ... Mr Davies ... and I have not seen him from that moment to this. In the proverbial puff of smoke.'

Davies got up and paced to the window. The day had the sheen of spring but he could see a sharp wind riffling the sea and the loose sand. 'Then his shoes were found on the beach,' she said behind him. 'There was no doubt they were his. Expensive brown shoes. London made. He had worn them for years and he used to have them stitched and repaired when necessary. They were always gleaming. He was a fastidious person.'

'The remains found at sea?'

'No one could say for sure,' she sighed. 'It would have made life much simpler for me if they could have been identified. I would not be in this limbo now, unable to prove that I am a widow.'

He paused, then asked: 'Do you have a photograph of your husband?'

As he asked there came a swift knocking at the door and without waiting for an invitation, Mildred's white, round and urgent face appeared. 'Pardon me, Mrs Dulciman.' She transferred her attention to Davies.

'Dangerous ... Mr Davies, your dog is howling.' Her expression tightened. 'He's got the chambermaid in there.'

Davies made for the door with Mod, fumbling with his exercise book, immediately following. Mrs Dulciman said: 'Oh dear.'

They rushed through the hotel and up two flights of stairs towards Mod's door. 'He's stopped,' said Mildred with foreboding. 'I hope he hasn't ... *had* her.'

Mod was trying to find the key. Davies told him to hurry. He located it, unlocked the door and threw it open. Kitty was sitting on the bed licking the chambermaid's face. The girl, a rural-looking blonde, sat blushing. 'Oi think 'e loikes me,' she said.

Davies left Mod to take Kitty for a walk. He returned to Mrs Dulciman's room. She called for him to come in. When he entered he found she was standing facing the window and was looking far out to sea as though expecting a ship. 'The widows used to stare out like this,' she turned smiling a little wistfully. 'Waiting for the fishermen who would never return.'

She sat down and smiled quietly. 'My ship won't come in now, Mr Davies.'

He took the chair opposite her. 'Why is it so important?' he asked firmly. He was glad Mod was not there any longer. '*Why* do you have to know?'

'I told you that I *needed* to know, for my own peace of mind. It's very strange, very strange indeed, not knowing whether or not you are a married woman. I would like to know for certain what happened to my husband. If he went away and is still hiding somewhere I would like to know where and, more importantly perhaps, *why* he did it.' She glanced up carefully, almost primly. 'But you will have ascertained that there is another reason,' she said.

'I thought there might be.'

'Money,' she said simply. 'A lot of money. Goodness knows where he got it, Mr Davies, but it transpired that he had a great deal, all unknown to me. It's tied up in business deposits and I have been refused access to it. Until I can prove that he is dead. Or the statutory seven years have gone by and a court can presume he is dead.'

'If he is not dead and he just vanished to a plan, for whatever reason,' said Davies, 'it's odd that he left so much money behind.'

She nodded. 'I have thought that too,' she said. 'But for all I know he may still be drawing on those assets from wherever he is. His financial arrangements were so complex, a veritable spider's web, all over the place, London and elsewhere. And I have no means of knowing or finding out. Until he is officially declared dead, all that is forbidden territory to me. I would never be able to find out. Two years from now is a long time to someone of my age.' She smiled ruefully. 'A long time and a very short time also, believe me. I must get this matter done. If this money remains where it is and I die in the meantime ... and let me not put too fine a point on it, Mr Davies. I am not only elderly, I have an illness. If it's a race between my illness and my age, then I think the ailment will win.'

Davies said, with the inadequacy of such moments: 'I am sorry to hear that, Mrs Dulciman. I really am.'

She leaned and touched the back of his hand with her frail fingers. 'I am sure you are. You are a very kindly man. I knew that from the start.' A bright look suddenly replaced her introspection. 'Shall we have a sherry?' she suggested. 'It's almost noon and it will cheer us up.'

'Please,' he said. 'A nice sherry would go down a treat.'

She rose and went to a cabinet, selecting two flimsy and finely engraved glasses. 'Do you prefer it dry?'

'Er ... oh yes. Dry please.'

'This is Fonseca seventy-one,' she said. 'I hope you like it.'

He took the slender-stemmed glass in the hand that was more accustomed to holding the thick handle of a beer tankard and assured her that he would.

She sat down again, opposite him, and crossed her slight legs, arranging her lace-trimmed dress carefully. She lifted her glass. 'There,' she said beaming a little. 'That's better.' They smiled and toasted each other.

'They sell a lot of sherry down here,' mentioned Davies remembering the people at the Moonlighters Club.

'Mr Davies, it is warm and it's sweet. Even the dry is sweet, if you understand me. It makes an older person feel ... warm and sweet.' She regarded him apologetically. 'But enough of this. You want to know why I need the money.'

He was about to shake his head and say that it was her private business but she went on: 'I don't. Not for myself. But my husband had a son, Gervais Dulciman, by his first marriage. He is middle-aged now. And more hateful than his father was even in his latter years. He is a cheat and a bully, a thoroughly unpleasant man. He left a sweet, good wife and two children destitute. Went off abroad to some warm beach where he could not be traced. Now he's back, still denying them. She has had to struggle, believe me, and she has done it very bravely.

'Mr Davies, I want her, Anna, to have that money. I want to make sure she has what is her due. If I cannot prove my husband's death and I die in the meantime, as I may well do, then it will drop very nicely and neatly into Gervais Dulciman's lap.' She paused and added: 'The rat.'

Davies felt his eyebrows lift. He concentrated on the sherry. 'I was asking you before we went to sort out the dog ... I was asking if you might have a photograph of your husband,' he said.

'I was about to get it.'

'Sorry about the diversion.'

'That's perfectly all right. This hotel could do with a little livening up sometimes.' She rose and moved towards a small, fine bookcase. She unlocked one of the lower drawers. 'This is where I keep all my secrets,' she smiled looking back at him.

She sorted through the drawer but quickly returned to him holding a photographic folder: 'It's a self-portrait,' she said. 'It was taken some years ago.'

With a small flourish, almost a little ceremony, she opened the folder, and displayed the black-and-white photograph. 'Vernon Dulciman,' she announced. It was like a picture of an old-fashioned film star; handsome regular features, a firm nose, carefully parted hair, thoughtful forehead, and light, slightly amused eyes.

'Artistic and arrogant, one of his friends called him,' she said.

'Who was that?' asked Davies.

She appeared surprised at the question. 'Let me see,' she mused. 'I can't actually remember. A woman I expect.'

'He had a lot of women friends?' he remained looking at the photograph so that he would not have to face her. But she replied easily: 'You imagine right. In the London days there were certainly. But I'm not the jealous type and I was certainly not inclined to spend all day keeping track of him. I had one or two flings myself. Strange to think of it now. But we went home together more or less every night. I was the one he took to Ascot and I wore the diamond bracelet he bought in Aspreys.'

'Have you still got it?'

She flushed. 'No I sold it. I had to sell it. Why do you ask?'

Davies said honestly and a little abashed: 'I don't know. I'm always asking questions for reasons I don't know.'

'Yes. I suppose it's something you would do. Anyway I sold the bracelet. Here in Bournemouth.'

He returned to studying the photograph. It was signed in a flowery script across one corner: 'Vernon Dulciman. Mayfair.'

'That was his normal trade mark, as it were,' she said.

'Even for a self-portrait?'

'It wouldn't be strictly a self-portrait. I mean I cannot imagine him setting a time switch and then rushing to the other side of the studio to pose. He was not that sort. One of his assistants would have done it.'

Davies returned the photograph to her. She looked at it with no particular expression and only briefly before closing the folder with the finality of someone closing a book.

'I'm afraid I have to pry a bit,' said Davies.

'Naturally. I'll tell you anything I can.'

'Not in that way. But I'd like to see any documents he left behind.'

She shrugged. 'He didn't, that's the point.' She walked towards the bookcase again, unlocked the drawer and replaced the photograph. 'There are a few bits and pieces here but very little. You can see them if you like.' She took a small sheaf of papers from the drawer. 'But there is nothing of any note.'

'That's a bit surprising, isn't it?'

'Yes, I was surprised certainly. When we came here he had a whole archive of things. After a life in business you are bound to accumulate aren't you. But there was nothing left. It was as if he had taken them elsewhere.'

'The action of a man running away,' he began.

'Intending to make an escape,' she agreed almost dreamily. 'But I wonder where? Where would he have gone, Mr Davies? Where?'

Seven

As they shuffled along the damp and resounding pavements to the Moonlighters Club to drink their lunch, Mod observed: 'There's some funny characters down here, Dangerous. Very odd.' The wet sea air seemed to have given extra weight to his overcoat. He peered below the dripping brim of a black sou'wester.

'You look like the coxswain of the lifeboat,' said Davies. 'I've never seen you wear a hat before. You don't wear one in Willesden, even in winter.'

'Salt,' muttered Mod his eyes still on his feet. His bootlace had become undone. He decided to leave it. 'This saline sort of rain, drizzle, Bournemouth mist, or whatever you wish, is very bad for the balding scalp.'

'You're not balding,' corrected Davies mildly. 'You're bald.'

'Most observant. But the fact remains that the salt corrodes the pate. Glance around at a few hairless heads down here and see how they have become pitted. I don't wish to spoil my appearance.'

They trudged on. There was an incline towards the club and Mod began to puff. 'There are some funny characters,' he repeated as they gained the top. He stopped to take in breath. 'All this exercise,' he complained.

'Which funny ones in particular?'

'I saw that woman on the beach hitting bread to the seagulls with a tennis bat,' Mod answered. 'The one Mrs Dulciman mentioned.' He commenced walking again. 'She had me throwing the crusts up so that she could whack them as they came down.'

'Mrs Nola Cloudsley-Clive,' nodded Davies. 'She's a lady I'd like to talk to.'

They paused at the foot of the final steps rising to the entrance of the Moonlighters. It afforded a further opportunity to regain breath and for Mod to raise his scattered eyebrows. 'She's a suspect?'

'I have a number of suspects,' corrected Davies. He shrugged. 'Well I have to have, don't I? I've got to start getting a few names together. Any names. You've got to start somewhere.'

Mod conceded the point. 'She could have battered him with her bat, I suppose,' he nodded ponderously. 'She knew him, then?'

'Everybody knew him, the dapper Mr Dulciman,' said Davies. They were at the club door. 'Everybody in here, for a start.'

They went in. Mod, who rarely strayed beyond the Babe In Arms, looked critically around the large, worn, all but empty room. The same couple as Davies had seen last time sat at one end drinking their twin glasses of Amontillado. It could have been the same glasses. Orville, the barman, polishing his counter, greeted them.

'This is Mr Lewis,' introduced Davies. 'Is it ... all right?'

'Of course,' returned Orville genially. 'I'll sign him in. You're a temporary member anyway. I thought you'd gone home.'

'I came back,' said Davies. 'I missed it.'

They had two pints and retreated to a table near the smeared window. After testing the beer Mod inquired quietly: 'What about the old lady?'

Davies was nodding with exaggerated amiability towards the Amontillado couple. They recognised him and raised their tiny glasses, each taking a minute sip.

'What about her?'

'After I'd gone to my duties as police dog handler. Pleasant young chambermaid that.'

Davies said: 'Well, Mrs Dulciman showed me a photograph of Mr Dulciman. I nearly said "the late" Mr Dulciman but it may well be "the absent Mr Dulciman".'

'You think he may have just gone off? Left his shoes in the sea and scarpered. Well, it's been done before. What did he look like?'

'Matinee idol type,' said Davies. 'There are some pictures of him on the wall over there. On our way out we'll have a quiet look at them.'

He drank his beer half-way down the tankard. 'He left no documents behind, or hardly any. Not a passport, nothing. Which sounds like someone who's doing a runner.'

'Why do a runner?' asked Mod.

Davies said: 'He was a ladies man, our Vernon. He may have had a piece of stuff and gone off to Honolulu or Ilfracombe or somewhere. But, on the other hand, he left a lot of money behind. It's all in various accounts and she can't lay her hands on it. That's why she wants to know if he's alive or dead.'

'She needs the dosh,' sniffed Mod.

'Not for herself apparently. The object is to stop a son by a first marriage, Dulciman's that is, getting his hands on it. This bloke is not very popular with Mrs D. She wants the money to go to his impoverished wife and kids.'

'I see. And you think Dulciman was carrying on. I hope it wasn't with the old bat with the bat.'

'There are more reasons for carrying on, as you put it, than the obvious,' pointed out Davies. 'Our Mr Dulciman was a devious gentleman.' Mod went to the bar and with a flourish bought two pints. He asked the barman to have one. To his relief the offer was declined.

'I've never understood why you haven't been more interested in women,' ruminated Davies examining the texture of the ale. 'You admired the chambermaid. The stirrings are obviously there.'

Mod exhaled hugely. 'What woman could I ask to share my regime of study and contemplation?'

'It wouldn't suit everyone,' agreed Davies.

'Celibacy', continued Mod, 'is a reward in itself. Not that even now I don't experience the rumblings of desire in this great body.'

'I've heard the odd rumbling,' acknowledged Davies. He grinned at his friend. 'Well, this afternoon you are going to have the opportunity to begin, or continue with, your sex life. We are going to the tea dance.'

Josef and the Nineveh Six were well into a set of foxtrots. The room was commodious and there were not many dancers, although more were coming in as the waitresses began to serve the tea trays.

'Shall I pour?' inquired Mod primly.

'You've eaten both the eccles cakes,' complained Davies. 'Yes, go on, you pour.'

The two big men were sitting at a dainty table next to a lolling rubber plant and almost as close to the band. The Nineveh Six appeared likely to be reduced to five at any moment for the drummer was doubled up with a coughing fit during the course of which he had poked his own drumstick in his eye. Josef glared, then sighed deeply, and tapped the rhythm with his patent-leather shoe.

They were playing 'I'll See You Again (Whenever Spring Breaks Through Again)'. Two ladies in dresses bursting at the busts cruised by. Although supported by each other's arms they contrived to turn both faces towards Davies and Mod.

'You two should be on the floor,' admonished one.

'Yes, come on. There's never enough men.'

Davies eyed them apologetically. 'We're just drinking our tea,' he said.

'Just had the first sip,' confirmed Mod his eyes lame.

'It will cool off while we're dancing,' said the first of the ladies. 'Up you get, the pair of you!'

The women broke apart like a large tree splitting down the trunk. There was no denying them. Each had chosen her target and now the two men found themselves confronted with the formidably overhanging bosoms topped by glittering eyes. Final desperate protests were pushed aside and Davies and Mod were towed into the dance. The floor was more populated now. Most of the people were middle-aged or elderly, but there was a young couple in pastel shellsuits, ducking and diving, whirling and twirling, and then swooping across the floor with an intricate embroidery of steps.

'Bobby and Mandy Brennan, Southern Champions,' identified Davies' partner with a touch of spite. 'They wind them up like clockwork.' Her dress felt warm and loaded.

Mod's partner clutched him close, like someone pleased with protection. He could feel her heart banging below her ribs. 'Do you come here often?' Her smile was pearly.

'No. No. First time,' he confessed. 'Don't go in for dancing.'

'I can tell that,' she answered her attitude changing. 'Why couldn't you have had a shave? Your chin is like a hedgehog.'

'I'm growing a beard.'

'Why?'

'Disguise.'

She appeared to find this acceptable. When the dance finished he led her gallantly back to her chair as Davies was doing the same with his partner. The two men performed old-fashioned half-bows and then returned across the floor. 'Didn't like yours,' muttered Mod.

'Nor me,' agreed Davies. 'Like pushing a bag of damp washing.'

Mod poured the tea. His hand was shaking. 'I don't really see where this is getting us, Dangerous.' He surveyed the room. 'No booze and not a decent-looking woman in the place.'

Davies was looking over his teacup towards the door. 'Now, this is where it's getting us,' he mentioned. 'Look who's come in.'

Mildred, wearing a big denim dress, was standing looking around the room. Mod peered at her. 'Well, she's younger but not much thinner,' he said morosely.

'She's the receptionist at the hotel,' said Davies. 'Didn't you recognise her?'

'Ah, right. Well I only saw the top half of her when I went in. Wonder what she's doing here?'

'It's not for the band,' said Davies.

He stood up and brushed cake crumbs from his front. The Nineveh Six had started a wheezy waltz, a favourite because there were twitters of approval, and the floor began to fill. Davies walked around the edge of the dancers and lightly tapped Mildred on her fleshy shoulder. She was looking the other way and she turned suddenly and flushed when she saw who it was.

'Waltz?' invited Davies with another little bow.

'Love to,' she said.

They shuffled into the revolve of the other dancers. 'What are you doing here?' she asked carefully.

'Basking in the social scene,' said Davies. 'And what about you?'

'Looking for someone,' she answered. Her frowning face came around to him. 'Anyone.'

'Oh, I see. Well, it must get a bit lonely for a young person in the afternoons.'

They were dancing awkwardly; she was not much better than him. 'Not only the afternoons,' she corrected. 'There's young people around. Students and plenty on the dole. They come down from the north, Liverpool especially, because they get some idea that it's warm down here.'

'The warm south,' agreed Davies. He was aware that other dancers were looking at them. 'It's because we keep barging into them,' Mildred whispered. 'They like to do all the silly steps. Sod them, I say.'

He grimaced. 'This is the best I can manage,' he confessed. 'Do you want to sit down?'

'Oh, no.' The words were almost urgent. 'We're all right.' She surveyed the dancers. 'Silly old farts.'

'You don't mix with the younger people then?'

'There's a pub I go to sometimes. But, generally speaking I haven't got that much in common. I'm not studying anything and I've got a steady job, so I haven't got a lot going for me.' She looked almost sulky. 'And I'm big,' she said.

'And lovely,' he said kindly. She smiled her thanks and said: 'I had a boyfriend once. Well, a fiancé more or less. He was a soldier. But he's dead.'

Davies was shocked. He stopped dancing and regarded her with sympathy. 'That's rotten luck,' he said.

'Bloody rotten,' she said.

'Was it ... on active service ... ?'

'Sort of. Salisbury Plain. He went on a survival course and he didn't survive. Broke his leg and was lying out there for God knows how long. Got pneumonia, exposure, the lot. He died. He was only twenty-five.' She glanced at him. 'We can sit down if you like.'

Davies took her plump elbow. 'Come and meet Mod,' he said. 'Have a cup of tea. We'll get an extra cup.'

She walked slowly with him. 'Mod,' she repeated reflectively. 'MOD. Ministry of Defence.'

They reached the table. Mod, who had been looking around like someone expecting an ambush, was relieved to see them. 'I remember when you checked in,' said Mildred shaking hands.

'I only saw the top half of you,' Mod told her cheerfully.

'Is the rest any better?' she asked.

'You're lovely,' put in Davies. 'All of you.'

Quietly Mod said: 'Dangerous. There's that old thing who hits bread with the tennis bat. I think she's seen me.' His voice dropped. 'God, she's coming to get me.'

The angular Mrs Cloudsley-Clive approached the table with a craggy smile. 'Ladies' invitation, Mr Lewis,' she smiled. 'Hello, Mildred.' She looked at Davies. 'And it's *you.*

How nice to see you again. Come, Mr Lewis. Let's hit the floor.'

Mod started to protest but she had a grip on him. She almost levered him from his seat and setting him in front of her, and placing his hands in the correct position, she led him into the dance. 'I can't do this one,' they heard him plead haplessly. 'I don't know how.'

'She's determined,' observed Davies.

'They are,' answered Mildred with a grimness that surprised him. Her face had hardened. 'When they get on in years,' she said, 'they do things you'd never dream. It's like as if they don't care any more. They're up against it. Time. And nothing gets in their way, Dangerous.'

She said she would not have tea but she took the remaining cake, a cream horn, and ate it fiercely. Then she wiped the crumbs from her mouth and said: 'You're trying to find out what happened to Mr Dulciman, aren't you.'

He nodded. 'Who told you?'

'No need for anyone to tell,' she said shaking her head. 'Anything like that gets around like wildfire. I bet everyone in this room knows.'

He sighed and then said: 'Maybe that's not a bad thing. Maybe they'll start telling me things.'

'They won't be able to wait,' she forecast. 'They'll all have their opinions and their theories.'

'Some of them might even know something,' he said. He looked into her plump face. 'What did you think of him? I might as well start with an objective opinion.'

Her expression filled up. 'Oh, Dangerous, he was a nasty man. The most terrible turd, if you'll forgive the expression.'

After four days Mod shamefacedly announced that he was homesick. Davies feigned surprise. It was a bright morning, the window full of sky and the sky full of wind; waves sharp and white at their fringes were running exuberantly up the slope of the beach. 'You're homesick?' Davies whispered. 'Homesick for Willesden?'

'I can't explain it,' agreed Mod. His face dropped and then he turned and swept his hand across the view from the window. 'But all this fresh air has been too much for me. I miss the Babe In Arms, Dangerous. I miss the library, my studies …' He regarded his companion realising the next excuse would be dumbfounding. 'I even miss our lodgings and … everybody …' His hooded eyes rose guiltily. '… Even Mrs Fulljames.'

Davies patted his arm as one might to a dear one who had revealed a dread illness. 'Well … it's what you are used to, I suppose. Bournemouth has been a bit of a culture shock.'

Mod anticipated the next question: 'I'll take the dog back, if you like. He'll be all right with me.'

'On the train?'

'Kitty will be fine. He'll behave,' repeated Mod without much conviction.

Davies saw them off in a taxi and turned a little disconsolately back into the hotel. 'They've gone off then,' said Bertie the hall porter. 'But you're staying.'

Everyone knew why he was staying. Bertie said: 'I've got all the newspaper reports if you want to see them. About Mr Dulciman.'

Davies felt as though a small, difficult door had been half opened. 'You have?' he said. 'I'd certainly like to.'

'I'll show you now,' offered Bertie. 'It's my elevenses. I'll make you a cup of coffee and leave you with the stuff if you like. It might help.'

Curiously, he locked the door of his glass booth although there was nothing in it. 'I kept them out of interest,' he explained. 'Nothing like that ever happened to this hotel before.' Surveying the lobby, mundane and musty, he let out a brief snort. 'They're always talking about getting some publicity for the place. Well they certainly got it then.'

Bertie unhurriedly led the way down the stairs to his basement room. 'It was just the local papers at first, then the big boys got interested. Television, everything. When his shoes turned up they showed them on one of those *Crimewatch* programmes.'

'Strange about his shoes,' observed Davies.

'It was too. I took them to the police.'

Davies stopped on the stairs. '*You* found them, Bertie?'

Bertie carried on to the bottom before turning around. 'Well, in a way. Some lad came up and said he'd found them down by the sea. He was only a kid but he was bright and he thought he should tell somebody, although he didn't know anything about Mr Dulciman.'

'A pair of shoes floating about looked suspicious,' nodded Davies. 'One shoe and he would not have bothered. And you handed them to the police.'

The porter unlocked his door and let Davies into the crammed room. It seemed he locked and unlocked everything possible. 'I showed them to Mrs Dulciman first,' he said. 'But I recognised them anyway. Good shoes from London. Brown and stitched. I would have known them anywhere. When I showed them to Mrs Dulciman she told me I should take them to the police.'

'She was upset, I expect.'

The statement seemed to give Bertie doubts. 'No, not really. She just sort of stared at them and said they were his all right.'

He sat Davies in one of the heavy old armchairs, then went to his alcove kitchen and began to prepare the coffee. Davies heard the kettle whistle and Bertie's head appeared around the door. 'She did a funny thing, though,' he said. 'Now I come to think of it.'

'What was that?'

The porter walked into the room rubbing his chin. 'I was holding the shoes and she just reached over and tied the laces up. They were hanging loose, soaking wet, and she tied them in bows. Then she said to me: "You must take them to the police, please Bertie." '

'People do odd things at moments of stress,' Davies called to him when he had returned to pour the coffee. 'All sorts of little bits and pieces come out of the backs of their minds.'

'I know a woman', said Bertie, 'who knew her husband was dying when he told her to treat herself to a tumble drier.'

They sat drinking the coffee. Davies said: 'What did you think of Mr Dulciman, Bertie? Just between ourselves.'

The porter pursed his lips as if making an effort to be fair. 'Not my type, Mr Davies,' he said decisively. 'Very arrogant, used to strut around. Never walked, strutted. Aloof is the word.'

Davies said: 'What did he *do*? What did he occupy himself with? He was out most of the time, I gather.'

Bertie ruminated again. 'Well, he was supposed to be retired. But, you're right, sir, he was not indoors very much. He went out every day more or less regular.'

'Do you have any idea, any theory, of what might have happened to him?'

The porter seemed surprised but pleased to be consulted. 'I've given it a bit of thought, of course. Those shoes, Mr Davies. Why only the shoes, I ask myself? If you're going to walk out to sea to end it all, why take your shoes off? You drown better with them on.'

'You think they were just left purposely to make it look as if that was what had happened?'

'That's what I think,' confirmed Bertie. 'Those remains that was brought out of the bay, they wasn't him. I never have believed that.' He hesitated as if undecided whether to go on.

'Go on,' encouraged Davies.

Bertie appeared troubled. 'I've never said this to anyone,' he went on slowly, 'because it didn't seem to have any direct connection to the case. No bearing. And I didn't want to upset Mrs Dulciman.'

'But …'

'But I saw him one day about six months before he vanished. He was with a youngish woman in a car. Up on the East Cliff.'

'Ah, a love affair.'

'I don't know about that. The woman was crying her eyes out.'

On Friday evening Jemma telephoned, sounding pleased. 'Dangerous, I'm coming down to see you tomorrow. We can have a whole weekend together.'

'How many of us?' he inquired cautiously.

'By myself,' she promised. 'We can take Kitty for walks on the beach. Mod can come back to Willesden if he likes. I bet he'll be getting homesick by now.'

There was a silence. Then Davies spelled it out: 'Mod should be back there now. And Kitty. They left here two days ago, Jemma.'

There was another pause. 'That's ominous,' she said eventually in a low voice. 'They've not arrived back here yet. I was in the Babe In Arms at lunchtime. I had to go to court. Nobody mentioned that they had seen Mod. We were laughing about him and the dog and the hot-dog stand, so somebody would have said if he had been in.'

'They might be at the house,' Davies said. 'Mod may be ill. Perhaps he had a hard journey with the dog.'

'He could be in shock.'

'Well, you know Kitty leads him a dance. They were all right when they left here. I put them in a taxi for the station. I'd better call the house.'

'I'd do it from here,' said Jemma dubiously, 'but you never know who is going to pick up the phone. It might be Doris.'

'I don't particularly want to ring either,' he said, 'if I ask for Mod and he hasn't turned up. And I certainly don't want Doris answering either.'

Jemma said: 'Listen, I'm going to Kensal Rise to sort out a

kid who keeps running away. I'll go in the Babe and ask. I'll call you in about an hour. Stay in the hotel.'

'I won't move,' he said. 'I'm very worried about my dog.' He went thoughtfully into the bar. He had already eaten dinner and now he sat reading the local evening paper but he could not get engrossed in complaints about exorbitant local car-parking fines nor that another late goal had beaten The Cherries. It was almost an hour before she rang. Mildred came into the bar and made a mime of holding a telephone to her ear. He followed and went into the booth in the lobby.

'He's back,' said Jemma breathlessly. 'What a relief. He's just got here apparently.'

'Is Kitty all right?'

'As far as I can gather Kitty is fine. But Mod is on the edge of a breakdown. I haven't seen him myself so I don't know what it's all about. I've left a message at the Babe that he's to call you as soon as he comes in.' Her voice softened. 'Don't worry, Dangerous. It's nothing serious, I'm sure.'

'They've taken two days on a four-hour trip,' pointed out Davies.

'Well, they're okay. I'll be down there by lunchtime tomorrow. How are you getting on with Mr Dulciman?'

'He's still missing, presumed drowned,' said Davies. 'But a few niblets are turning up. I'll tell you when I see you. I'll wait for Mod to ring.'

It was a further hour. He went into the residents' lounge and alone watched moodily as a Los Angeles television cop, with a choice of blondes, cleared up a multiple murder between coition and commercials.

He had left the door ajar and Mildred's pale round face appeared once more. 'Phone, Dangerous,' she said. She stood still and regarded him. 'You look ever so solitary there.'

He smiled at her. 'These cops on television,' he said. 'They're either picking up clues or picking up women.'

'It's not like that, is it,' she said.

'Not for me,' he smiled. He patted her on the broad arm as he went towards the phone. 'Is Jemma coming down?' she asked suddenly. She knew because she had been eavesdropping.

'Tomorrow.'

'Oh. That will be nice.'

He went into the box. 'Oh God, Dangerous, have I had a bloody time,' Mod moaned.

'Where have you been with my dog?' asked Davies evenly.

'Where *haven't* I been. Dangerous, don't ever ask me to take that animal anywhere again. There's a limit.'

'I'll make a note. Is he all right?'

'He's fine. Sleeping like a child. It's me that's shattered.'

'Sorry about that,' said Davies composed now that he knew Kitty was safe. 'What happened?' He sensed Mod's hesitation. 'I'll pay you for the phone.'

'Oh, thanks. This call is the least of the expenses.'

'Where have you been?'

'Hinton Admiral, Southampton, Southampton Airport,' Mod recited. 'Winchester, Lower Dever, Basingstoke, Frensham Ponds ...'

'You were supposed to go straight home. Waterloo, Willesden.'

'You should have told your dog,' grumbled Mod. 'We got on the train and everything was all right for a while, and then he tried to get this man's chocolate bar. He was on the man's lap, for Christ's sake. There was a terrible scene. The bloke called the guard, the guard was knocked over by Kitty, and we were ejected at this wayside station, Hinton Admiral ...'

'Kitty was just excited,' said Davies mildly. 'Being on a train.'

'The excitement spread,' returned Mod dolefully. 'We waited an hour and just to keep him occupied, I took him for a bit of a walk. That was when he had this woman off her bike.'

'That's not good news,' conceded Davies.

'Fortunately she was a dog lover and once we'd got her and the bike more or less straightened out she went off without a lot of fuss.'

'Then?'

'Then we got on a local train to Southampton and that was without incident. Kitty must have been tired by all the activity and he went to sleep. We changed at Southampton but by the time we got to Southampton Airport Station he had peed all over the floor. I just crept off the train, making out I hadn't noticed. But it was swirling around people's feet and the smell ...'

'He's a dog,' Davies pointed out. 'Dogs' water does smell.'

'By this time I'm wanting to pee myself but I couldn't go because I would have had to take the dog. Next time, try and get something a bit smaller, like an Afghan.'

'I'll bear it in mind,' promised Davies. 'What next?'

'Things took a turn for the worse,' intoned Mod. 'Serious. He got off the lead and ran from the platform and went tearing through the damned airport which is right next door to the station. He got over the fence and went haring across the grass and then the runway ...'

'Oh, shit,' breathed Davies.

'Oh shit, indeed,' echoed Mod. 'Police, security men, ground staff, women, the lot, chasing him. They wanted to shoot him, Dangerous.'

'They didn't!'

'They did. And by this time I was all for it, believe me.'

'I left that dumb animal in your care,' accused Davies.

'I stopped them shooting him in the end. Somehow I managed to get on a bus. I didn't care where it was going. I just wanted to get away from the place. Kitty seemed to like the bus but it only goes to this village, Lower Dever, and that's as far as it went. It was dark by now. It had taken all day. I'd had nothing to eat ...'

Davies sniffed down the phone. 'Neither had Kitty.'

'He had the man's chocolate bar.'

'Well, that's not much. What did you do then?'

'Found a bed-and-breakfast place. I was a jangling wreck by this time. There were some children in the house and they loved the dog. He let them pull him all over the place. I very nearly left him there.'

'I'm glad you didn't,' said Davies sombrely.

'Well, I was seriously thinking of it,' admitted Mod. 'Just asking them to keep him while I went and got help. Bed and breakfast was ten pounds fifty, by the way. And two pounds for Kitty.'

'Did he get breakfast?'

'He got breakfast.'

'What then?'

He heard Mod sigh. 'Then I decided to get a bus to Basingstoke. Kitty seemed to be more at home on buses.'

'And he was?'

'Loved it. Loved it so much he tried to get on top of the driver. He very nearly caused a crash, Dangerous. The man was trying to control the bus and the dog was all over him. It was horrifying.'

'So you got off the bus.'

'They made us. I tried walking the rest of the way to Basingstoke but it was miles. My feet wouldn't go any further. Kitty was tugging me along. Then this chap, farmer type, stopped and we got a lift. Kitty was in the back seat with me and he leaned over and took a bite out of the man's hat. So that was that.'

Davies said: 'Don't tell me any more. I've heard enough. You're back there now anyway.'

'Yes. We got back,' replied Mod dolefully. 'It cost another night's bed and breakfast. Then I thought I would try the train again. But he howled ... Jesus, have you heard your dog howl?'

'Of course I've heard him howl,' muttered Davies testily. 'He does it when he's upset.'

'He upset the whole train. Howling, loud as anything and he wouldn't stop. The train was packed as well. It was terrible. They put us in the guard's van. And I had to sit with him while he howled.'

At the end of the conversation Davies put the phone down and dejectedly went back into the lounge where the Los Angeles cops had now been replaced on television by an alternative comedy show. He sat glumly watching. He did not detect Mildred's approach until she sat heavily on the arm of the chair.

'Funny?' she asked nodding at the screen.

'Not that I can tell,' he answered.

'What's the matter?'

'Oh, that Mod ... he's taken two days and two nights to get back to home with Kitty ...'

'What did he do, walk?'

'Quite a lot of the way, apparently.'

'Tell me ... no, wait. Do you want a drink, Dangerous?' she whispered. 'I've got the keys.'

'Oh all right, love.' His eyes came up. 'I'll have a scotch.'

'Good idea. So will I.'

She went to the shuttered bar and unlocked the door. She emerged with a bottle of whisky and two glasses.

'You drink scotch?' he asked as she returned to the chair. She sat on the arm and he took the bottle from her and opened it. 'Put this on my bill,' he said.

'I will *not,*' she said firmly. 'Let them pay for it. I do enough unpaid overtime.' She regarded the level of whisky in her glass. They toasted each other with two mutters and two tight smiles. She made a face as she took the first swallow of raw scotch and shook her hair fiercely as though to dispatch it. 'Went down the wrong way,' she excused herself. She pushed her shoulder against him in the chair. He leaned forward and turned the television off. 'Tell me about Mod and Kitty,' she said.

He began to laugh silently, shaking his head, and recounted the journey as Mod had described it. She began to giggle. She took the bottle from him and poured two more big drinks.

When the story was ended she said sadly: 'I really enjoyed that, Dangerous. It was funnier than the box. It was like listening to a story. My dad used to tell me stories.'

'What happened?' asked Davies.

'At home? Oh, everything changed. It all seems all right, then you hear them rowing in the middle of the night. I thought they were going to kill each other. It frightened the hell out of me. He didn't used to drink much but then he started and he made up for lost time. She pushed him down some stairs in the end. Concrete stairs.'

'What happened?' said Davies again.

'It killed him.'

'Christ.'

'Exactly, Christ. I was only about twelve and I had to tell the police that I saw him fall down when he was drunk. To back up my mother. Fat lot of good it did me. A couple of months and she was off with some man, and I've never seen her from that day to this.'

'You haven't had a lot of luck, have you,' he said. 'What with your boyfriend ...'

'No I haven't, I suppose. When I say "it's just my luck" I really mean it.'

He thought she was going to cry. 'I think it's time we put the bottle away,' he observed. She handed it to him and replacing the stopper, he took it back to the bar, taking the keys from her and locking the door. Then he guided her towards the lobby.

The ungainly young woman and the shambling man climbed the stairs together. When they reached the landing she turned and pressed herself to him, her eyes full of tears. 'You'll be all right, will you,' he said.

'Take me to my room, Dangerous. Just to the door.'

They went stumbling along a corridor until they reached a low white door at the end. 'This is it,' she said. 'Home sweet home. I have to duck my head to get in.'

She pursed her lips and he kissed her gently and briefly.

'Good night, Mildred,' he said.

'And you, Dangerous. Good night. I hope you find Mr Dulciman. Or what's happened to him.'

Eight

Bournemouth looked very nearly like Rio that night; almost balmy despite the time of the year, the sea luminous and docile, the land lit with lamps.

They sat at the window in the Ritz Hotel, on the clifftop. 'I've never seen you look so smart, Dangerous,' she whispered.

'Oh, I can when I want. I'm a chameleon I am. Most of the gear I normally wear is disguise, you know. I can't walk around Willesden done up like a dog's dinner.'

They were drinking coffee and brandy. 'Why did she tell you, do you think?' she asked.

'Mildred. About her old man being pushed down the stairs? I don't know. Maybe she's been waiting for years to tell someone. Telling that lie to the police is probably the only thing she's done in her life that she's quietly proud of.'

Jemma regarded him quizzically. 'In an unofficial way she *was* telling the police – you. Owning up.'

He grunted. 'Could have been. But her secret is safe with me. I've got enough on my plate without going back years to find out whether some woman in Newcastle pushed her drunken mate down some stairs. And then disappeared forever.'

'At least you're getting to know your way around,' she said. 'Any ideas?'

'None of them valid,' he said. 'I thought the press cuttings might have something.'

'Fancy the porter keeping them.'

'Biggest thing that's ever happened in *his* life.'

'That hotel seems full of people that nothing ever happened to.'

'Well, something happened to Mr Dulciman, that's for certain. Mildred hated him. Bitterly. He was not a popular guest. He was arrogant, overbearing, all the things that people *really* hate.'

'What about Mrs Dulciman. Did she really hate him?'

'They were all right, she says, when they lived in London, but the minute they came down to Bournemouth, his attitude changed. They ended up despising each other.'

'Something happened.'

'Seems like it. It may have been he was upset at getting on in life, having to retire. People do, you know.'

'It's like they're blaming someone for their age,' she agreed.

'Or there could have been another reason. He seems to have had a mistress, perhaps more than one. There were dealings with women. About six months before he disappeared Bertie saw him in a car on the East Cliff with a young woman. She was crying.'

He picked up the menu and almost absently began to make a list, writing between the courses. 'Vernon Dulciman, aged sixty-two. Last seen on the evening of 14 September 1988. He was at the Moonlighters Club, one of his regular haunts. He had left the hotel about eight. Phineas, the man with the one leg, told me Dulciman left the club about eleven to go home. He had been drinking scotch. Mrs Dulciman did not wait up for him. She went to bed and she did not miss him until the next morning. And she never saw him again.'

'And his shoes were found by the edge of the sea.'

'By a boy. He brought them up to Bertie.'

'Oh?'

'Yes. Oh? Who the boy was, God knows. His name does not appear in the press stories nor the report of the inquest. Bertie says he doesn't know and the only place I'm going to find out is in the police records.'

'And that's difficult.'

'Very. I can hardly breeze up to the Bournemouth police station and say I'm a copper from London doing a bit of moonlighting. I could get it easily enough on the computer from the Willesden end, making out it was part of something I was doing officially. But if someone wanted to know why, I'd be right in it.'

'They *were* Mr Dulciman's shoes?'

'No doubt about that. But there's a question mark against the bones in the sea. It was a male roughly the same size, but it could have been anyone. And he had no teeth, the one sure way of identifying people who turn up in bits and pieces.'

He looked at the list he had written on the menu, glanced guiltily towards the head waiter, and folded it into his inside pocket.

'But who could have sent his teeth to Mrs Dulciman?'

'How about Mrs Dulciman?' he replied simply.

'You're joking!'

'Why did they suddenly turn up now? He's been gone five years and suddenly his gnashers appear.'

'Just when you have been told about the case.'

'And decided *not* to take it on. It was either someone who was aware that she had asked me to get involved and sent them as a sort of tease. ... A variation on the old returning-to-the-scene-of-the-crime syndrome. ... Or it was the old lady herself sent them to give me an extra push, to make me decide to take the thing on in spite of myself. The package was stuck with sealing wax.'

'The sort of thing she might use.'

'Or others in this town. It's a sealing wax sort of place.'

'Where do we go from here?'

'Back to bed, hopefully,' he smiled at her.

She touched his wrist. 'Apart from that. With the case.'

'Well, I'd like to have a chat with Nola Cloudsley-Clive, the dotty one who bashes bread to the gulls with a tennis racquet. But first I think I ought to see if I can get something out of a man named Pengelly, the private detective Mrs Dulciman got on the case.'

'You won't be able to tell him you're a police officer,' she said. 'All you can say is you're another private investigator.'

'Or a relative with a bee in his bonnet,' added Davies. 'We'll have to see which one he will swallow.'

The address in the telephone directory for Pengelly Associates, Private Investigators, was in Boscombe. On the Monday afternoon, after Jemma had gone, Davies got a bus and alighted at Shore Road. On one side of the street were old-fashioned houses and shops, descending to the beach. On the other, brick streets led one from another. The entrance was at the side of a greengrocer's shop. He went up some dusty stairs to a bare landing upon which was a single door paned with opaque glass. There was a blocked-off window with a dead and dust-covered mouse on the sill. There was a plaque with 'Pengelly Associates' written on it beneath which was pinned a square of paper. 'Apply upstairs.'

Davies retraced his slow steps along the landing and climbed another flight. There was an identical door, this time with a light behind it. Hearts were painted on the middle panel and the words 'Goodtime Escort Agency'.

He was still taking this in when the door opened and a sly-looking man in his thirties came out. He was almost bald, a few strands of hair stretched across his head. His eyes were red. 'Did you want something?'

'Er ... yes ... an escort,' said Davies.

'It's done on the phone,' responded the man but less aggressively. 'Customers don't call here.'

'I didn't know. I haven't done this before.'

'You'd better come in,' said the man cautiously. He still looked disgruntled but reluctant to turn down business. 'I'm Pengelly,' he said and led the way into the tight, grubby office, with a desk and a chair, with another chair piled with yellowing newspapers. He looked at Davies as if wondering whether he was worth a seat but then put the newspapers on the floor. 'Have a chair,' he said. He sat behind the desk. His back was to the grimy window framing the grimy sky. Illumination came from a single overhung light. On the wall was a calendar showing February and a naked woman on a donkey. 'You need an escort,' said the man.

'I'd *like* one,' answered Davies.

The man seemed to miss the point. 'Clients usually phone,' he said again. 'We don't have personal callers.'

'Well, I didn't know whether it would be all right,' Davies told him. 'Whether I'd be acceptable.'

The man looked up with a slow scorn. 'They're not particular, most of my girls,' he said. 'As long as you've got the dosh.'

'What does it cost?' said Davies. 'I've got no idea.'

The man studied him. 'A hundred quid,' he said firmly. 'For that you get to go home with the girl as well.'

'As well as what?'

'Well, *escorting* her. Taking her out somewhere. Then you can have the other. You'll have to give the girl something extra.'

'It works out expensive.'

'It depends what you want,' replied the man impatiently. He seemed to think that Davies might change his mind so he quickly pulled a plastic photo album onto the desk and opened it. He swivelled it around so that Davies could view the photographs. Two young girls were on the first page, no more than eighteen, Davies thought, plain girls trying to look coquettish, their mouths open and their tongues slightly protruding. 'They do a double,' said the man.

'Twice as much?' asked Davies.

'We could come to some arrangement,' said Pengelly. 'I could knock a bit off, I expect. I'm not greedy.'

'But I'd have to take *both* of them out?' queried Davies.

'Of course. You have to *talk* to them.'

He turned the page. An older woman in a swollen sweater smiled artificially. 'More your type, perhaps,' suggested the man. 'She's been around for a while but she's good. And she's very presentable, clean to look at.'

Davies sniffed. 'Any more?'

'I can't be here all day,' complained the man. 'I'm busy.'

Davies said mildly, 'I expect you are. All right. The last one, the one who looks clean. She'll do.'

There was another moment's hesitation. 'It's just for yourself is it?' asked the man.

'Yes, just me.'

'Right, I'll give her a buzz.' He looked up. 'Would you mind stepping outside for a minute.'

'I'll take a bit of a walk,' said Davies. 'I'll come back in ten minutes.'

'I'd like a deposit.'

'I'll be back.'

'It's usual to have a deposit. Before I ring her. Fifty quid will do, then you give the other fifty to her. And whatever you decide for ... extras.'

Davies counted out five ten-pound notes. The man checked them carefully and, saying 'ten minutes' picked up the telephone.

'Do I get a receipt?' inquired Davies.

Pengelly banged the phone down and impatiently scribbled a receipt on a blank-paged pad. He handed it to Davies with ill grace. 'I've built this business on trust,' he said.

'I'm sure you have,' said Davies. 'You have to, don't you. I'll be back.'

He went down the stairs past the detective agency landing. Swiftly he went to the door and tried it but it was locked. He glanced at the dead mouse on the sill, picked it up by the tail and put it in his pocket. He descended the second flight of stairs and went into the chill afternoon.

'It's just for yourself, is it?' he mimicked below his breath. 'What's he think it is, a regimental reunion?'

It took five minutes to walk to the beach and he had five minutes to sit on a bench, looking at the sad sea, almost invisible in the afternoon gloom. The signature on the receipt was F. Pengelly. He stood up and retraced his way to the stairs and the office.

The man called for him to go in as he knocked. He was just replacing the phone. 'She's very busy,' he said.

'She would be,' acknowledged Davies. 'Looking like that.'

Pengelly laughed, a sour, short laugh. 'She'll meet you outside the Ritz at eight.'

'The Ritz Hotel?' said Davies apprehensively.

'The Ritz Cinema.'

'She wants to go to the pictures?'

Pengelly looked at him in amazement and scorn. He produced a pink comb and began combing the thin hairs on his bald head feverishly. 'That's where's she'll *meet* you,' he said. 'You won't get away with taking her to the pictures, mate. She'll want to go somewhere nice. Michelle is very particular.'

'Ah, it's Michelle is it. Right. I'm glad she's particular. I am too.'

The Ritz was showing *Postcards from the Edge.* Davies smiled at Michelle and said awkwardly: 'Good picture for Bournemouth.'

She looked puzzled. Plump mouth pursed, she looked first at the sign above the cinema and then unsurely at Davies. 'You're not an intellectual, are you?' she asked warily.

'Me? God, no. I just thought it was a bit appropriate. Seaside, postcards, edge of the cliff, sort of thing ...'

'Oh yes, now I see,' she nodded with another glance at the sign. 'I wouldn't have thought of that.'

Pengelly had not exaggerated when he said she had been around. She tried to smooth herself down, rubbing her pink, ringed hands down the sagging artificial furs of her coat, and blinking her made-up eyes. 'Had a hard night last night,' she explained adding frankly: 'And I can't take them at my age. Not like I did once. I wouldn't have come out at all but Pengelly said you were desperate.'

They were walking along the damp pavement, lit by the windows of the closed shops, towards the taxi rank. Davies winced at the information but made no comment. 'What would you like to do?'

Her frown did not improve her appearance. 'Dinner,' she said emphatically. 'I'm always taken to dinner. Nearly.'

'Anywhere special?'

'Pengelly said you wanted to take me to the Ritz. That's why I came out.'

Glumly Davies nodded. He might have known. They got into the taxi and drove around the one-way system and then east. She pushed herself familiarly against him in the back seat and he smiled at her in the merciful dimness.

It was not far. Davies helped her out of the taxi and paid the driver. She was wearing red stockings on fat, though shapely, legs. Ten years before she had probably looked passable.

The doorman studied Davies oddly, confirming his worst fears. Two nights before he had gone there with Jemma, beautiful and black, who could not help but be noticed, and now he was back with a big, blousy blonde. ''Evening,' he said as blithely as he could.

'Good evening sir,' returned the doorman and with a short stare towards Michelle, 'Good evening madam.'

'I'm going to like this,' confided Michelle as she took Davies' arm going into the foyer. 'When he said it was the Ritz I thought it was one of his lies. I've never set foot here before.'

Davies was not surprised but he did not say so. 'I thought it was your stamping ground,' he said.

'Me? No, I generally stamp elsewhere.'

He led her into the bar. She had a double vodka and tonic followed quickly by another. Over the third he told her he had been ill and was considering early retirement from his job as a tax inspector. His wife had gone off with a man from Ipswich.

'Fancy you being in Income Tax,' she said, adding slyly: 'Oh, you just *wait* till later. I'll get my own back on you.' She puffed her cheeks in a plump giggle and looked around with an almost winsome expression. 'It really is nice,' she said. 'Thank you for bringing me, Lol.'

He had told her his name was Laurence Durrell. He had failed to prepare an alias and had panicked when she asked. Laurence Durrell was in his head because a man had been reading one of Durrell's novels in the hotel lounge that afternoon. He mentioned to Davies that Bournemouth seemed, in a roundabout way, like Alexandria, and Davies politely agreed there were resemblances although he did not understand the reference. Durrell remained in his mind, however, and it was the first name that came to him when he introduced himself to Michelle. She showed no sign of recognition. He thought she was probably not a reader.

She was, however, an eater, ploughing with increasing enjoyment through the most expensive dishes on the menu. 'Are you sure you haven't run off with all our tax money, Lol?' she smirked through a mouthful of partridge. She drank in quantity, becoming flushed and content.

The restaurant manager had joined those looking surreptitiously askance at Davies, once his attention had been drawn to their table by the waiter who had recognised him from the Saturday, a sighting confirmed by the wine waiter. He was obviously being listed as a man who enjoyed women in variety. Inwardly he groaned. He consoled himself by pouring the wine extravagantly.

'The bloke what I had last night wanted to pretend we was in a tent,' she confided leaning towards him with a surge of scent.

'Really? I bet you get some funny requests, don't you.' He was aware that his words were slipping. She giggled fruitily. 'Funny's not in it, Lol. How about another one, had me done up in a ballet dancer's gear? *Me,* in my state. And he brought his own kit. He was an opera and ballet maniac apparently and had fantasies about some of those big fat opera ladies dancing in the ballet. It was exhausting believe me. I was knackered. But he paid up all right and went away happy. That's the main thing.' She regarded him with dampish eyes.

'I like to send them away happy,' she told him throatily. She pressed his crotch below the table.

Startled, he poured some more wine. It wobbled into the glass. This was the end of the second bottle and she was already eyeing the liqueur trolley. He thought he had better get to business before it was too late for both of them. 'What's that bloke Pengelly like?' he asked.

'Odd bugger. Don't care for him at all,' she said. 'But I need him. It's not fun walking the streets at this time of the year.'

'You don't ... er walk the ... ?'

'Streets? No. Well, not if I can help it. But there's a recession on and it's hit our industry like everything else.' She leaned over, heavily confiding: 'I saw one girl I know standing in front of a shop window the other night in Southampton. There was a sale on and they had notices on the window, saying: "Big reductions", "Half price goods" and I thought to myself, that's just about right.' She looked at him pessimistically. 'The bank rate goes up and down but we don't.'

She made a visible effort to cheer herself. She put her arms around herself, across her large bust, and gave herself a hug. 'This is nice,' she repeated. 'I'm really enjoying this.'

Davies tried pouring some more wine but the bottle was empty. The wine waiter approached with a swift step. 'I'll pour it shall I, sir.'

'It's finished,' said Davies examining the waiter accusingly as if he might have drunk it.

The man frowned and examined the bottle: 'So it is, sir,' he confirmed. 'I wonder where that went. Would you like another?'

'No, no,' interrupted Michelle her mouth bulging crème caramel. 'No, let's have a few brandies, shall we precious.' Davies glanced around to see who she was calling precious but realised it was him. While he was hesitating she said to the waiter: 'Bring the bottle.'

'Any *particular* bottle, madam?' he inquired.

'Anything but Greek or Spanish,' she told him swallowing

her mouthful. She turned to Davies. 'Makes me sick as a bloody rat that Spanish brandy. Too much of it does anyway.'

He brought the bottle and Davies asked for cheese and biscuits. 'That's right,' encouraged Michelle. 'Bit of oozy cheese would go down a treat.'

Over their first two brandies he returned to his question. He would have to ask it now, before it was too late. 'What about Pengelly?' he said rolling his eyes at her. 'You were going to tell me about him.'

She blew a spray of cream-cracker crumbs over the table-cloth. 'I shouldn't use language like this ... not in here, Lol,' she said when she had composed herself. 'But he's a real bumhole. That's the only word for him ... bumhole.'

'You don't like him,' he said inadequately. They were now the only people left in the restaurant. The waiters were grouped at the end of the room observing them.

'He runs that racket, that so-called agency of his ... well, it's *crinimal....*' She tried to correct herself but only said '... *crinimal* ...' again. She managed a compromise. 'It's not right,' she said.

'In what way?'

'It's highway robbery. Percentages for this and that. We're just slaves.' To his consternation she began to weep, the tears rolling down her coloured cheeks. 'I'm just a sex slave,' she snivelled. Davies glanced towards the waiters and hurriedly said: 'Don't cry' and wiped her cheek with his napkin. She smiled bravely into his face and said: 'You're so nice, Lol. I've really fallen for you.'

Davies tried to appear pleased. She then volunteered the opening for which he had been so clumsily manoeuvring. 'He's a detective as well, that Pengelly,' she sniffed. 'Well, by his reckoning he is.'

'Good God, a detective!' He shook his head: 'Who would have guessed.'

'Pengelly Associates, although who's going to associate with him I don't truly know.' She sniggered wetly. 'Have you seen him comb across his bald patch trying to arrange about three bloody hairs?'

'Fancy him being a detective,' repeated Davies as if he could not get over the information. 'A private eye.'

'Well he doesn't do anything very big. Sometimes he hardly does anything at all. The office is closed mostly. All he does is a few divorce things, you know spying on people.' She sniggered with satisfaction. 'The bugger fell out of a tree once,' she said.

The brandy bottle was diminishing at the same rate as the wine before it. Davies was struggling to keep his senses together. Michelle was lounging over him now, her powerful scent going up his nose, but her speech, to his admiration, remained lucid.

'I had to do an investigation down here once,' he said carefully. 'Inland Revenue sent me down. Big Income Tax fraud.'

'Oh,' she said. 'I forgot that's what you do.' She became alarmed. 'You're not after me, are you?'

'Not in that way,' he returned roguishly. He was quite proud of the lie and the way she smiled as she accepted it. 'No, I came down, a few years ago this was, to take a look at a man who was on the fiddle in a big way. What was his name? He had a funny name ... Ah yes, Dulciman. That's an odd ...'

'Dulciman?' she said immediately with a start. 'Well, I knew about *him.*'

'You did?'

'Everybody did around Bournemouth. He was a pig. Another one. He disappeared you know.'

'Did he? Disappeared? No, I didn't know that. You mean he left the area on the quiet.'

'Left the earth,' she corrected grimly. 'They reckon he walked into to sea like the MPs do. Left his shoes on the side and just walked in.'

'Fancy that,' he said shaking his head. 'Only his shoes left.'

She shook her head. 'I could never understand why he *left*

them. Except as a sort of signing-off, you know what I mean, like goodbye.'

Davies acknowledged the point. 'So they reckon he did for himself, did he?'

'Or did he?' she queried. 'I don't know, Lol. Anything could have happened to him. Pengelly might know more than he tells.'

'He was involved with the case, Pengelly?'

'Oh, I'm sure. I heard him talking on the phone one day.'

The head waiter padded towards them. 'Would you like your bill, sir? I happen to have it here.'

Davies blinked. 'That's a stroke of luck. Are we keeping you up?' He took the bill and preferring not to look at it handed over his Visa card. Michelle said she was going to the ladies. While she was away the man brought back the docket to be signed. Michelle's heady aroma was still present. 'Sir was in here on Saturday,' said the head waiter. His eyes remained unblinking.

'You're right,' said Davies as if the man had won a quiz. He nodded sideways to the empty seat with the debris from Michelle's meal scattered across the table. She had spilled her brandy as she had attempted to get up. 'I thought I'd give the old lady a treat.' He nodded sideways again. 'My mother.'

'Oh, quite sir.' Michelle was returning, waltzing heavily between the tables. The waiter said: 'Thank you Mr Davies ...'

Davies glanced up in alarm but she had not heard. He picked up his credit card. 'Durrell,' he corrected.

'Oh, yes. Of course. Thank you Mr Durrell.'

The sleepy cloakroom attendant helped Davies on with his coat, assisting him to remain upright as he did so. Michelle had collected her tatty fur but had insisted on putting it on herself and had done so back to front. As they went out towards the main exit, where the attendant eyed them apprehensively, Davies put his hand into his overcoat pocket and detected an unfamiliar object which he privately extracted.

It was small and soft and turned out to be the dusty dead mouse which he had picked up from the window sill in the corridor outside Pengelly Associates. He blinked at it in the palm of his hand and then, with a guilty glance around the lobby, placed it on a brass tray on an ornamental table. 'Sleep well,' he said quietly to the mouse. It looked out of context there, however, and he imagined it would end up inside a dustpan so he retrieved it and put it back in his pocket.

In the taxi he showed Michelle the mouse. She produced a bottle of brandy, half-full, from the folds of her coat and two glasses from the pockets. 'Couldn't get the proper glasses,' she apologised hazily.

'Where did you obtain it?' he asked squeezing his eyes at the bottle.

'It ... Well, it sort of became attached to my hand as we left. They won't miss it. We paid enough.' She cuddled fatly into him. She had told the driver where to go and the lit and deserted streets travelled by the window. Davies tried to focus on the buildings but could not. 'You're ever so nice, you know,' she confided. 'For an Income Tax man.' Her big face worked reflectively. 'Fancy her going off with a bloke from Ipswich.'

'Who was that?' he inquired blearily.

'Your wife.'

'Oh, *that* Ipswich,' he said trying to remember the lie in full. 'Well, she was no loss. I'm better off on my own.'

'You are *now*,' she gushed. 'Now you're with *me*.' She attempted to embrace him extravagantly but with a soft groan slid onto the floor of the cab. She was too heavy to retrieve so she remained propped up there for the rest of the journey. He poured the brandy lavishly and handed it down to her.

He had no idea where they arrived. Nor did he remember its location later. It was a house in a terrace with a single light behind curtains in the bedroom. 'I always have that on,' she mumbled as they stumbled towards the door and she attempted to lift her keys from her handbag. 'It lights me home.'

The contents of the bag spilled on the pavement and they spent some minutes trying to collect them. A lipstick had rolled into the gutter and was the last object to be found. A window opened along the street and a voice shouted for them to shut up since he had to go to work.

'It's a bleeding change then!' Michelle bellowed back uncompromisingly. She completed restoring her goods to her handbag. 'Hasn't done a stroke in years, that bugger,' she said.

With difficulty they got inside the house but the stairs proved too much for them. They sat at the bottom finishing the brandy and that is where Davies awoke with the first insipid daylight seeping through the fanlight above the door. Michelle was not with him and he decided to remember her as he had last seen her. Groaning, quietly he unhinged his limbs. God, he felt terrible. The empty brandy bottle was standing upright on the stairs, half-way up, with the two glasses set neatly beside it. He still had all his money so he put fifty pounds under the bottle and made for the door. Some things were not meant to last.

It was late afternoon before he thought he could face the outdoors. He crept out of the hotel and went again to the Goodtime Escort Agency. He could see Pengelly moving behind the glass door. He walked in.

'It's usual to knock,' said Pengelly.

'Sorry,' returned Davies. 'I didn't mean to frighten you.'

Pengelly pondered this and then said: 'Wasn't she any good? You can't have your money back. We have no facilities for dealing with complaints.'

Davies waved a dismissive hand. 'Don't worry. I'm hardly likely to take it to the Ombudsman, am I?'

'What did you want then?'

'A bit of a chat really.' Davies smiled a broken smile. He moved the newspapers from the chair and pulling it sideways sat on it in front of the desk. 'Oh,' sniffed Pengelly. He produced his comb and began to run it nervously through his sparse hair. 'What about?'

'You're not really Cornish, are you?' said Davies as though it were the most important thing. He leaned towards Pengelly. 'You don't sound all that Cornish.'

'It's a trade name,' the man answered sulkily. 'I'm from London.'

'Go on!' enthused Davies. 'So am I!'

Pengelly regarded him narrowly and nervously. Fumbling he put his comb away. 'There's a few million of us,' he suggested.

'But only two in this room,' returned Davies.

'What do you want?'

'A natter really.' He hesitated but then produced his warrant card. 'Metropolitan Police.'

'So?'

'I wanted to question you about Vernon Dulciman. You did some private eyeing didn't you. I just wanted to ask you what you'd got.'

Pengelly appeared astonished. 'Dulciman?' he said. 'What the hell ...?' He became firmer. 'What's got the Met involved?' he asked. 'Or am I not allowed to know? I can find out. I have my contacts.'

Davies' heart sank but he said: 'I bet you have. This is a private investigation. On behalf of Mrs Dulciman.'

Pengelly laughed outright. 'Private? Off your own bat, is it? Christ, that's bloody rich, and you come in here flashing your warrant card. Maybe I ought to have a quick word with my contacts. You'd be right in it then.'

'Not as much as you'd be in it, Pengelly,' said Davies with a little menace. 'Pimping. Living on the earnings ...'

'Michelle ...'

'Michelle nothing. I've got plenty on you without her telling me. And unless I get your co-operation I'm going to shop you. And if you try to take it out on her I'll shop you as well.'

'What's your wife going to say?' suggested Pengelly but unconvincingly.

'My wife went off with a man from Ipswich,' recited Davies.

Pengelly sighed. 'All right. Dulciman's no skin off my nose.' He went to one of the desk drawers and took out a key. 'The file's downstairs. In the other office.'

Again he nervously combed his sparse hair. They went to the door. He locked it after them and led the way down the bare stairs. While he unlocked the door of the lower office, Davies, on a thought, felt in his pocket and produced the dead mouse. 'I brought your mouse back,' he said replacing it on the dusty window sill.

'Thanks. I wondered where it had gone,' sniffed Pengelly. He led the way into the office which was almost identical with the room upstairs except that the naked-girl-and-donkey calendar was replaced by one showing a London policeman directing traffic. Davies studied it: 'Makes me feel homesick,' he said.

'That's why I keep it,' said Pengelly. He sat at the desk and opened a drawer. 'There's not a lot,' he said taking out a file. 'He just vanished. End of story.' He made to pass the file across to Davies but then withdrew it.

'You're on a fee,' he said. 'You wouldn't be doing it out of the goodness of your heart.'

'Believe it or not that's how it stands at the moment. I get a fee at the end. When I've found him or whatever.'

'The old girl's crafty,' said Pengelly.

'It was my suggestion,' said Davies. 'No solve, no money.'

Pengelly had become more assured, as if he had feared much worse. He turned the pages in the folder. 'When you get paid, if you get paid, I'd like a little cut for this,' he suggested. 'I had to do all the work.'

'Two hundred quid,' said Davies as if he had thought it through.

'How about three? I can get the official police report as well.'

'Three,' agreed Davies. 'Where is it?'

'My auntie's looking after it,' said Pengelly. Davies felt his eyebrows rise. 'I don't like things lying around here.' He smiled craftily. 'Make it five hundred.'

'I'm already blackmailing you,' Davies pointed out. 'Don't try my patience.'

'My auntie might have thrown it away,' said Pengelly combing his bald pate again. 'She's always throwing things away. She's houseproud.'

'Another hundred then,' said Davies.

'Now.'

'When I get the file.'

'She only lives around the corner. I could go and get it,' said Pengelly. He was confident now, confident and relieved. He handed the first file across and rose from the desk. 'I'll leave you with this while I go,' he said. 'You can sit and read it here. There's nothing special kept in this office.' He rose. 'I hope auntie's in,' he said. 'Do you need to go to the bank?'

'I've got enough,' said Davies.

Pengelly laughed unpleasantly. 'Michelle left you with some then?'

'I've no complaints,' said Davies.

Nine

Nola Cloudsley-Clive changed her location in the afternoons. She was poised at the fringe of the ornamental lake propelling bread to the ducks. Davies, who had been directed to where she might be by Phineas at the Moonlighters, approached as she was in mid-serve. He waited until she had projected a crust some distance into the water and the gratified recipients had gathered quacking around it.

'Play much tennis?' Davies inquired.

She was startled but smiled a little when she saw who it was. 'Good practice for the summer months,' she said. 'It keeps me out of trouble, I get some fresh air, and the ducks and the gulls look forward to it. They're not half so enthusiastic if you merely toss the bread into the water.' She gave him a swift sizing up. 'Here, you have a go,' she said offering the racquet. 'You'd better take your overcoat off. You won't get any distance.'

Davies climbed out of his overcoat. He took the racquet and made a show of testing its weight, the tautness of the strings with the nub of his hand, and its feel in the swing. She handed a piece of bread to him and he tossed it into the grey afternoon bringing the racquet down ferociously and completely missing the crust which fell at his feet. Nola Cloudsley-Clive and the assembled ducks watched with scarcely concealed disdain.

'Timing's a bit out,' said Davies embarrassed.

'Completely out,' she corrected. She eyed him like an already lost cause. 'You don't appear to have any co-ordination. I thought policemen were supposed to be co-ordinated.'

Davies looked shamefaced. 'Well, we are. But not with tennis bats.'

She appeared sorry that she had been critical. 'Here, have another go,' she encouraged. 'This time bring the racquet around in a loop.' She looked him over again. 'And your stance is wrong.' Tentatively she leaned forward and moved him into position, getting her long, elderly hands around his knees to put his legs into place and then revolving his arm with the racquet. 'There, at least you're facing the right way,' she said surveying him again. 'Now first look towards your target and measure the distance.'

Davies peered into the middle of the lake. The ducks were floating impatiently, looking at him and uttering short, grumbling quacks. 'All right, all right,' he called to them. 'Here it comes.' He threw the bread into the air and brought the racquet over in a loop striking the crust with the metal edge and splattering it over his head and Nola's face.

'No, no,' she said crossly. 'No, you're not doing it *at all* well.' She peered at the paper bag on the ground. 'And we're running out,' she said.

With a sigh Davies handed the racquet back to her. She took it silently and retrieved some bread from the bag. The ducks were visibly encouraged. They nudged against each other and quacked in anticipation. She struck the missile accurately among them and followed it with another. They squabbled and thrashed the choppy water.

'There,' she said with finality. 'That's sufficient for today.' She picked up the bread bag, screwed it up, and, as if to give Davies something to do, handed it to him. He put it in his pocket. They began to walk away from the lake. 'You realised that I am a policeman then,' he said.

She looked surprised. She was very tall, taller than he was, and her face inclined towards him. 'But, of course. *Everybody* knows that. All the ladies from the luncheon club.'

'Ah, yes.'

'You were sitting in the dining-room at the last Sunday lunch, weren't you,' she said.

'That's right. It all looked very jolly.'

'Widows are often jolly,' she said. 'They have to be.'

'All the husbands passed on?' he said.

'A bad habit husbands seem to have,' she said. 'You were with that lady of colour and that little boy.'

'That's right,' agreed Davies steadily. 'She is ... my ... girlfriend.'

'Very beautiful,' she said with a little sadness. 'Some of them.'

They had reached the stone gate of the park. 'I live just along here,' she said. 'That damp-looking block of flats.'

'Oh.' He hesitated. 'I wanted to ask you some questions about Mr Dulciman. Do you mind?'

'I don't,' she said firmly. 'My hope is that you do not succeed in finding him. He's better lost – or dead. Come and have a cup of tea.'

He walked alongside her past the row of flats, four storeys high. 'Not very opulent but at least they have a view of the ducks,' she said. 'I used to live at Branksome.'

They went up a flight of damp concrete steps and she unlocked the front door. 'Very exciting having a gentleman to tea,' she said.

'Even one who can't serve for toffee,' he added.

She laughed quite girlishly. They had walked into the tight hall. The walls were covered with tennis photographs, teams, tournaments, trophies.

'You've always been keen,' he said examining them.

She sat him on a chintz settee in the old-fashioned room. There were gilt mirrors, tapestries, a painting of Poole Harbour, bits and knick-knacks of a former life. She said: 'Keen, yes.' Her tone dropped. 'People around here really *believe* I played at Wimbledon. These sort of rumours get about in a place like Bournemouth. There are so many people with nothing to do.' She put her finger dramatically to her lips. 'And I've never tried to scotch it,' she said. 'Why should I? It gives me some sort of distinction.' She went into the kitchenette. He could see her through the partly open door putting the kettle on. 'I expect you spend most of your life dealing with stories, Mr Davies,' she called.

'Some of them highly unlikely,' he answered.

She came back and looked through the damp window at the darkening park. 'My story has not had much of an ending.'

'What is your story?' he encouraged gently.

'Oh, a sort of comfortable life. Nice husband and house. You could see the whole sweep of the sea. Then Trevor died and I had to sell up.'

She returned to the kitchen as the kettle whistled. She brought the tea in on a tortoiseshell tray with a silver sugar bowl and milk jug and a plate of neat biscuits. There was a woollen cosy on the pot.

'So you want to know about Vernon Dulciman?' she said, pouring the tea.

'That would be interesting.'

She poured the milk and handed the delicate cup and saucer to him, inviting him to help himself to sugar. 'As I told you, I hope you never find him, Mr Davies. At least, alive. He is better wherever he is. Anywhere other than here.'

'Mr Dulciman does not appear to have been all that popular,' mentioned Davies. 'I haven't heard anyone say a good word about him yet.'

'Oh, but I *loved* him,' she said dramatically. Her faded blue eyes moistened. 'Deeply.'

'And what happened to change that?'

She did not answer at once. Then she said decisively: 'He used to come here and we would go to bed for the whole afternoon. He would go to sleep and snore and I would lie awake listening to the children in the park and think how lucky I was to find love again. You see, I had known him before.'

'And where was that, in London?'

'Exactly. Almost thirty years ago. When he had his own teeth. Before he married ... And afterwards.'

'And you renewed the association in Bournemouth?'

'Yes,' she replied a little wistfully. 'I was doing my silly thing hitting bread to the seagulls when someone called. I was in mid-serve as it were. There he was, larger than life than ever. Except that his teeth were more pronounced.'

She took her teacup to the window and stared out over the darkening park.

'I thought it was so wonderful at the time but later I came to regret it bitterly. Vernon Dulciman was someone who should have remained firmly in my past. I was, and still am, a foolish woman.'

Davies looked into his tea-leaves. There was a strainer on the tray but she had not used it. 'What did he do?' he inquired as gently as he could.

'He robbed me,' she sighed simply. 'Robbed me rotten. Twelve thousand and thirty-four pounds. Every penny I had. He even made me cash in my little Premium Bonds.'

Davies regarded her with solid sympathy: 'What was his story?'

'A business opportunity. Something not to be missed. I believed him, naturally. He could make me believe. He said that we would go away together. ...' She sighed. 'I wonder how many times that hollow promise has been made? I wonder how many times he made it?' Davies thought she was going to cry and hoped she would not. 'Acapulco,' she mumbled. 'Mexico.'

'And he took off with your money.'

'Took off is the right phrase, Mr Davies. He positively flew out of here. I looked from the window. Even now I can see him bouncing along the street.'

'You saw him after that?'

'Oh yes. Most certainly. Eventually I made inquiries about the business deal and regarding my money but he seemed to have forgotten all about it. He brushed me aside. It was very painful. Humiliating. Naturally I would not, could not, tell anyone else. But then it emerged that he had taken money from others. Silly women like myself. Goodness knows how much.'

She turned slowly still holding the teacup like a small third prize. 'And that's all I can tell you,' she muttered sadly. 'Except that he vanished.'

Davies had spent an hour picking his way through the files handed to him by Pengelly. Back in his room at the hotel he examined them again. Nothing noted by the police nor by Pengelly himself added anything to his knowledge of the case. The end of Vernon Dulciman, if it was his end, remained as unsolved as ever. Pessimistically, he began to suspect that it might well remain so.

That day he had to leave. He took a reflective lunch in the hotel dining-room. Mildred came in and sat with him while he drank his coffee. 'When will you be back?' she asked. Then anxiously: 'You will be back, won't you?'

'Oh, I will,' he assured her. 'Of course. I've got to get this done if I can. Lots of people haven't told me the truth. Or not all the truth.'

'Am I one of them?'

'You could be.'

'Don't you believe it,' she said enigmatically. She leaned forward confidingly. 'Next time you come down we'll go for a walk. Up along the coast. It's terrific up there. Dangerous. You can see for miles.'

He smiled and said: 'We'll wait for a nice day.'

'I always am,' she said.

Davies finished his coffee. He had only drunk a solitary light ale with his lunch. He went to see Mrs Dulciman before he left.

'Any clues?' she asked. She was almost jovial. She told him she had won the club bridge championship the previous evening, and he congratulated her. There was *something* he wanted to ask her but he did not know what it was; something simple that had been touching his thoughts without making itself clear. In the end he shook hands with the old lady and she gave him a scented kiss on the cheek.

'I look forward to seeing you again soon,' she said.

'I'll be down as soon as I can,' he promised. 'In the meantime if there is anything I want to ask, anything that occurs to me, is it all right if I telephone you?'

'Yes, of course,' she said. 'I do hope you think of something soon.'

'So do I,' he said.

He had the gravest fears that the car would not reach home. On the motorway he twice had to pull it onto the hard shoulder to give it a rest and by the time they reached Hammersmith it was groaning. With a sense of achievement he finally coaxed it into the yard behind Bali Hi where it stood wheezing on the cobbles.

It was strange how he felt at home there. He looked around the walls, bleak and enclosing, with the yellow light of a street lamp leaning over from outside. 'Davies of the Yard is back!' he called out. Davies of the Yard; his favourite joke against himself. He would never know Scotland Yard, only this one. Within the garage Kitty began to howl extravagantly, the noise echoing in the enclosed space.

'All right, all right Kitty,' he called soothingly. 'Your master is home!'

The howls turned to snarls as Kitty recognised his voice. He scraped open the door with caution. The dog remained in his deep basket, apparently deciding that a full frontal attack was not fully warranted.

'Your master is back,' repeated Davies in honeyed tones: the dog's reply was a low growl. Nevertheless, and to his surprise and gratification, the animal appeared grudgingly pleased to see him. He allowed Davies to pat his tousled hair and to smile into his face.

'Has that Mod been looking after you properly?' he

questioned the dog, risking giving his hair another ruffle. 'We've got to get you ready for Crufts.'

Outside he met Mod stumbling across the yard with Kitty's dinner bowl. 'Good old Mod,' he encouraged. 'No trouble, I take it.'

Mod's customary pallor was thickened by the edgy hue of the street lamp. His chins folded doubtfully. 'I don't truthfully know, Dangerous,' he said.

'Why is that? Why don't you know?' frowned Davies.

Mod paused, the bowl hanging heavily in his hands. 'He's been up to something, but I don't really know what.' He looked as though Davies really ought to be told. 'He had a pair of ladies' knickers in his basket two evenings ago,' he reported sorrowfully. 'God knows who they belonged to.' Further seriousness creased his face. 'Mrs Fulljames, perhaps. I have no means of identifying them.'

'That's serious,' muttered Dangerous. 'Nicking knickers. Has he still got them?'

'No. I managed to remove the evidence.' His head shook miserably. 'They're in my room.'

'Maybe she won't miss them,' said Davies without much hope. 'That's if they are hers.'

'They could belong to your wife.'

'I have no means of knowing that.'

He waited until Mod had given Kitty the food and returned with him to the house.

'Did you solve the big mystery?' asked Mod.

'Not a clue,' said Davies. They wandered into the house.

'There's a new lodger,' said Mod. 'A Mr Leadbetter. To do with gas.'

When they were seated at the evening table Mrs Fulljames introduced Mr Leadbetter, who looked as if he would rather be elsewhere. 'I don't know why they've sent me,' he grumbled over the brown windsor. 'There was them on the list before me.'

'Oh, but you'll like it down here in London,' enthused Mrs

Fulljames as though they were dining in Mayfair. 'There's so much to do and see.'

'February', intoned the newcomer, 'is the time for a man to be in his garden. There was others above me on the list for detachment. There must have been a reason.'

Doris, who had been quietly spooning her soup from one edge of the dish to the other, watching the brown waves, said to Davies: 'Mr Leadbetter takes the *Country Landowner*.' She addressed the remark as someone pointing out how well a man could do if he really tried. Mod turned his big, questioning head towards Davies and Minnie Banks emitted an envious squeak. 'Oh, it must be lovely to have land.'

'How many acres do you have?' asked Davies wondering how much the gas board paid its employees.

Mr Leadbetter looked around the faces as though cornered. 'Only the garden and a bit of allotment,' he confessed decently. 'I get the *Country Landowner* from my sister who works in a dentist's.' He surveyed the company again. 'She gets me *Autocar* and *Our Pets* and sometimes *The Lady* as well if the other cleaner don't grab it first.' He swallowed heavily and a riverlet of soup came from the corner of his mouth. Then like a man who has decided to come completely clean said: 'I like to read the small ads. Especially the Lonely Hearts.'

'Lonely Hearts in *Our Pets* must be worth reading,' mentioned Mod heavily. 'Man with big dog would like to meet lady with small pus ... cat.'

'Is Mr Leadbetter a single gentleman?' inquired Minnie looking directly at the person in question. She blushed narrowly down the edges of her nose. Doris extended her chin, reinforcing the inquiry. Mrs Fulljames paused in collecting the plates, balancing them like a poor circus act. Mr Leadbetter said: 'Mr Leadbetter is not but wishes it was otherwise. Mrs Leadbetter is not exciting enough for me.'

When they were walking down to the Babe In Arms, Mod said: 'I wonder what Mrs Leadbetter's like then?'

They had a couple of pints and then walked to Jemma's

flat. Davies was carrying the police file and Pengelly's file on Vernon Dulciman. They spread it on Jemma's kitchen table while she brought them sandwiches. After dinner at Bali Hi they were frequently hungry.

'There he is,' said Davies putting Mrs Dulciman's photograph of her husband in the centre of the papers. 'The man they love to hate. Vernon Algernon Dulciman, aged sixty-odd, five feet ten inches, of upright almost military bearing, although he may have slumped when nobody was looking, small moustache, false teeth, bright challenging eyes, and lots of charm when he needed it, like when he wanted money. Walked out of his wife's life on 14 September 1988, never to be seen again.'

'Who sent his teeth?' asked Mod.

Davies said: 'Well ...' Jemma glanced at him. 'The consensus of opinion about the teeth is that Mrs Dulciman sent them to herself.'

Mod looked astonished but quickly understood. 'To give you the "come on",' he nodded. 'That's clever.'

'She's a bright old lady,' responded Davies. He turned the sparse pages of the police file saying: 'I had to use a little blackmail on Mr Pengelly.'

'What's he like?' asked Jemma, looking over his shoulder.

'Claims to be a private investigator but he earns his bread from a decidedly dodgy escort agency.' He glanced sideways at Jemma. 'I had to take one of his escorts out.'

Jemma lifted her calm eyes. 'Was she fun?'

'I can't remember. She drank me under the table. But I got enough on Pengelly to get this file ... and this police file which he had as well.' He turned the pages of the second file. 'The trouble is that there's something missing. When Dulciman's shoes were found on the seashore, more or less floating, some lad brought them up to Bertie at the hotel and he took them to the police.'

'That was a trifle convenient, wasn't it?' asked Jemma.

'Maybe, maybe not. They were found on the beach right

below the hotel, presumably where Dulciman went into the sea or wanted to make it look as though he had. The boy who found them took them up to the hotel and gave them to Bertie the porter. The trouble is that Bertie didn't ask the kid's name so he couldn't tell the police and they didn't think it was important enough to make further inquiries. A bit sloppy.'

'And this boy is important, you think,' said Mod. 'Well, maybe next time we go down I'll try and track him down for you. You know I'm good at legwork.'

'And booking your next holiday,' mentioned Davies.

Mod grimaced. 'I don't want to be left with your dog any more,' he said with doleful firmness.

'When are you going down again?' Jemma asked carefully.

'As soon as I can get a couple of days off,' said Davies. 'Without sick leave if possible.'

Jemma said: 'Remember our music evening. It's this Friday. Valentine is looking forward to it. Because you're coming. We're doing our duet.'

'I can't wait,' said Davies. 'Is he okay?'

'For the moment,' she sighed. Her white teeth gritted. 'There are times when I could do a few murders of my own.'

At the Babe In Arms Auntie Trudie, a ruddy old woman who drank only rough cider, said she remembered Bournemouth from her girlhood. Mad Maggy said she had been there or it may have been Brighton; Scotty, who boasted a medical background, had memories of Poole. They were talking of distant countries.

The mystery of Julie Willis, the girl buried on Wormwood Scrubs, remained unsolved, nor had anyone been charged with stealing the library hatstand.

Davies walked Jemma back to her front door and they kissed there like teenagers in the dark. 'So what was the escort lady really like?' she asked in her offhand way.

'Like I said,' replied Davies. 'She could certainly put it away. I woke up on her front stairs.'

She laughed and said: 'I believe you, Dangerous' and he thought that she did. She had paperwork to do before the morning. They kissed again and he promised that he would be at the Music Evening to hear the duet. Then he trundled off through the familiar streets, shadowed and wet, back to his home at Bali Hi.

As he was opening the door of his room, Mod's door opposite eased ajar and the round, creased face emerged like a doused lantern. It was followed by a hand holding a pale scrap. 'The knickers, Dangerous,' muttered Mod. 'You said you'd take charge of the knickers.'

Davies frowned but accepted the torn garment. They became aware of a dim face looking over the banister above. 'What knickers?' inquired Mrs Fulljames.

There was no escape. Davies stood with the incriminating evidence in his hand and Mod's attempt to withdraw his face from the scene was thwarted by Mrs Fulljames descending the stairs and growling: 'Mr Lewis.' Davies felt himself blushing in the dark. He looked at the ragged material in his hands. 'These are the knickers,' he muttered helplessly. 'They're mine.'

'They're his,' confirmed Mod disloyally.

'Evidence,' Davies said desperately. The landlady was now face to face with him and scarcely a step distant. 'Evidence in a case.'

She thrust out her hand and he obediently put the remnant into her hands. 'My silk panties,' she said, her voice low and threatening.

'My dog ate them,' said Davies hopelessly.

'After stealing them from the laundry basket,' grunted Mrs Fulljames. 'I've told you, Mr Davies, that I will not allow that overgrown, dirty, mischievous animal in this house. It stays in the garage where it belongs.' She rolled her knickers in a bundle in one hand. 'I've had these years,' she said her voice trembling. 'When my dear husband was alive. Now look at them.'

'Sorry Mrs Fulljames,' muttered Davies. 'I will of course replace them ... In a manner of speaking.'

She glared at him. 'I am certain of that. I shall purchase

another pair. And if that dog of yours so much as shows his nose in Bali Hi again I shall hit him on the head with my meat cleaver. The one I keep for burglars.'

'He doesn't *mean* any harm,' he said.

At last a clue had emerged in the case of Julie Willis. A girl who walked the Edgware Road with her recalled that on the night when she last saw her she was wearing a brooch in the shape of a swastika. It was a red swastika, the eastern emblem of luck, not the Nazi version. It was not attached to her clothes found in the grave and was not among the tin and trinkets of the box where she kept her jewellery.

Davies spent his first two days back on duty door-stepping once more, asking the same questions and showing a photograph of a similar brooch. No one recognised it. Some looked at the photograph closely and conscientiously and others barely gave it a glance before closing the door on him as though he were an unwanted salesman. He trudged on through the February streets, his step getting slower, his head lower. In the evening he had to muster all his energy and bathe his feet before taking his dog for a walk along the steamy canal bank, the park and the cemetery both being closed by that time.

By day, as he walked from door to monotonous door, he tried to think of what might have happened to Vernon Dulciman that night five years ago. Over and over again he mentally ticked off the facts and the theories. He still felt that something was staring him in the face.

On his third day back on duty he was glad to be relieved of the door-stepping and transferred to a series of petty burglaries all in one street, the usual loot of break-in thieves, televisions, videos, portable radios, stereos. So much of this type of stuff was stolen, he sometimes wondered where it all went.

One unburgled house was clearly next in line. The owner was a worried Sikh who opened the front door with a caution his forebears might once have used when ambushing the British in their homeland mountains.

'You see,' said the Sikh. 'Many televisions are here. In this room, two, in every other room, one. Even in the lav I have one.'

'Well, you wouldn't want to miss anything,' acknowledged Davies. He tried to appear convincing, prowling around the terraced house, peering out onto a back-garden jungle, deep enough to hide a tiger. In a small clearing was a shed.

'What's that for?' he asked.

'It is my garden shed,' said the Sikh. 'For my garden tools.'

'Oh, right,' nodded Davies surveying the jungle. 'It would be I suppose.' He sniffed around as if seeking some final clue, then bade the man goodbye.

The Indian seemed displeased and asked: 'Will you be making arrests?'

Davies studied the fierce face. The deep eyes burned among their wrinkles. 'I can't give you an exact time,' he said. 'But arrests will be made. Just as soon as we know who to arrest.'

This seemed at least partially to satisfy the Sikh. Davies went towards the door. 'Keep the doors locked and windows bolted,' he said, looking around at the evident precautions. He tapped his nose. 'I have a plan.'

They were already singing when he got there, the voices rising from the ugly church hall into the damp Cricklewood night. The windows were bright with yellow light and a glow issued from the front entrance lobby.

Davies was late because Detective Superintendent Harvey was delayed getting back to the station and all CID men had to await his arrival for a briefing on the Willis case. Harvey was not in a kindly mood. It had not been so much of a briefing as an harangue followed by a bad-tempered casting around for ideas. The street traipsing of the swastika photograph had come to nothing. Harvey surveyed the hapless faces and said: 'Thank Christ we've got a computer. We can always blame that bastard.'

Hurrying from the station Davies caught a passing bus to Cricklewood and got off outside the church hall. The singers, musicians and the entire audience were black. His was the sole white face. His eyes went at once to Jemma who was wearing a long grey dress and standing in front of the choir all in white. She had a well-known voice and there was a murmur from the audience as she stepped forward with the introductory music. She sang 'For He Shall Feed His Flock' from the *Messiah.*

Then she was joined by the diminutive Valentine who stepped forward shyly from the choir, grey suited, and they sang 'I Can Feel It All Over', with 'I Just Called To Say I Love You' as an encore. The little boy had a buoyant voice and he and Jemma enjoyed the duets. The audience loved it.

Afterwards, as they went back towards Willesden in Jemma's car, Valentine was inclined to be modest. 'Anybody could 'ave done that,' he said while they smiled in the dark. 'But I got chosen.'

Three hours later Davies woke up at Jemma's side. 'That's *it*!' he exclaimed. He sat up heavily in the bed. 'That man Leadbetter said the same thing.'

'Dangerous,' mumbled Jemma turning over, 'it's three o'clock in the morning.'

'Leadbetter *said* it and tonight Valentine *said* it. *Anybody could have done it but they were chosen.* Leadbetter was grousing that the gas board had sent him down to London when he wasn't even the next one on the list. And Valentine said he was just picked out when anyone else could have sung.'

Jemma replied sleepily: 'I still don't understand what you're going on about.'

Davies looked at the clock. 'Five past three,' he muttered. 'Well, it's too early to ring them now anyway.'

*

He waited until eight.

'Hello. Is that you Mildred?'

'Dangerous! It's you! When are you coming back?'

'Soon.'

'I'll get a day off,' enthused Mildred. 'The weather's turned lovely. Just like summer ... We could go for our walk.'

'Oh, yes. All right. Now Mildred, look in the Bournemouth Yellow Pages for me will you, love. Under ...'

'Bertie's got them,' she said sounding disappointed. 'I'll get ... Oh here he is.' Davies heard her call for the Yellow Pages directory. 'It's Mr Davies.' Bertie insisted on taking on the task himself. 'Hello sir. I've got them here. What was it you wanted?'

Davies said: 'Look under Private Investigators, will you, Bertie. That's right ...' He heard Bertie mumbling. 'Private Investigators, got it,' he said.

'How far down the list is Pengelly Associates?' asked Davies.

'How far down? Well, there's not many, sir. Only five. Pengelly Associates is number four. After that there's only Zodiac Inquiries.'

'Four,' repeated Davies. 'Right, thanks Bertie, that's all I wanted to know.'

'Good sir. Glad to help. Coming to see us again soon?'

'Next week, probably.'

'Lovely. That Zodiac Inquiries, sir. There's a horse called Zodiac running at Kempton this afternoon and another called Inquirer. Looks like a hint for a double.'

'Right,' said Davies. 'I'll remember to put a few thousand quid on.'

'Me too, sir. Goodbye.'

By Sunday the spring-like weather had moved north-east from Bournemouth to Willesden. The dour water of the canal took on a sheen and clouds of instant midges buzzed; there were primroses in the park and the tombstones in Kensal Green cemetery gleamed.

Even the old car seemed to react to the change. It stood almost purring in the cobbled yard as Davies prepared Kitty's blanket on the back seat. He beamed with satisfaction as the pale sun shone on his dog who sat with every appearance of a smile on his shaggy face. Jemma arrived and tousled him and the dog, who was always delighted to see her, grinned more widely.

Davies was glad to see her too. She had been at a two-day seminar on single-parent families. She got into the car and Davies climbed in beside her. They kissed and sitting upright in the back Kitty growled. 'I don't know whether that's approval or jealousy,' observed Davies.

'Why did you wake me up in the middle of the other night?' Jemma asked when they were driving out of the yard and into the Sunday street. 'You were going on about Valentine and a Mr Leadbetter.'

'They both said, in different ways, that other people could easily do what they were doing at that time,' Davies told her. 'Valentine singing, Mr Leadbetter with his gas pipes. They were not the *only* ones on the list.'

'So?'

They moved from the traffic lights. Two Indian boys jeered at the car and Davies gave them the finger. 'So it made me think, something that has been in the back of my mind since I came back from Bournemouth. *Why* was Pengelly chosen to try to find out what happened to Mr Dulciman? *I* had to look him up in the normal telephone directory. Pengelly Associates. But anyone trying to find a private detective from scratch would naturally look in the Yellow Pages. And Pengelly's name was last but one next to Zodiac Inquiries.'

He acknowledged a round of cheers from some men standing in the sun outside a public house. 'The point is that Pengelly was not *asked* to undertake the investigation *at random.* He must have been *known* to Mrs Dulciman before.'

They turned along the North Circular Road towards the Welsh Harp. 'Pengelly may have been recommended by someone,' put in Jemma. 'Why didn't you ask Mrs Dulciman? You could have phoned her.'

'I like being there when I ask questions.'

They drove alongside the lake. The air was warm through the car windows. The boot sale was in its usual Sunday site. They parked the car and Jemma put Kitty on the lead. Davies moved towards a table laid out with junk jewellery. He took out the photograph of the swastika brooch and showed it. 'Nah, never seen the like of that, Dangerous,' sniffed the man. 'I'd know if I did.'

Davies showed the picture to two other sellers but they both shook their heads. Then he saw the library hatstand.

It was standing, unattended, in the space between several cars. 'Whose is that then?' he asked. The nearest vendor, a man with a bright red shirt under an unbuttoned waistcoat, like a cockney bullfighter, shook his head. 'Gawd knows, Dangerous,' he said. 'Never set eyes on it before.'

Helpfully he called out, as loud as a warning: 'Who's that 'atstand belong to? Mr Davies wants to know.'

There were blank expressions, suddenly rough and devious faces became cherubic, and several men crept behind cars. 'Nobody,' reported the red shirt. 'It just got there.'

'I have reason to believe it's stolen property,' said Davies amiably. 'Nicked from the library.'

Jemma was running her fingers along the varnished wood of the hatstand. It seemed that the waistcoated man would never recover from the shock. 'What? From a *library*?' he said hand to mouth. 'Who, I ask myself, would do a thing like that?'

Ten

That afternoon, as they sometimes did, Davies and Jemma went to her flat and spent a couple of hours in bed, making love and talking. The hatstand was in the corner of the room. The man who lived all by himself in the next flat was watching football and when a goal was scored they heard his lonely shout of 'Goal!'

They remained until the unaccustomed sun faded from the window. At six he got up. 'I've got to spend the night in a garden shed,' he said. 'Surveillance.'

'I'll make you something,' said Jemma. Nothing he had to do surprised her.

She was a good cook and he lay in the bath savouring the smells from the kitchen. 'You watch that Mildred,' she called through the ajar door. 'She's a poor frustrated girl.'

She sat while he ate. She had to go to a buffet for the deprived that evening. 'Why do you have to hide in a garden shed?' she asked.

'Every telly and every video in this street has been burgled and this Mr Khan is expecting his to go any minute,' he said. 'He's going to a big Sikh night out, and they may try to turn over his house tonight. I'll be in his garden shed.'

'They may beat the life out of you.'

'I've got back-up. I can call for reinforcements.'

Jemma kissed him and said: 'Take care.' The early night had turned chill. She turned up his overcoat collar for him.

'There's not a lot of difference between a copper going off to work and a burglar going off to work,' he observed.

'What about the library hatstand?' she asked.

'Ah, yes. I'll take it with me. Tomorrow I'll return it in triumph.'

He went back into the flat and picked up the unwieldly hatstand with its long polished stem and its ornate hooks curling out like antlers. In the street again he half swung around and almost knocked her off her feet. She staggered back into the doorway. 'Don't swing it when there are people about,' she suggested. 'Or in front of shop windows. And be careful tonight, Dangerous. In the shed. Please.'

'Nothing to worry about,' he assured her. 'Cheers.'

He turned painstakingly but still caught the doorpost with the foot of the stand. 'Steady,' he warned himself. He staggered a little, then, like an ill-founded ship finally settled on a course, he set off down the street.

Jemma watched him go with a touch of sadness. She loved him but she often wondered where it would all end. She watched his slightly comic staggering along the pavement, the hatstand swinging like a derrick. His overcoated arm detached itself and waved. She waved back slowly.

'Oh, Dangerous,' she said to herself. 'Whatever am I going to do with you?'

'It is a good shed,' said Mr Khan leading Davies into the dark and tangled garden. He waved the small stool he carried. 'You will be most comfortable.'

He opened the creaking door. Davies peered in. 'You'd better get going to your gathering of the clans,' he advised. 'Leave a couple of lights on in the house.'

'So that burglars know we are out but pretending to be in,' said Mr Khan.

He placed the stool and then, as if it made any difference, moved it a fraction. 'Most comfortable,' he repeated.

Davies sat on the stool and looked about him in the close gloom. He produced a half bottle of whisky from his overcoat pocket. 'I've got something to keep me warm.'

The Sikh waved a large hand and set off to return to the house. It was seven thirty. Davies took a preliminary swig at the whisky and tested the walkie-talkie. The ponderous tones of Police Constable Westerman sounded from the other end. Everything was ready. Everything was fine.

Just before the Khan family left, Mr Khan's mother noticed from the kitchen window that the shed door was open. She had not been told that the shed concealed a police officer and, knowing how her son feared intruders, crept fearfully out into the garden and quietly shut the door, bolting it from the outside. Davies had dozed off. The sunny day and his lovemaking had tired him and before he could fully rouse himself he was trapped in the musky dark.

He banged on the metal door but nobody answered. He called up PC Westerman. Only a ghostly crackle replied. 'Good old Westerman,' he muttered. 'Hope he hasn't gone off with one of his nosebleeds.'

Westerman had, however, suffered a copious discharge which left him confused and embarrassed. He was taken off duty and, in the ways of even the best organised police forces, nobody was sent to replace him. Davies' attempts to contact his back-up became more hopeless. He had a couple more swigs of the whisky.

He was asleep, uncomfortably propped on the stool, when the burglars arrived. They were noisy burglars, three young fellows gaining experience, and their clatterings and voices awoke him. He pressed his ear against the door, grinding his teeth. He tried calling up Westerman again but only the crackle came back. Cursing, he tried pushing at the door. Nothing.

With a sudden surge of anger he banged on the door of the shed and bellowed and bawled as loud as he could. 'Police! Police!' Then, pathetically: 'Let me out of here.'

The thieves, having almost finished their task, paused. 'Somebody's in that shed,' said one.

'Trying to get out,' added another.

'Police,' echoed the third. 'There's a copper locked in there.'

'Get the stuff and then scarper,' said the first. He tiptoed to the shed which had begun to rock perceptibly as Davies tried to force his way out. He returned to his accomplices. ''e won't get out of there easy,' he forecast. 'It's all metal.'

They cleared the house deftly, carrying their loot to a van parked outside. It was still only ten thirty but the next day was Monday and people went to bed early. The street was dumb.

As they were about to leave Davies launched his most frantic assault on the door. The shed was rocking on its foundations. 'Come on,' said the leader of the criminals. 'Give him a hand.'

The three went on swift tiptoes to the moving shed. With a nod from their leader they heaved it once. It fell forward, door foremost, onto the ground. Then they left.

'Dangerous,' whispered Mod. 'A word.' He rolled his fat, creased eyes. 'In private.'

'What is it?'

Mod lowered his voice further. 'I think I have solved the mystery.'

'Which one?'

'The disappearing hatstand. From the library.' He leaned closer. 'It could be Mrs Fulljames.'

'What makes you think so?'

'It's in the front room. Concealed behind the door.' He looked swiftly both ways. 'I've seen it.'

Davies sighed. 'I put it there. It turned up at the Welsh Harp car-boot sale.'

'Amazing. Did you make an arrest?'

'There was nobody to arrest. It was standing there with lots of space around it.'

Delight spread across Mod's face. '*I'll* take it back this morning,' he said. 'The Librarian will be pleased.'

'*I'll* take it,' Davies told him firmly. 'It might be a bit heavy for you.'

'You appear to be out of sorts, Dangerous.'

'I spent two hours last night trying to kick my way out of a garden shed.'

Mod examined him closely. 'I noticed a discoloration on the forehead. Hospital job?'

'I didn't bother them.' Davies walked into the front room and returned holding the cumbersome hatstand with both hands. 'Are you coming down with me?'

'Oh no, Dangerous. I don't want to steal your thunder.'

'Right,' said Davies firmly. He opened the front door and manoeuvred the hatstand outside. 'I hope this is something I might get some thanks for.'

People stopped as he walked into the main street with the hatstand on his shoulder. 'Doing a bit of totting, Dangerous?' called a man from a car. Davies half turned and the long stem of the stand struck a rack of newspapers outside the Pakistani shop. He bent to try and pick it up striking the emerging owner of the shop a blow in the midriff.

He was almost at the library when a car drew up behind him. 'Hey you! Where are you taking that?'

He knew a police voice when he heard it. 'Buckingham bleeding Palace,' he called over his shoulder. 'I thought the Queen might like it.'

They jumped from the car and he turned almost striking the leading constable. 'Oh God, it's you, Dangerous,' said the policeman.

'We had a call that somebody was hiking stolen goods down the street.'

Davies said patiently: 'It *is* stolen property. Nicked from the library. And I am restoring it.' He paused. 'Last night when I needed a copper there wasn't one for bloody miles.'

'That's what they all say, Dangerous,' said the constable cheerfully getting back into the car.

Davies swore to himself and stumped along the street to the library. There he straightened himself up and, adjusting the stand on his shoulder, marched in. Inside there was only a woman sweeping and the girl behind the desk.

'Is the Librarian in yet?' inquired Davies looking about him.

'It's Monday,' said the girl as if that were a complete answer.

'Oh,' he said his voice dropping. 'Well, I've brought back your hatstand.'

'Right,' said the girl. Her eyes had dropped to something on her counter. She pointed vaguely. 'Put it over there will you.'

On Thursday he got an early train and was in Bournemouth by noon. Mildred was behind the reception desk at the hotel. Her round face lit when she saw him. 'Dangerous, we could go for our walk *this afternoon.* I can get off.'

He regarded her guiltily. 'I have to see Mrs Dulciman,' he said. Mildred bit her lip. 'You can't, she's in hospital.' Davies' face clouded. 'Oh ... I didn't know ...'

'She's all right. She'll probably be back next week. Every now and then they take her in.'

'I'll go and see her.'

'We're going for our walk this afternoon,' Mildred repeated. 'You promised. I've got the time off. You can see Mrs Dulciman this evening.'

He smiled at her, a child anxious for a treat. 'Right, that's fixed then,' he said.

'Have you brought your car?'

'Er ... no.' He shook his head. 'I didn't think it could manage a second journey.'

'Don't worry, there's a bus from right outside.' She looked at her watch, tiny on a broad wrist. 'We could catch the two o'clock. The forecast is fine, rain later.'

Bertie, the porter, ambled into the lobby and made towards his cubicle like an old dog making for a familiar kennel. 'Oh hello sir,' he said when he saw Davies. 'You're back then.'

'Is the bar open?' asked Davies craning around the lounge door.

'She's away sick,' said Bertie. 'But I'll open up. Sorry about Zodiac and Inquirer. At least Inquirer was third.'

'We should both know better,' Davies said patting his arm. As he walked from the lobby he said to Mildred: 'I'll be there at two.'

'It's a bit of a climb,' she said.

'I think she was warning me not to have too much beer,' said Davies when Bertie had gone behind the bar.

'It's quite a way,' Bertie confirmed. Davies ordered a scotch. Bertie said he would have a beer because he was not climbing. 'I can't understand why she goes up there. Something to do with that boyfriend she had, I suppose. The little soldier.'

'Was he little?'

'Undersized. Goodness knows how he got into the army. He was in the medics though. They probably take them a bit shorter and thinner.' He paused and then added cautiously: 'It's all Ministry of Defence up there, you know sir. Officially closed to the public. Some of the villages have been unoccupied since the war. They just use them for manoeuvres. You can hear the guns going off sometimes even from here.'

'Mildred seems to think it's safe,' Davies said uncertainly.

'Oh, I expect it is. She goes up there regular. She's a funny girl.'

Davies leaned a little closer over the bar. 'Bertie,' he said. 'You remember when you told me about Mr Dulciman's shoes, how that lad found them on the beach and brought them up to you?'

'And I took them to the police. Yes sir.'

'There is no way you can recall the boy's name is there? Or anything about him.'

Bertie looked puzzled and doubtful. 'None at all, sir. It was five years ago, wasn't it. He was just a lad. I can't remember anything about him. I took the shoes from him but I didn't get his name. I didn't think to. After I realised they belonged to Mr Dulciman, I took them to Mrs Dulciman and she said to take them to the police. They asked me the boy's name but I said I didn't know.'

Davies said he would have a sandwich. He ate moodily, then took his bag upstairs and arrived back in the lobby at five to two. Mildred was already waiting. She wore a large pair of jeans, a green sweater with a roll neck and a drab brown anorak. Her face was round and pretty like a pleased Eskimo.

'I'm glad you've brought your mac,' she said as they walked to the bus stop. 'It's almost khaki. That's why I wear these colours. You can't be spotted from a distance.'

'I feel as though I'm going on a commando raid,' grimaced Davies.

She laughed and gave him a push. 'It's all right. It's not dangerous, Dangerous.'

The bus arrived and they boarded it and went on the top deck. As they travelled she provided a commentary. They went along the sea, up into the town and, eventually, out into the Dorset countryside, to villages and heathland and a distant prospect of the English Channel lying in the cradles between low hills. She put her arm into his and wriggled. 'I'm enjoying this,' she said. 'I've been looking forward to it all week.'

'You like company,' Davies told her. 'I don't understand why you don't mix with younger people.'

'I told you before, they're all students or on the dole, and I don't have anything in common with any of them. And the staff in the hotels are always shifting jobs and they work funny hours. And Alfie dying like that, it really put me off.'

After thirty minutes they came to a hamlet with a pub, a few cottages and a telephone box. 'This is it.' She tugged his arm. They clambered heavily down the stairs. The bus drove away leaving them in the middle of the deserted place. She strode off between the pub and the telephone box. 'Come on, it's this way.'

There was only room for him to follow behind her. At the end of the lane was a notice, black letters on a white ground with a red and grinning skull at its centre. 'Keep Out!' it ordered. 'Danger of DEATH.'

'That seems pretty clear,' muttered Davies.

'It's nothing. There's another up here. But I know a way,' she said.

They climbed a stile which had barbed wire across its horizontals. Davies looked at the palms of his hands. 'Keep close to the side of this field,' she advised from just ahead of him. 'As near to the hedge as you can.'

He frowned across the ploughed field. 'It's a minefield, don't tell me,' he said.

'No. The minefields are over there. Just beyond those trees. We can dodge them. See along here ...' She pointed ahead. 'This is where they've been shelling. See the craters.'

Davies swallowed and kept close behind her. They reached a clearing and she stood upright from her crouch. 'It's all right from here,' she smiled. The sun was glistening on her round face. He was sweating down his neck. 'It's up there,' she said pointing. 'See at the top of the hill. That's where we're going.'

Panting and stumbling he followed her to the summit where they almost fell on top of each other on the warm grass. Still fighting for breath she rolled sideways and ended sitting up on a green ridge. Regaining his breath he straightened and sat beside her. 'There,' she exclaimed throwing out her arms. 'Look at that view! Did you ever see anything so beautiful?'

The green land fell away to the hedged fields below and then over another rise to the bright crinkled sea. Below one side of the ridge, only part of it visible, was a stone hamlet with a church tower. A soft wind brushed across the landscape.

'See the village,' said Mildred. 'Nobody's lived there for fifty years. It's just empty, used by the army.' Her eyes surveyed it carefully. 'Alfie knew how to get into the houses. Once we went into the church and pretended we were getting married.' She frowned. 'Actually he was married already but I didn't know that then.'

'When did you know?' asked Davies.

'When he was dead,' she mumbled. 'I didn't find out until then. Her name was Georgina. I was so shocked and miserable, Dangerous. He never let on and I couldn't understand that. Married. But I'm sure he liked me best.'

He thought she was going to cry and he put out his hand awkwardly to pat her. 'We had a house in the village,' she said pointing at the roofs. 'We used to play at it being *our* house. It had a bed and everything. Alfie knew when it was safe although once ...' She giggled sadly. 'Once we were in bed there and we heard some soldiers and some shooting. We didn't half move, Dangerous, I can tell you.' Again she nodded towards the settlement. 'Our house is still down there, just like it was. I went and had a look one day.'

'You ought to be a bit more careful about coming up here,' he suggested. 'The army might start an unscheduled battle and what would you do then?'

'Scream, I suppose,' she answered smiling tightly. 'But I love it up here. I got the whole country to myself. Just me and the wind.'

'We ought to go soon,' he told her. 'It's getting cold.'

'It's getting a bit dark too,' she agreed. 'All right.' She turned to face him. 'Will you just kiss me, Dangerous. Just once.'

He was about to say something but her plump, pretty face came close to him. The wind was blowing her hair forwards over her forehead. He leaned towards her and kissed her on the lips. 'Is that all right?' he asked unhappily. 'That'll do,' she said. She stood up and pushed her hair back. 'For the time being.'

Davies never felt comfortable carrying flowers but it was a change to go to a hospital to visit someone else. He cruised through the various corridors and past the entrances to wards, with the aplomb of a veteran.

Mrs Dulciman was pleased to see him. She was sitting brightly in bed wearing a lacy cape around her nightdress. 'Still on the trail, Mr Davies?'

'I certainly am,' he assured her. He looked around for somewhere to put the flowers and a nurse appeared and took them from him.

'Tell me all about it,' said Mrs Dulciman. 'I'm feeling much better. I'm not going to pop off yet. But if you wish I would be more than willing to honour my original suggestion and pay half the fee to you now.'

Davies held up a refusing hand. 'When I've done will be the time,' he said. 'I'm enjoying it.'

She smiled mischievously. 'Moonlighting becomes you. There was once a song like that.'

'It's a nice change from walking the London streets knocking on doors, showing people photographs,' he said.

'What's that for, Dangerous?'

'A murder. We have a body but we haven't a clue, not as far as I know. The top brass may have but they don't confide in me. I just do the footwork.'

She folded her hands across her chest. 'Well, at least you have *our* case to yourself.'

'I must ask you something,' he said. 'How did you come to choose Pengelly as your private investigator? He wasn't a random choice was he?'

'Oh no. Vernon knew him.'

Davies stared at her. 'He *knew* him?'

'Yes. I don't actually know how. But on two or three occasions when I went to the Moonlighters Club, I didn't care for it very much so I did not go there often, only for special events when I could not avoid it ... When I did go there I met Pengelly. Vernon knew him quite well, I think, although I don't know how or why. When I needed to employ an investigator it was just natural that I went to him.'

'So you knew he was a detective?'

'Of sorts,' she said a little scornfully. 'But I did know. I suppose Vernon must have mentioned it.'

Davies looked thoughtful. 'Have I given you a clue?' she asked eagerly.

He smiled at her. 'I don't know,' he said. 'But you've given me one or two ideas.'

Eleven

The Moonlighters Club was more crowded, with the everlasting sherry couple still in their corner. They greeted him with neatly raised glasses. Other members looked at him with the curiosity of regulars for newcomers. Phineas was at the bar and waggled his missing leg at him.

They drank amiably. 'You're practically a resident,' observed Phineas. 'This place is like a desert island, once you're here it's difficult to get away. Like being shipwrecked.'

'It's busy tonight,' mentioned Davies.

Orville, the barman, leaned over confidingly. 'There's been a funeral today. It's always busy after a funeral.'

'Mrs Sowerby,' put in Phineas. 'Ninety-two. She said she was seventy-five.' He eyed Davies. 'She knew your Mr Dulciman.'

'Now you tell me.'

'He did a bit of wheedling with her, so they say. Got some money out of her.'

'He seems to have done the rounds of elderly ladies fairly efficiently.' He inclined his head and his beer tankard towards Phineas. 'Did you ever see him in here with a man called Pengelly, a younger chap?'

'Oh yes,' returned Phineas. He spoke over his shoulder to the barman. 'We know Pengelly, don't we ...'

The barman blew out his cheeks and said: 'I'll say.'

'What do you think of him?'

Phineas sniffed. He put his empty tankard on the bar. It was Davies' round. Phineas said: 'Shifty customer, I'd say. Reckons to be a detective.'

Davies ran his eye over the members of the club. Some of them still wore the funeral black but others had been home and changed. The conversation was quite jolly. Ninety-two was a good age to live and to die. A few small toasts were raised to the memory of Mrs Sowerby but they were not demonstrative.

'Did Pengelly know Dulciman *closely*, do you think?' asked Davies.

Phineas ruminated. 'They certainly got together a bit. They drank in here and seemed to have a lot to talk about.' He became thoughtful. 'And once I remember seeing the pair of them in the gardens, across from the Royal Bath Hotel, sitting on a bench together. It was wintertime and I remember thinking it was a bit funny for them to be out like that. Then they saw me coming and they got up quick and went off in different directions. But it was them. I might only have one good leg left but I've got two good eyes.'

'You've never heard what their association might have been?' suggested Davies.

'No. Just business,' said Phincas. 'I don't know what sort.'

Davies wandered over and looked again at the snapshots on the wall. One of the sherry drinkers stood up and, to his surprise, came over to stand at his shoulder. 'Those were the days,' said the man. He pointed to one photograph. 'That's Mrs Sowerby that we saw away today. Before she went potty.'

'Who's this chap?' asked Davies casually. He pointed at Dulciman.

'Vernon,' said the man reflectively. 'Dulciman. He vanished, you know. Walked out to sea so they say.'

'Really?'

The sherry drinker nodded. He had left his glass on the table. Davies saw the woman steal a sip from the glass. She caught his glance and smiled in a way that suggested they shared a secret. 'Yes,' continued the man. 'Walked. It's a wonder he didn't walk *on* the water because he thought he could do everything else. Women, charm, business. Full of it all. I wouldn't be surprised if somebody *dragged* him out to sea.'

'He wasn't popular then.'

'Not with me, he wasn't. It's his fault that me and my missus are living in a rented flat. One bedroom. We even have to sleep together.'

'What did he do?'

'Borrowed money from her, an investment he said. And she, silly old tart, believed him. Women did. It was our savings and he never gave any back. He never did. To anybody. No wonder whatever happened to him happened to him.'

Davies had another two pints with Phineas and left the club. It was windy after the sunny day but there was a mild touch to the air. A moon appeared momentarily from ragged channel clouds. Thumping sounds came from a disco. Davies had the sudden urge to see some young people. He went down the steps and spoke to the bouncer at the end. 'You can come in if you pay,' the man assured him. 'There's no age limit. Just don't have a heart attack on the floor.'

'I'll dance the slow numbers,' rejoined Davies. He paid his four pounds and went into the dim cave of a room. Figures were moving and weaving on the central floor. It was hot in there, fetid. Davies made for an illuminated corner that he imagined was the bar. His instincts did not let him down. There were three youths standing against it and he ordered a double scotch. The barman looked pleased in the sickly light. 'At last somebody who can afford a decent drink,' he said loudly. The youths, sharing a beer between them, moved away.

'Haven't got a bean between them, mostly,' sighed the barman as he handed over the scotch. Davies bought him one. 'These kids just hang on here,' he said lifting the glass in thanks, 'from the end of one season to another. Living on the dole and whatever they can pick up.' He leaned across his bar. 'And when I say "pick up" that's exactly what I mean.'

A girl approached and, fumbling in her purse minutely,

eventually produced enough small change for a Coca-Cola. 'It still costs four quid to get in,' pointed out Davies.

'For you, mate, it might. But half of this lot don't pay anything. They're the "can't pay, won't pay" generation.' The girl glared at him but he ignored her. 'Everything's been put in their laps.'

'Except a job,' mentioned the girl as she turned and shifted away.

'Jobs. They wouldn't know one if they saw one,' sniffed the barman.

Davies turned and immediately saw Mildred dancing, merged with the dim crowd but still discernible. She saw him watching her and came towards him. 'Looking for me, officer?' she asked. The barman gave them an odd glance.

'Could be,' Davies replied. Blatantly she pushed her big soft body towards him.

'Didn't know you came in places like this.'

'I thought it might keep me young,' he smiled. 'Would you like a drink?'

She said she would have a Coca-Cola, then added a rum and poured it into the glass. 'I thought you didn't mix with the younger set,' he said.

She pouted. 'I wasn't mixing. I was dancing by myself. Didn't you see?'

'I can't tell who's with who.'

'Do you want to dance?'

'I'll wait for a waltz.'

'I was ready to go anyway,' she said. 'Are you ready too?'

The barman shook his head as they left. He did not understand what went on these days.

Outside they walked down the slope towards the hotel. There was a fretting wind and clouds ran swiftly across the long sky.

'They always seem to be in a rush, clouds,' she observed. 'I wonder where they're rushing to?'

Davies studied the sky briefly. 'Boscombe I'd say,' he

suggested. Mildred laughed richly and squeezed his arm. 'Oh, Dangerous, if I was older,' she said.

They went around to the back entrance of the hotel. She had a key and she let them in. They walked silently up the stairs. On the landing he kissed her on the cheek and she kissed him on the lips. 'I'm married,' he said uncomfortably. 'And I have a regular girlfriend. What used to be called "spoken for".' She hugged him again and turned towards the corridor leading to her room.

''Night then,' she said.

He said good night and went up the short flight of stairs to his room. He felt sad for her. 'It was lovely having a walk today,' she called after him in a whisper.

'I enjoyed it,' he replied hoarsely.

She vanished in the half light of the passage and he went to his room closing the door with a sigh. He undressed, put on his flannel pyjamas and climbed into bed. He was just dozing when he heard his door open. Standing in the dimness wearing a wide faintly luminous nightdress was Mildred.

'Dangerous,' she whispered. 'Can I come in bed with you?'

He turned on his bedside lamp. He could see she was crying. 'Just for a cuddle,' she said. 'Nothing else. I only want to be cuddled.'

He said nothing but opened the bedclothes. She padded forward and slid into the double bed turning away from him so that her large backside was in his lap. He put his arms around her.

'Oh Dangerous,' she croaked, 'I'm ever so lonely.'

'Hello. This is Pengelly Associates.'

'Oh, hello. I need some help. I've lost my pussycat.'

'Who is this?'

'It's Davies.'

'Oh, you. I might have guessed from the rich humour. What did you want?'

'Just a bit of a chat, really.'

'We've had our chat.'

'I enjoyed it too. I want another one.'

He heard Pengelly draw a deep breath. 'I can't tell you anything more.'

'You could try,' said Davies.

'I don't want you in this office. These offices. Either of them. My auntie is coming in today.'

'I'd move the dead mouse on the window then.'

'Listen. I haven't got all day ...'

'Neither have I,' said Davies. 'I have to catch a train. The escort game must be frantic at the weekends but I won't keep you long. We could meet in a pub. I think I owe you a drink.'

'I haven't got a lot of choice, have I? All right. There's a pub called the Sugar Loaf along the street from this office. Fifty yards down. I'll see you in there at midday.'

'Fine. A chat might do us good. Public bar or saloon?'

He thought he could hear Pengelly's teeth grinding. 'Saloon,' he said.

Davies replaced the phone. He went to the bathroom. There was a plastic shower cap in a container on the shelf. Thoughtfully he took it out and, after briefly trying it on and making a face in the mirror, put it in his pocket.

He got the bus to Boscombe and retraced his steps to the doorway by the greengrocer's shop which gave entrance to Pengelly Associates and the Goodtime Escort Agency. Along the pavement he could see the sign hanging outside the Sugar Loaf.

He went into the saloon bar. It was barely noon and there was no one in there except for a motionless woman framed by the bar. He wished her good morning and bought two double scotches. He placed one on the bar and moved a yard away. As though he had been lurking, Pengelly came in. He looked impatient.

'I can't stay long,' he said.

'Is your auntie afraid to be by herself?' asked Davies. 'I bought you a scotch.'

'Thanks,' grunted Pengelly. To Davies' relief he picked up the glass and took a drink. 'Now what is it, this time?'

'You had a business association with Vernon Dulciman, didn't you?'

Pengelly grinned savagely. 'And we quarrelled over the profits and I threw him in the sea.'

'Is that how it happened?' asked Davies looking into his face.

'Listen,' sighed Pengelly. 'I had nothing to do with whatever happened to Dulciman. He was an arsehole but I didn't kill him for business or any other reason.'

'But you had an association.'

'What association? I just knew him, that's all. So did a lot of other people.'

'What was he like?'

'A randy old pest. He wanted to get a woman from the agency. She didn't fancy him. She'd had one experience with him apparently and that was enough for her.' He stared into Davies' interested expression. 'You get my drift?'

'What was his business then?' asked Davies. 'Why did he keep cheating old ladies out of money?'

'Some old ladies are all too eager to get rid of their money.' He looked at Davies slyly. 'You should know that.'

Davies moved his face towards him. 'Say that again.'

Pengelly looked frightened but he said it again. Slowly Davies' hands went out. They paused a fraction from Pengelly's collar. 'I told you *I'm* not taking any money', he said deliberately, 'until it's finished. Until I know what happened to Vernon Dulciman.'

The woman who had been serving came around the corner of the bar and saw their attitudes. 'No fighting,' she said stoutly. 'Out you go if you start fighting.'

Pengelly picked up his glass and finished the whisky. 'Don't worry. I'm going.' He looked at Davies. 'I'm not going to fight.'

The barwoman said: 'I should hope not. This time of the morning.' Without another word Pengelly went out. Davies watched him go. The woman went around the corner of the bar again.

He picked up Pengelly's whisky glass, took a hotel napkin from his pocket and wrapped it up carefully, then he put it in the shower cap he had brought from the bathroom. 'Bye bye,' he called to the barwoman.

She appeared and said: 'Good riddance.'

He went out of the door smiling.

'Hello, is that you, Fingers?'

'Who is that?'

'It's Davies, Fingers. At Willesden.'

'Hello, Dangerous.' The voice mellowed. 'And what are you after?'

'Can you do a few dabs for me?'

'Of course. Send them over.'

'Fingers, I don't want to make a fuss over them.'

'No problem. I'll do them after work. Nobody will know.'

Davies thanked him and put the telephone down. He was at his desk, a sandwich now shaped like a large piece of jigsaw, three bites taken out of it, was displayed in its wrapping on the desk. The CID Room was empty. He bit into the sandwich, again in a separate place, making a fourth indent. The telephone on the desk rang. He picked it up saying 'Davies' with his mouth full.

'Ah, Mr Davies. It's Bertie here. From Bournemouth.'

Davies sat up in his chair. 'Yes, Bertie.'

'You know you was asking me about the shoes and the boy that brought them in?'

Slowly Davies put the indented sandwich on the desk. 'Yes, Bertie. Have you remembered something?'

'Yes, I have. I've had it on my mind. And last night, three this morning actually, I thought of it.'

'Yes,' encouraged Davies.

'There was a bit in the *Echo* last night and it reminded me,

I suppose. There was a photograph of some kids that they're going to have going along the beach this summer wearing special caps picking up litter and telling people to keep the beach tidy. They have sweatshirts as well with some slogan written across them.'

'Yes.'

'Well, they've done that sort of thing before, every year I think, and when I was lying awake I suddenly remembered that the boy who found Mr Dulciman's shoes had one of those caps and shirts. Is that any help?'

'I'll say it is, Bertie,' enthused Davies. 'It will help no end. Remember anything else?'

'No.' Bertie sounded a little disappointed. 'But I thought it might be something.'

Davies thanked him again and put the telephone down. He sat back thoughtfully, finishing the sandwich. So engrossed was he that he ate part of the wrapping without noticing until it was in his mouth. He got up from the desk and went out into the street. It was a mild, grey morning. Willesden was going about its weekday business. He went towards the library.

Mod was sitting in his accustomed place, a pyramid of books in front of him. His look was only one of mild surprise. 'You probably already know, Dangerous, that the present-day Australian accent may well be the genuine sound of how people spoke in Georgian England.'

'And I never realised,' breathed Davies.

'Language travels in mysterious ways,' said Mod. 'Like God.' Davies took the chair opposite him.

'I want you to travel, Mod.' His friend's slow, unkempt eyebrows rose. 'Not in a mysterious way. By British Rail.'

'To the seaside, I take it.'

'To the seaside,' confirmed Davies. 'Bournemouth. Tomorrow.'

Mod pursed his lips and fingered his ponderous books. 'I am right in the midst of *Language and the Masses*,' he pointed out. 'It may take some weeks.'

'I can't wait,' Davies said. 'Who got you the library hatstand back?'

'No one appears to have noticed,' complained Mod. 'Only when it was taken. Librarians are not given to appreciation, Dangerous.'

'Bournemouth – tomorrow,' reiterated Davies. 'You can go early and be back at night. What I need you to do is to check the newspaper files, the Bournemouth *Echo*, for five years ago. I'll give you the dates. The porter has remembered about the boy who found Dulciman's shoes. He was part of some campaign to keep the beach clean. He had a special cap and sweatshirt. If we can get the names of the kids who took part in the campaign five years ago, then we can really narrow it down. One of them will remember who it was picked up the shoes. If you don't have any luck with the paper then try the council. Put on a clean shirt, will you. The paper probably has a picture every year of the lucky lads. There's a train from Waterloo at eight forty-five.'

Elvis was trudging down the slope of the street as Davies left the house in the morning. The youth was dragging some pieces of rotten fencing. 'For my fire,' he explained. 'Getting short of stuff.'

'There won't be anything left to burn around here soon,' suggested Davies. 'You'll have to open a branch in Hammersmith.'

Elvis looked interested. 'Branches burn like anything,' he said with the voice of the expert. 'It's paper what you can't get. You know that bloke that's your mate. 'im what carries them books.'

'Mr Modest Lewis,' said Davies formally. 'The books belong to the library.'

'D'you reckon they got any old ones they don't want?'

'They tend to hang onto their old books,' Davies told him.

A glow came to Elvis' face, as though the thought in itself had started a small fire. 'They wouldn't 'arf burn good,' he said wistfully.

Another, neater, youth came down the street earnestly carrying an armful of pamphlets which he pushed into letterboxes. He had a laden bag around his neck. Elvis took a quick interest and again his face began to glow. 'Look at that,' he whispered almost to himself. 'Wasting all that paper.'

He left Davies and hurried back up the street. Davies could hear him pleading to be allowed to assist the earnest youth with his distribution. By the time Davies had reached the top of the street, Elvis was standing, looking half happy, and holding a fistful of fliers. 'That's all 'e give me,' he groused. 'Lot of good that is. Look at 'im sticking them through front doors, annoying people.'

'Elvis,' suggested Davies, 'why don't you try and get a job with the council. Refuse collection operative.'

'Nah,' returned Elvis. 'I 'ad a go at that. But they won't let you 'ave your own fire. Anyway I likes working for myself.'

'Ah, you're a freelance.'

Elvis wrestled with the meaning but brightened once more and agreed. 'Yeah, that's what I am. A freelance.'

As he walked on, down the main street, past the Babe In Arms, where a not disagreeable scent of stale beer was issuing from an open door, Davies repeated to himself: 'A freelance. That's what I am, a freelance.'

An old woman threw half a bucket of water from the open pub door, swirling and swilling across the pavement and splashing Davies' shoes.

'Sorry, Dangerous,' she croaked, throwing the second half. She apologised again.

'Any time, dear,' he responded. How many policemen had a bucket of water thrown over them so early in the day? He walked along the street towards the police station. The Italian who ran the Spaghetti Junction restaurant was also washing down his area of pavement but spared the bucket as Davies walked by. There were buses and cars nudging towards the traffic lights. He could remember when trolleybuses ran along there, when people cared for each other except on occasional Saturday nights; when crime was rarely more than a misdemeanour. Those were the days.

At the police station the desk sergeant greeted him affably. 'They picked up the bright sparks who nicked those televisions, Dangerous,' he said.

Davies professed relief and satisfaction. Inside the CID Room Detective Sergeant Burrows, newly promoted after his course, grinned as he entered. 'I hear you've nicked the telly-burglars,' said Davies before Burrows could tell him.

'I'll say,' nodded Burrows, still beaming. 'And guess what?'

'What?'

'We also fingered your friend Mr Kahn.'

'Receiving stolen goods, i.e. television sets,' guessed Davies glumly.

'Right first time,' said Burrows. 'You must have wondered where he'd got all that stuff.'

'It did cross my mind,' admitted Davies. 'But you never think that a receiver would be so worried about having stuff pinched, would you.' He shrugged. 'Well, there it is. You'll be detective inspector next, Bunny.'

'Give me time, Dangerous,' said Burrows.

Heavily Davies sat at his desk. The telephone rang. It was Jemma. 'We've got a date tonight,' she said. He smiled at her through the mouthpiece.

'The Savoy wasn't it?'

'If you like,' she answered blandly. 'I think I'd prefer a curry.'

Davies was preparing to lower his voice but Detective Sergeant Burrows got up from his desk and made for the door waving a silent farewell. Davies said to Jemma: 'I've sent Mod to do a bit of legwork at Bournemouth.'

'You're getting somewhere?'

'I keep thinking I'm not. But I think I could be wrong. I often am.'

'Tell me,' she urged.

'I'll tell you tonight.' He replaced the telephone and it rang again.

'Hello, DC Davies here.'

'Dangerous, it's Marsden. Good morning.'

''Morning, Fingers. Get anything?' Davies picked up a pen.

'Your bloke's got a bit of form. Theft from a bookmakers. I suppose there's a case for saying that's poetic justice. And intent to defraud.'

'What's he call himself?'

'Page. William Henry Page. Aged thirty-three. Lived in Marylebone at one time. Want the address?'

Davies said he did and wrote it down.

'When were the offences?' he asked.

'Let's see. Some time ago. The theft was 22 November 1984. From Winner and Co., Marylebone High Street, fined three hundred quid.'

'They're still there,' said Davies. 'And the other?'

'Intent to defraud, not proved. That was in 1981, 3 July.'

'Thanks very much, Fingers. Keep it to yourself, will you.'

'I'll not say a dicky-bird. Do you want the whisky glass back?'

'No thanks. Keep it and I'll put a double scotch in it next time I see you.'

There was a 999 call from a butcher's shop in Kensal Rise reporting an armed raid. Davies was sent with two uniformed officers. The butcher, a tearful man, reported the theft of a leg of lamb, six pork chops, and two pounds of best liver. 'Nothing's safe these days,' he wailed. 'What my dad would have said I don't know. He had this business thirty-three years and never anything like this. There's no morality, Mr Davies, no morality.'

'There's not a lot of it about,' agreed Davies. The robber, a man variously described as in his thirties, forties and fifties, bald, sparse gingery hair or straight black hair combed across his brow, with menacing, wild, crossed eyes, of medium or short height, quite tall, stocky or thin build, had rushed in waving something which most witnesses described as a gun, an automatic pistol of sorts, but which might well have been a lamb chop picked up from the window display as he entered. In moments of crisis, as Davies knew well from experience, few people could get a description or a sequence of events in order.

Routine inquiries were initiated. One of the constables earnestly asked Davies what he thought the man's motive might have been and Davies told him: 'Gluttony.'

One positive benefit came from the interlude, however, for Davies left the scene of the crime with a plastic bag full of meat scraps which Kitty devoured later with growls of satisfaction and a violently wagging tail. He returned to the station and put in his preliminary report. 'No ideas?' asked Detective Sergeant Burrows who was put in charge of the case. Davies sniffed and said: 'I think we're looking for a non-vegetarian with a deep freeze.'

It was getting dusk but he thought he would still have time to go to Winner and Co., Turf Accountants of Marylebone High Street, before they closed. It was out of his area, in the next division, so he would need to proceed with caution. He took a bus down Harrow Road and another along Euston Road. The bookmakers' premises were lit encouragingly with windows full of photographs of horses and greyhounds, footballers, tennis players and cricketers, all in the course of winning.

He went inside. There was the usual late-afternoon fuggy smell, much like the morning scent of a pub but warmer. He pretended to be studying the lists of runners on the wall. The place was empty except for a man preoccupied with an adding machine behind the counter. The man looked up and Davies thought disconcertingly that he recognised him. 'What chance does Little Dorritt have,' said Davies conversationally.

'None at all,' responded the man. 'It fell in the two-thirty this afternoon.' He paused. 'I know you, don't I? Are you a copper?'

'No, not me,' lied Davies at once. 'No. I work for Sainsbury's. Just on my way home. Well, cheers.'

'Cheers,' returned the man amiably enough. 'I could have swore you was a copper.'

Quietly Davies cursed as he stood at the bus stop. He pulled his collar up so that nobody else would recognise him. Working another police patch was not so frowned upon officially in the Metropolitan Police these days but the local nick did not like it. Policemen were inclined to be jealous of their own preserve. Inquiries might be made.

He went back to Bali Hi and took Kitty for a walk around the lit streets. The dog kept burping but behaved well, apparently trying to keep friendly with him now that he had a source of good meat. He called into the Babe In Arms for a pint and wondered how Mod had progressed that day in far-off Bournemouth.

Mildred was on his conscience. They had slept together all night, with their arms innocently looped around each other, first his around her from behind and then, as though by some rehearsed manoeuvre turning to reverse the embrace. In the morning she had left silently while he still snored. Now he had the problem: should he mention it to Jemma?

As so often happened he made the wrong decision. They were enjoying their curry in Kilburn and he had drunk several lagers. During the meal he had gone through every aspect of the Dulciman case, pulling it apart, as he pulled apart chicken on his plate. Teasingly she leaned towards him over the table. 'And how was Mildred?' she asked sweetly.

'Fine, fine,' he returned amiably. 'We went for our long walk in the country.' He decided to take the risk. He was innocent anyway. Fairly innocent. 'She came into my room when I was in bed and she was lonely and crying and ...'

'And?'

'Well, it was all innocent but I was half asleep and I let her share the bed.'

He knew he had made the wrong decision. 'You *what*?' she demanded with sudden menace. 'You slept ... ?'

'*Slept,*' he argued. 'Just slept.' He did not like the look in Jemma's eye. 'Proper sleep, bye-byes, nothing happened ...'

She was livid. 'Like the escort tart you took home and slept on her stairs,' she said through her teeth.

'Well, now, come on, Jemma ... That was ... And as far as Mildred is concerned ... she's only a kid and ...'

'She was lonely and crying,' mimicked Jemma. Her Caribbean eyes were like lightning. 'That's the lousiest excuse I've ...' Words failed her. She stood up and picking up her plate of curry turned it onto his head. The plate cracked in two equal halves and he ended up with one in each hand while she went out of the door. The Indian staff and the other diners had watched the assault with growing interest and now the manager came diffidently to the table and inquired, 'Is sir finished?'

Davies was trying to scrape the curry from his head. It ran down his forehead and continued onto his nose, it made his eyes smart. He looked at the manager through the mess and said: 'I think you could say I have.'

Slowly he stood up, wiping the curry from his hair and his eyes. The manager looked helpless but anxious to please: 'Not a very hot curry,' he ventured wringing his hands, his eyes rolling. 'Quite mild.'

The other customers were entranced, forks hovering, pieces of Tandoori chicken falling onto plates, rice tumbling. A staring man bit through a popadum with a resounding crack. 'Where's the toilet?' asked Davies grimly.

Pointing the way the manager said: 'I will procure towels.' He surveyed the other eaters and announced: 'Incident is finished.' Obediently they returned to their plates.

In the confined lavatory Davies managed to scrape most of the curry from his hair with toilet paper. The manager, his arm only appearing around the door, like someone who fears an explosion, pushed in the towels. Grunting and cursing Davies threw water over his head from the basin. 'Rotten cow,' he complained almost sobbing. 'Bloody women!'

'Bloody women,' echoed the manager when Davies returned to the restaurant. 'Most bloody some of them.' The other customers were trying to keep their eyes down but some of them were smiling. The man who had cracked the popadum did it again.

'How much is it?' asked Davies morosely.

'This much,' said the manager handing him the bill. He regarded the plate cracked cleanly in two and still lying embedded in the red-brown mess on the table. 'No charge for damages.'

'Thanks,' returned Davies. 'Best news I've heard all night.' He paid and made for the door. For once, just when he could have done with it, it was not raining. He stood reeking at the bus stop. When the bus came he went on the top deck and sat at a distance from the scattering of other passengers. Two West Indians got up and went downstairs holding their noses. At the Jubilee Clock he left the bus and hunched along the street. The conductor leaned from his platform and called: 'Love the scent.'

Davies shook his fist and muttered: 'Funny bugger.' He plodded around the corner from the High Street. Another bus coming from the opposite direction stopped and Mod alighted heavily. He saw Davies and waddled towards him. Davies stood truculently and Mod stopped. 'You smell very exotic, Dangerous,' he observed. 'A touch of the sub-continent if I'm not mistaken.'

'You are not,' grunted Davies. 'It's Chicken Madras.'

'You're supposed to eat it,' said Mod. 'Not wear it.'

'That Jemma put it on my head,' muttered Davies.

'Ah, a hot-blooded lady.' They both peered towards the Babe In Arms but it was irrevocably shuttered and dark apart from the single light left glimmering over the bar. 'Let us see if the hot-dog stand is open,' suggested Mod. 'Now that we have made our peace with the vendor.'

'Come on then,' agreed Davies. 'I've never had so much food and still been hungry.' He glanced sideways at Mod as they turned their steps around and went back towards the clock. 'How did you get on?'

Mod nodded weightily, his head going with his steps like a carthorse. 'Not at all badly, in the circumstances,' he replied.

'What happened?' asked Davies at once eager. 'Did you find the kid's name?'

'I shall tell you while we dine,' insisted Mod. 'I feel this is a two-hamburger night, with double chips for me.'

They saw the stall in the distance, lit like a craft in dark space. The man stood in his oblong of illumination and watched them approach. 'You haven't got that dog have you?' he called.'Not on you.'

'Not on us,' repeated Davies. 'You've got nothing to worry about, mate.' They came up to the counter. With a continental touch the man had placed a scruffy wooden table and two collapsible chairs under the plastic awning of his cart. 'Another attack like that would finish me,' said the vendor. 'And the business. That dog is mad.'

'Four hamburgers and double chips twice,' said Davies determinedly. 'The dog is at home, in his basket, sleeping the sleep of the innocent.'

'I bet,' said the man, but mollified by the unexpected size of the late-night order. He sniffed. 'Something smells like the Ganges,' he said.

Davies glared but said nothing. He retreated to the small table and he and Mod sat down, Mod carefully testing the strength of the chair first. 'It must be a niff if he can smell it over his rotten onions,' grumbled Davies. Mod went to the counter and picked up the paper plates with their steaming and greasy contents. 'And two teas please,' he added turning to Davies and saying: 'The teas are on me. On expenses.'

They sat down and hungrily ate the hamburgers and chips. The vendor regarded them with the expression of one who knows more than he says. 'Nice are they?' he asked.

'Brilliant,' returned Davies. 'I must tell Egon Ronay.' He said to Mod: 'All right, what happened?'

Mod disposed of a bulging mouthful of hamburger and then took another bite before replying. 'I got down there at ten forty-five,' he related. 'It was a pleasant day for the time of the ...'

'Don't give me a weather up-date, for God's sake. Did you get the names of the kids who were cleaning up the beaches on that day?'

'No,' admitted Mod firmly, 'but I made some progress. I went to the newspaper, as you suggested, and they were very friendly and helpful ...' Davies rolled his eyes. A piece of onion was caught on Mod's lower lip and hung there perilously, eventually falling into his lap. '... but the man in charge of the archives had gone off on holiday and taken his key with him.' He looked at Davies thoughtfully. 'He went to Brighton on holiday,' he said. 'From Bournemouth.'

'Really,' sighed Davies. 'So what did you do, go to the council offices?'

'I did but they were not very helpful. Indeed they were a mite suspicious about a man turning up and inquiring about lads who clean up beaches.'

'You surprise me,' said Davies looking at Mod's bent form over the steaming chips. 'So then what?'

'I returned to the newspaper because they had said they must have a duplicate key somewhere, but they couldn't find it. I told the chap that I was looking for a long-lost relative and he came up with an idea. He remembered that all the youngsters who helped to clear up the beaches came from youth clubs and he put me in touch with a Catholic priest who was in charge of the whole operation for several years.'

Davies brightened. 'Ah, and what did he say?'

'Not much. He was dead.'

'Oh, sod it,' said Davies.

'Probably his own sentiment,' observed Mod disapprovingly. 'Another priest had taken over the parish but he was in Rome, an audience with His Holiness.'

'I'll go down again next week,' said Davies. 'At least that's something to go on.'

'I am glad I was useful,' said Mod looking sadly at the last crescent of his second hamburger. His eyes went to Davies' chips, pale in the night, and Davies pushed them towards him. He picked some up in his fingers. 'Why did Jemma throw the curry over you?' he inquired mildly. 'That large girl at the hotel?'

'You should be a detective,' suggested Davies sourly.

'Have you been romancing that young lady?'

'Not at all. She climbed into bed with me because she was lonely. She was crying and ...' He saw Mod did not believe him either. 'But nothing happened. It was just company.'

'Two's company,' agreed Mod sagely.

Davies changed the subject. 'I've got another little job for you,' he said. The man with the stall looked up and down the yawning street, yawned himself and prepared to close for the night. 'Tomorrow,' said Davies. 'Today, that is.'

Mod looked a little peeved. 'But my studies are suffering,' he complained.

'Today,' insisted Davies. 'I'd like you to go to a bookmakers. It's not far, only in Marylebone. I can't go. The bloke in there knows me.'

'All right,' sighed Mod. 'What do you want me to do?'

'Put a bet on the favourite in the two-thirty.'

Davies loitered as inconspicuously as he could in the shadow of the bus shelter while Mod went into the betting shop and looked melodramatically in both directions along the street before entering. There was still a streak of Welsh probity in him. Once he had entered the premises, his big untidy head appeared again and he treated the street to a further scrutiny before giving a blatant thumbs up sign to Davies who was doing his best to remain at least half hidden. Davies sighed.

It was not Mod's signal which caused him to come to the attention of the bag lady. She was heading in his direction anyway, muttering, examining the gutter, and rearranging her burdens. Davies saw her coming and hovered, undecided whether to break cover or remain where he was and hope that she would ignore him. He knew she would not.

'You waitin' for a bus or waitin' for the Queen to go by?' she inquired gummily.

'Is the Queen coming down this way today then?' he asked interestedly. To his discomfiture she put her bags on the pavement carefully one at a time and then, after a glance at the sky, moved them under the canopy of the bus shelter, obviously prepared for a long conversation.

'The Queen will be along before the bus comes,' she cackled. He smiled tightly at her, keeping an eye on the betting-shop door. She seemed pleased at her joke and cackled louder, spraying spit and squeezing up her eyes. 'A lot bloody before,' she embellished.

'I expect so,' said Davies glumly. Why did they always pick him out? Worse was to follow.

'You're a copper you are,' she said prodding him with a filthy finger. 'I seed you up in Willesden. I seed you with that dog. Is that a police dog?'

Davies could feel himself sinking. Why could he never hide like other police officers. 'No, he's my personal dog,' he said keeping his voice low.

She looked around speculatively. 'What you whispering for?' she inquired. She pointed accusingly: 'You're waiting to nick somebody.'

'I'm busy,' he said winking, hoping she would enter into the spirit of the moment. 'Very busy.'

'I 'spect you want me to piss off then, don't you.'

'If you wouldn't mind,' he said pleadingly.

'You're watching that betting shop,' she concluded after giving the street a further scrutiny. 'That's what, ain't you?'

'Look ...' pleaded Davies feeling in his overcoat pocket. 'Do me a favour ...'

Her hand was out for the money before his was out of the

pocket. She looked anxiously at what he might produce. He gave her a pound coin. 'Go and buy yourself a drink,' he suggested.

'Too early,' she pointed out. 'Not open yet.'

'Go and buy a sausage roll then,' he urged. He thought there was some movement in the betting-shop doorway. 'Or another bag.'

'If you want then I'll piss off,' she said haughtily. She took and examined the coin and dropped it disdainfully into one of the large carrier bags. 'I got things to do anyway. Places I got to go.'

She started to gather her bags and he made to help her but she pushed him loftily aside. 'Hands off my property,' she said. Her eyes were like liquorice. 'I don't trust coppers.'

With a deep sniff she heaved up her bags and proceeded along the street only pausing to stop several passers-by and point out Davies to them. 'Copper!' she called back belligerently. 'Trying to bribe an old woman!'

To his immense relief Mod came out of the betting shop. A bus arrived simultaneously and Mod had to trundle across the road to get out of its path. They got on the bus and went to the top deck. 'So what happened about Pengelly?' he said gritting his teeth.

Mod said: 'Why were you talking with that old bag woman?'

'I thought I might take her for a fortnight's holiday,' groaned Davies. 'Tell me what happened about Pengelly.'

'Well, fortunately, the chap in there remembered him. He was called Bill Page then, of course. As you said. It was some time ago but he recalls there was a theft or a misappropriation of money. Page was done for it and they threw him out.'

'And ... ?'

'Well, he didn't know a lot more. I told him I was a debt collector, which I thought was pretty astute.' He glanced at his companion for approval.

Davies said: 'Brilliant' and sighed deeply. 'And what about after the theft case? *Where* did Pengelly go?'

Mod had been puzzling the answer and now the uncertainty clouded his dark face. 'He went off to work with badgers,' he shrugged. 'That's what he said.'

Davies regarded him unbelievingly. 'Badgers?' he echoed. 'What badgers?'

'Goodness only knows, Dangerous. I thought it might mean something to you. All I could think was that it was something to do with shaving brushes.'

Then Davies realised. A large, rough grin filled his face. 'Badgers,' he said. 'Not Badgers. *Beavers.*'

'Ah, that's right,' said Mod relieved. 'I stand corrected. Wrong animal.'

The conductor came up the stairs for the fares. Davies was still smiling as he paid. 'Beavers,' he ruminated. 'Why didn't I think of that before.'

'What's beavers got to do with it?' inquired Mod whispering in case the conductor had loitered on the stairs.

'The Beaver Trade,' said Davies. 'You've never heard of the Beaver Trade?'

'Something Canadian?'

'No. The Beaver Trade, Mod, is photographic. It refers to pubic hair, usually female. Our friend Pengelly was in the *pornography* business. And I bet his mate, Mr Dulciman, was too!'

Twelve

Years before, Davies had been on a course concerning burglary and breaking and entering. The optimum time, and criminals were well aware of it, for breaking into business premises was six o'clock in the evening. Now he was going to try it.

Even Boscombe had a rush hour, early in the year though it was, and the main street and its tributaries were busy when he surveyed the premises of Pengelly Associates and the Goodtime Escort Agency from the café across and slightly along the street. Cafés, in his experience, were rarely sited conveniently for surveillance, rarely directly opposite the place under observation, often a difficult fifty to a hundred yards to the left or right resulting in some odd postures having to be adopted by the watching officers and frequently cases of cricked necks.

Both the offices he was observing were now unlit. There had been a light in the lower of the two rooms, until five thirty when it had been extinguished. He had seen no one leave the building but they may well have done so because a funeral procession had occupied his field of vision for some time, the hearse having had a blown tyre.

At six o'clock he made his move. He could not have stayed for a fourth cup of tea because it would have looked suspicious and the tea was terrible. As it was, the woman with the urn had made remarks about how thirsty he must be. 'It's your tea, love,' he said. 'Never tasted tea like it.' She blushed and said she would tell her husband.

Davies strolled across the street. He had often thought that nobody ever looked so furtive as a policeman, nor so suspicious, and he felt so now. But Boscombe was hurrying and no one stopped and stared at the secretive man. He sidled through the held-up traffic (the funeral had caused a long tailback which even now was not cleared) and quickly entered the door at the side of the greengrocer's shop.

The passage and the stairs were dark. He went up on the edges of his shoes, poking his head as far around the top bend as he could. The landing was dark also. He had already decided to break into the escort agency first. He had studied the lock on his previous visit and he did not think it would cause him many difficulties. He produced the clever instrument which he had taken from a cat burglar called Jennings several years before, and had kept for moments like this. Jennings, in exchange for some fair treatment and food in the police station, and a guardedly favourable mention in court, had tutored him in the use of the tool. He had often used it when returning to Bali Hi late at night when he had forgotten or lost his key. It could be worked on locks of all different sizes and the door was no match for it.

The lock surrendered with a brief click. He eased the door open. Sitting in the semi-darkness, in a chair, was one of the biggest men he had ever seen.

''Evening,' said Davies swallowing. 'Mr Pengelly about?'

'You're breaking in,' said the man, his voice as threatening as his size. He stood up and stepped towards Davies.

'I'm an old friend,' Davies tried desperately. 'Haven't seen him for years, and I thought I'd ...'

'... Just pick the lock and see if he was here,' finished the man.

'You're the security chappie, are you?' chatted Davies desperately.

'You got that right,' said the man punching him in the stomach. Davies doubled up and fell back so that he was sitting on the floor. 'Stop it,' he said as if his assailant were playing some sort of joke. 'Pack it in, will you.'

He used up all his remaining breath on the plea. The guard stood over him like a stormtrooper. Davies clutched his stomach and leaned forward with the action. The boots of the security guard were each side of his body. Davies reached out and catching the boots at the heels, pulled sharply, sending the man toppling back onto the desk. He rolled sideways falling onto the chair in which he had been sitting. Davies clambered awkwardly from the floor and, as the man regained his feet, hit him with both fists at once. The result was disappointing. The man's eyes blinked.

Davies moved in to close quarters. He tried to remember what you did, apart from the obvious with the knee. Every fight he had ever had as a police officer had been of the roughhouse variety where there was no opportunity for theory. He brought his knee up towards the guard's groin, but the man, who was left-footed, was doing the same thing to him and their knees collided. 'You … you …' bellowed the guard as if searching for a phrase for foul play.

'You … you,' howled Davies.

They closed against each other, rocking body to body, a ridiculous ballet of large and unfit men in combat. Davies tried a punch to the chin but only struck his opponent's chest. 'You …' the man shouted. 'I've been in 'ospital.'

'Are you better now?' asked Davies repeating the punch. Doubly enraged, the guard rushed into Davies and, taking him in a bear hug, wrestled him to the door.

The force of the onrush took them onto the landing and Davies hung on. But the banisters of the stairs were weak, and with a doomful crack they gave way. Both men toppled over.

They hit the stairs separately. Both howled in pain and shock and sprawled moaning in chorus until Davies summoned strength enough to stagger to his feet, step over the doubled form and stumble into the street.

'Well,' philosophised Mod wandering to the window. 'At least it's a change of hospital.' He peered out, his big back bent. 'Better outlook than Willesden. There's a view of the sea.'

Davies was nursing bruised ribs. 'It's the bump on your forehead I don't like,' intoned Mod turning and swaying. 'It's like an aubergine.'

'I've seen it,' said Davies. 'I won't be long in here anyway. For a change there's nothing broken.' He looked downcast. 'It's a pity you couldn't contact Jemma.'

'A message was all I could do,' said Mod. 'You are hoping that you might be reconciled?'

'It's possible,' said Davies miserably. 'I wouldn't mind if I was guilty. But I didn't do anything.' The emphasis made him wince.

'Apart from taking pity on that poor young woman and allowing her to share your bed,' Mod pointed out sagely. 'Nothing wrong with that.'

'Well there *wasn't*,' retorted Davies wincing again. He put both hands cradling his ribs. 'Nothing happened. We just went to sleep.'

Mod held up his large hands. 'I believe you, Dangerous. But I am not a woman.'

A bustling nurse came into the ward holding a telephone at arm's length. 'For you,' she said to Davies. She plugged it in at the bedside. 'Don't get excited. It will hurt.'

He picked up the receiver. 'Davies here.'

Mod watched his expression. His face lit. 'No, I won't talk too much. Yes, it's agony. You will? Oh, good. Thanks. Thanks very much.'

He put the phone down and grinned at Mod. 'She's coming down to get me.'

The telephone rang again. 'She's changed her mind,' muttered Mod. Davies picked it up.

'Mr Davies, can you take another call? It's a Mr Pengelly.'

Davies' eyebrows rose. 'He's an old friend.'

'Davies?' inquired the voice.

'This is he,' replied Davies primly.

'It's Pengelly. Why were you trying to burgle my office last night?'

Davies assumed an affronted tone. 'Now would I do that?'

'Yes,' said Pengelly emphatically. 'You picked the lock.'

'I merely wanted to see if you were at home,' said Davies ambiguously. 'And sitting there was a monster. He nearly killed me, Pengelly.'

'The monster has a fractured kneecap,' said Pengelly. Davies realised that the voice was different, low, uncertain, on the defensive. Pengelly paused. 'I think we ought to have a talk.'

Mod saw the expression brighten. 'When and where?' asked Davies.

'The sooner the better. This afternoon. In an hour say.'

'All right. On the bench in the park opposite the Royal Bath Hotel ... where you and Mr Dulciman used to meet.'

'All right,' said Pengelly sourly. 'In one hour.'

'You'll know me,' said Davies. 'I'm the bloke clutching my ribs.'

Smiling thoughtfully he replaced the telephone. Mod looked worried. 'You're going to just walk out of here?' asked Mod.

'I'll come back,' Davies promised. 'They won't know I've gone.'

He took Mod with him. 'I'm in no state to have another punch-up,' he said when they were on the bus. Calling a taxi would have aroused suspicion. No one had seen them walk out.

'Sit on a bench not too far away,' instructed Davies. 'Read a paper. If there's any violence ...'

'Run?' suggested Mod.

They left the bus at different stops; Davies first. By the time he was sitting on the bench Mod was concealed behind the public lavatories. Pengelly appeared on time, hard-faced, and slumped on the other end of the bench. Mod appeared, being berated by a council employee for hanging around the toilets. He shuffled away and sat on the next bench.

'Your bodyguard's been sussed,' said Pengelly.

Davies looked about him blandly. 'My bodyguard?'

'Forget it. I'm not going to do anything rough, even if you've got bruised ribs. I want to talk to you, Davies. I want to get you off my back for good.' He moved up the bench a foot towards Davies. 'I had nothing to do with Dulciman's disappearance, death or whatever.'

'You were in a dodgy business with him, Bill Page. Pornography.'

'So you've done your homework. All right, so we were. And we fell out, badly, but I still didn't do for him.'

'How long had you been taking dirty pictures together?'

'Years. Down here and before that in London when it was a risky business. Nowadays it's nothing like as much. Only kiddie porn and animals is asking for trouble.' He smiled grimly: 'No children or dogs allowed.' He went on: 'Every one of our models was over sixteen and they were all human.'

'How come then you were so shifty about it?' asked Davies moving his face a trifle closer.

Pengelly looked at him as if he knew he would not be believed. 'I didn't want my auntie to know,' he breathed. 'And I was standing for the council.'

'Shit,' said Davies. He looked wildly around as if seeking a witness.

'I knew you'd say that. But it's true. My auntie was rotten rich and I had every expectation of getting my hands on some of it when she snuffed it. Well, last week she did snuff it.'

'Get away,' said Davies quietly. 'And has she left you some loot?'

'Yes. That's why I want to get this straight with you.'

'Are you asking me to believe that you were *standing for the council?*' Pengelly nodded. 'There was some land an acquaintance of mine wanted to get his hands on. To build some flash houses. But then the bottom fell out of the building business, so that went by the board and I lost interest in local government.'

'Tell me about Dulciman,' said Davies.

'He was a terrible old shit,' volunteered Pengelly. 'Twisted as they come, theft, blackmail, conning. It was all the same to him.'

'But business was good.'

'You know what the beaver trade is like. Well, *was* like. The recession's hit that like everything else. But it used to be a goldmine. We did very nicely out of it. All studio stuff. Hard porn. As far as we could go. He wanted to do kiddies as well, but I didn't want to get involved.'

'Where did the models come from?' asked Davies. 'Not from your agency?'

Pengelly looked offended. 'Some of them did.' His eyes flicked around nervously. 'The younger stuff, well there's plenty of it around here. Unemployed teenagers. Mostly girls, of course. They were more than happy. They'd do anything. Anything.'

'Well, I suppose it's a job of sorts,' commented Davies thoughtfully.

'And well paid. We gave them fifty quid a session. Sometimes more depending …'

'You're not involved now?'

'No. I got out after Dulciman disappeared.'

'Do you think his vanishing trick may have been connected to the … er business?'

Pengelly nodded. 'It could have been. We started getting interest from the London boys. Moving in on us. We were getting threats. Then he vamooshed.' He waited. 'That's all I wanted to say. Just to let you know I had bugger all to do with it.'

He stood. Davies remained thoughtfully on the seat. 'Cheers,' said Pengelly beginning to walk away. 'Hope your ribs get better.'

'We've been searching for you everywhere,' the matron told Davies bitterly. 'You can't simply walk out like that.' She regarded him sourly. 'We really do not want your sort here, Mr Davies. If I had my way you'd never be admitted again.'

'I hope you're right,' mumbled Davies. The matron turned to Mod and regarded him with speechless scorn. Mod nodded humbly.

'I understand that someone is coming to collect you,' she said, revolving back to Davies. She sniffed as if he were someone who could *only* be collected.

'Yes, matron,' he said not meeting her eye. 'My lady friend from London.'

'Your lady friend?' Her voice was loaded with doubt.

'Here she comes now,' muttered Mod. They were in the reception area of the hospital and Davies half turned and saw Jemma coming through the outer doors. He smiled deeply.

The matron turned to see and her face altered. 'Oh ... I see,' she muttered.

Jemma walked in black and beautiful, then almost ran towards Davies and flung her arms crushingly about him. 'My ribs!' he cried. 'Oh, my ribs!'

'It's his ribs,' said the matron unnecessarily. 'He has bruised ribs.'

'Yes, yes,' said Jemma hurriedly to the matron. 'Of course.' She turned to Davies. 'Oh, Dangerous, I'm sorry. I shouldn't have tipped that curry on your head.'

Matron gave up. With a huge pouting sigh she whirled and strode off, her starched uniform crackling. 'This *is* a hospital,' she emphasised over her shoulder. 'There are seriously ill patients in here.'

Davies rolled his eyes towards the exit. He signed a book to say he was leaving at his own risk and ten minutes later they were driving from Bournemouth, east then north, towards London.

'We saw our friend Mr Pengelly this afternoon,' said Davies, his arms hugging his ribs.

'You did? What did he say?'

'He said he did not kill Dulciman, nor cause him to vanish, although they had fallen out over business.'

'What business?'

'Hard-core porn.'

She kept her eyes on the road. 'So that was it.'

'Giving much needed employment to young people,' he added.

'Children?'

'He said not. Dulciman wanted to do it but Pengelly said he wouldn't. Very sporting. Nor animals. No girl with guard dog stuff. He was frightened his auntie might find out and cut him out of her will. Oh, and he was standing for the council.'

'You believe all this?' asked Jemma.

'For the time being. It's all I've got. He was trying to get on the council to push through some crooked land deal. They were making a pile with the dirty pictures. Although he said the recession has killed a lot of it off.'

'Well done the recession,' she muttered. 'And that's why he stopped doing it ... ?'

Davies said: 'And Dulciman's disappearance plus the fact that the London nasties were moving in on them, two events which may be not unconnected ...'

Mod, sitting in the back, said: 'It doesn't do to mix it with toughs.' He paused. 'I trust we are not going to. In any case I'm getting behind with my studies. And I don't think you can put up with any further assaults, Dangerous. You'll simply collapse, like some gutted building.'

When they reached Willesden they dropped Mod at the Babe In Arms and Jemma took Davies back to her flat. He could not face Doris nor Mrs Fulljames with his ribs. Not immediately.

Jemma helped him up the stairs and into the bedroom where she stretched him out on her bed. She took his shoes off, then prised his overcoat away, hardly taking her eyes from his face. 'That bump,' she sighed. 'What a colour.'

'Aubergine,' said Davies.

He closed his eyes, then opened them again and saw her still regarding him with her deep expression, part sorrow, part exasperation. 'What *am* I going to do about you, Dangerous?' she said.

'Anything but the Madras curry,' he sighed. He closed his eyes. 'I didn't do what you thought I did. Honest, I didn't.'

'I know.' She sniffed back tears. 'I should have known. I'm sorry about the curry.'

He opened his eyes to slits and saw a touch of a smile on her pensive face. 'It was only a mild curry,' he said.

Jemma began to laugh and cry at the same time. She moved forward and lay upon him. He howled with pain.

Thirteen

Davies walked painfully along the High Street and to the police station. 'Drinking again, Dangerous?' called the desk sergeant cheerfully.

'In the call of duty, Francis,' responded Davies. He made to walk towards the CID Room. The sergeant called after him. 'Know a bloke called Weary Williams?'

Davies paused. 'Yes, I know Weary. What's he been up to?'

'Don't know. He's been in a couple of times but he'll only talk to you.'

'It's called popularity,' said Davies over his shoulder. 'I'll find out where he is.'

'No need to go far,' said the sergeant. 'He's down in the cells. Brought in last night. Drunk and aggressive.'

Weary Williams was not big enough to be truly aggressive; not without having to pay heavily for it. Looking through the grille Davies could see him hunched in the cell nursing a split lip. Being familiar with the injury he regarded it sympathetically. The door was not locked. Williams looked up as he entered.

'Watcha Dangerous,' he said, his rattish face lighting up. He shook hands eagerly. His hand like his face was small and bony. 'Can't smile,' he added apologetically. 'This starts pouring blood.'

'I know,' returned Davies feelingly. 'I know, Weary. What's your problem?'

'Usual,' sighed Williams. 'I got 'im first this time. Bang!' His miniature hand smacked into his small palm. 'When I punch 'em, they stay punched.' Davies was breathing painstakingly because of his ribs. 'You look like you've been in the wars too, Dangerous.'

'Nothing much, Weary. What's a few ribs.'

'Nasty I should think, mate. I been tryin' to see you.'

'So I heard.'

Williams wiped his face with his sleeve, skilfully avoiding his lip. 'Had breakfast?' asked Davies. 'You're entitled.'

'Don't I know it. Yes. Can't complain. The grub in this nick always was a bit of all right.' Davies sat on the opposite bunk and Williams leaned towards him and said: 'You 'member you was up at the Welsh Harp, that boot sale?' Davies nodded. 'Well, I was up there,' continued Williams, 'but you di'n see me. I do a bit of business there. Selling ... and buying like. But I was hangin' about there, behind somefink, when I 'eard you asking that bloke with the bits and pieces, I don't know 'is name, you was askin' him about a thing with like a German swastika on it. A brooch or somefink wa'n't it?'

Davies caught his breath as he leaned forward. It hurt again. 'Yes, Weary ...' he encouraged.

'Is there a reward?' asked Williams.

'There could be. It's a murder, Weary.'

The pale face went paler. 'Oh Gawd, is it. Well, I don't want to get anybody into trouble nor anyfink, but I 'membered you saying it and then a bit later I was down at Portobello Road, down the market. There's a geezer called Longo and what do I see on a stall, but this ...'

While Davies' eyes widened he produced from his pocket a brown envelope and from that took a red swastika brooch. Davies stared at it and then at Williams. Silently he held out his hand.

Williams put the brooch in his palm. 'Is that the one?' he asked tremulously.

He left Williams in the cell and went back to the CID Room. He telephoned Harrow Road Police Station and asked for a list of stallholders at the Portobello Road Market. They did not have one but they knew a man who did.

'Detective Constable Davies, Willesden CID here,' he said when he called the number.

There was a touch of anxiety: 'Oh, yes, Mr Davies. What can I do for you?'

'You hold the names of the stallholders at Portobello, I think.'

'I collect the rents. Who was it you wanted?'

Davies looked at the grubby piece of paper which Weary had given to him. 'Longo Burke,' he recited. 'Know him?'

There was a half laugh. 'Longo. Of course. I hope he hasn't been up to anything.'

'It's just some information,' said Davies.

'Right. Well he's got a place out in the country. In Essex. Here it is. Pickering's Barn, Saffron Walden. Shouldn't be hard to locate.' His voice gained in confidence. 'Not for a detective.'

'I'll try my very best,' said Davies caustically. He put the receiver down and glanced around to the Detective Superintendent's office. He could see Harvey's shape behind the frosted glass. He knew full well he ought to go in there now, produce the brooch and tell the story. But that would be the last *he* would hear of it. It would be taken out of his hands. Besides which, he consoled himself, Weary might be mistaken or telling lies, which was not unknown with criminals, or this was just another red swastika brooch. He had to take it – just a little – further.

He went out of the police station with Williams. On the front steps Weary surveyed the street, both ways. 'Sorry Dangerous,' he said. 'No offence but I got to be careful who I'm seen wiv.'

Davies said he understood and he glanced each way himself. 'I wouldn't want you in trouble with the Mafia, Weary,' he muttered.

They had a police driver and Weary ducked low in the back

seat until they were well clear of Willesden and on the M25 going east. They took the Saffron Walden road and Weary sat up and beamed from the window like a small boy on an outing. 'Cor, look at them *fields,* Dangerous,' he said. 'Green to hurt your eyes. And those cows.'

'You've seen cows, Weary,' admonished Davies from the front seat.

'Only on the box,' insisted Williams.

They turned into the old market town. The driver went into the police station and returned quickly. 'They know him,' he said with meaning. 'This Pickering's Barn place is on the main road out.'

It was two miles from the town. A broad, wooden building with a steeply sloping roof. As they arrived they heard gun-shots. At once the driver picked up his radio link. Davies touched him on the shoulder. 'Hold it a second. Let's have a look.'

The driver gave him a glance duplicated by Williams who had dropped to the floor between the seats. 'I ain't goin' in there, Dangerous,' he called up.

'I'll go,' sighed Davies. 'It's probably this bloke beating his carpets.' He climbed out of the car.

'Some carpets,' corrected the police driver to Williams who had remained under cover.

'What's he beatin' them wiv, I want to know,' Williams said.

They had brought the car onto a mud-and-stone drive in front of the barn. Davies went circumspectly along the track watched by the two men. He was ten yards short of the open barn door when there was another gunshot. He half dropped but immediately straightened and ran towards the wide door.

Putting his head around the post he saw that the firing was not coming from inside the barn. On the far side of the building was another open door. He could see drifting smoke. The barn was piled with junk, copper, brass, wrecked furniture, but standing in one corner were large objects neatly wrapped and apparently ready for removal. He went across the floor and out into the field. Another blast exploded. He bent his knees and peered around the corner. A very large man wearing jeans, a checked shirt, a leather waistcoat, and ear muffs, was firing a double-barrelled shotgun at a line of wooden chairs. He had lowered the gun but now he brought it to his bulky shoulder again and fired the second barrel. Davies waited until the sound had diminished and the blue smoke had cleared before approaching.

'What are you doing?' he inquired.

'Making antiques,' replied the man turning without hurry. His face was massive, the lower part festooned with a wide and unruly moustache and a thick ragged beard. 'Making them?' said Davies. 'I thought they had to *grow* old.'

'It's helping them do it,' explained the man unconcernedly. 'It's called distressing. What can I do for you?'

Davies told him who he was and produced his warrant card. 'Ho!' laughed the man. His voice was bluff, not quite upper class. 'You haven't come to arrest me for this have you?'

'It wasn't my intention,' admitted Davies.

'You'd have to prove a lot of things,' shrugged the man. 'What was your intention then?'

Davies produced the swastika brooch. 'Ever seen this before?'

Putting the shotgun onto a box, Longo Burke took the brooch between a large finger and an oily thumb. 'Oh, yes. Not long ago, either. I had it on my stall down at Portobello. I sold it to somebody.'

'I'll introduce you,' said Davies. He went into the barn and through to the other door, calling 'Weary!' towards the car.

Williams pushed his head out timidly. 'You all right, Dangerous? We was worried.'

'Weary, come on over, will you. The shooting's stopped.'

Williams, not particularly convinced, left the police car and walked towards the barn, eyeing it all the way. Timidly he looked around the door. 'Where?' he asked.

'Out the back,' said Davies. 'Longo is ageing some furniture.'

Williams kept behind Davies. They went out on the other side and Longo Burke grinned through his beard and said: 'Yes, that's him. Does he want his money back?'

Williams shook his head. Davies said: 'No, but I hope you can remember where you got this.'

'Don't tell me it's stolen,' said Burke. 'It's only worth a couple of pounds, if that.'

'Cost me a fiver from you,' said Williams.

'It *could* be important,' Davies said to Burke. 'In a murder investigation.'

The big man's whiskers fell. 'Oh, really. Well in that case I'd better check.' He made towards the barn taking the shotgun with him.

'Don't like shooters,' Williams whispered to Davies. 'Any sort.'

'Mr Burke only shoots at chairs,' said Davies.

'Sideboards and tables, cabinets,' corrected Burke. He picked up a grubby ledger. 'Keep everything on record,' he said. 'It makes holes, like woodworm. It gives it a bit of age.'

Burke was still studying the book running his fingers down the entries. 'Yoghurt is good for copper,' he said informatively. 'And a teabag stains documents and prints a treat.' He sniffed hugely. 'Here it is.' He handed the grimy ledger to Davies. 'At least I think so.'

'Assorted junk,' read Davies. 'Costume jewellery etc.' His eyes went along the line. 'Russian Mike,' he said. 'That's the bloke you bought it from?'

'Like I say, I think so,' nodded Burke. 'With bits and pieces like this I don't note every item. But I seem to remember this brooch being in that stuff I bought from him.' He took the ledger back. 'I gave him a fiver for the lot.'

'And *I* paid you a fiver,' said Williams indignantly. 'For one thing.'

Burke looked at him loftily. 'I have my overheads,' he said looking up at the barn roof.

'Do you know this man?' asked Davies. 'Russian Mike.'

'By sight,' said Burke. 'I don't know his real name. You know how they get nicknames in Portobello.'

'Do you know where he can be found?'

Burke shook his head. 'He's just "around" if you know what I mean. Can I ask who's been murdered?'

'I'll let you know,' said Davies shortly. 'When you say "around", around where? Portobello Road?'

Burke was becoming concerned. 'That's right.' He looked at Davies. 'This is a bit serious.'

'Murder often is,' said Davies.

'He may have got it from somewhere else, somebody else,' added Burke hurriedly. 'This sort of stuff circulates, you know.'

'Well, we'll have to ask him,' said Davies. 'Fairly quickly.'

He had gone as far as he dared. He knew he should have taken the swastika brooch to Detective Superintendent Harvey the moment Williams had produced it in the cell. His excuse that it was necessary to check it out first was hollow. So was the argument that it would not do to waste the superintendent's time with a trifle of evidence from a witness as unreliable as Williams. It did not even convince him. What would it do to Detective Superintendent Harvey? Davies sighed deeply.

There was, of course, the added excuse that he had needed to check the history of the brooch with Longo Burke. Swastika brooches were far from unknown. In the East the red swastika was a charitable emblem and plenty of people from Willesden were familiar with the East. It would not have done to have led the Detective Superintendent on a false trail. Would it? He sighed again.

Davies took the pin in its paper wrapping out of his pocket and studied it. Then he put it back, got up and walked through the CID Room. He could see Harvey's shape behind the frosted glass. He knocked. The invitation to go in was surly. Harvey stared up from the desk. He looked worn and unsuccessful. 'Can I have a word?' inquired Davies.

Harvey nodded at a chair. Davies sat down. 'I wouldn't mind', grunted Harvey, 'if I could get on with my work, my proper work of bringing villains to justice, without having to spend all my bloody time wading through this bumph.' He swept his shirt-sleeved arm over the piled papers on the desk. 'Look at it.' His head came up and then; as if realising for the first time who his visitor was, he sorted fiercely through the papers. 'Shit, I can't find it now,' he said. 'But you seem to have been having a lot of sick leave, Davies.'

'I keep getting duffed up,' pointed out Davies. 'In the course of duty.'

'Oh yes,' muttered Harvey as if trying to find a flaw in the argument. He examined the square figure in the chair. 'And you're nowhere near as fit as you were.'

'I don't wonder,' returned Davies in a hurt way. 'The way I get lumps knocked off me every time nobody else feels like getting lumps knocked off them.'

Harvey laughed as if to humour him. 'That's what they used to call you, wasn't it – Dangerous Davies?'

'The last detective,' Davies finished for him. 'They still do.'

'Perhaps we ought to think about a desk job. Fill up a couple of years before you retire.'

'If that happened I'd quit,' muttered Davies.

Harvey rose and patted him on the shoulder. It was a false bonhomie. 'You've got a good record, Davies,' said Harvey. 'You've just done things all the wrong way.' He regarded Davies with a sort of pity. 'In the Met there are ways of doing things. And there are ways of not doing things. You know that. Now what did you want to see me about?'

'This,' said Davies taking the swastika brooch from his pocket and unwrapping the paper on the desk. He enjoyed the moment as he had enjoyed few in his life. As the brooch tumbled from the wrapping onto the desk and lay there, cheap glittery clasp, red enamel emblem, Harvey's face became a mask. Then he choked. Choked so violently he could not produce words. Eventually like a man who has had a huge shock he descended heavily into his chair. 'Where the fuck did you get that?' he whispered.

'Little bloke called Weary Williams. He knew we were looking for it. He saw it in Portobello Road and brought it to me. It was on the stall of a man called Longo Burke, who makes antiques, and he got it from a character known as Russian Mike ...'

Harvey stared at the brooch and then at Davies. 'How ... how long have you had this?' he asked grimly.

'Twenty-four hours,' said Davies. He looked up into the hard, staring eyes. 'I thought I had better check it out first.'

Davies almost stumbled from Harvey's office into the CID Room and then the station lobby. The desk sergeant did not need to be a policeman to notice his state. 'What's the trouble, Dangerous. Somebody attack you?'

'Only the Detective Superintendent,' mumbled Davies. He was about to head for the door when three other plain-clothes officers hurried in from the street almost knocking him over in their urgency. Then Harvey appeared from the other direction and pushed the trio towards the street again. He ignored Davies, bellowing: 'Come on, we've *got* him! Come on, let's go!'

'*We*'ve got him,' echoed Davies dismally as they rushed out. 'I like the bloody "We".'

'What's up?' asked the desk sergeant.

Before Davies could answer a shabby and distraught man stumbled in from the street. His ash-stubbled face creased as he saw Davies. 'Ah, Dangerous,' he almost sobbed. 'Just the bloke.'

Davies turned on him but his anger dropped at once from his shoulders. He sighed: 'Hello Percy. What's your problem?'

'They done my bike again, Dangerous,' said the grey man, his face twisting. 'The same buggers gone and took it.' He was pleading. 'If I 'aven't got my bike I can't get to the 'llotment, can I?'

'Who's nicked it?' He could feel the desk sergeant grinning.

'Them what calls themselves the Angel Bruvvers. Lives at the end of the street. I know they got it, Dangerous. Get it back for me will you, mate.'

With a glance at the sergeant, Davies muttered: 'I'm glad somebody needs me.' He put his arm on the man's shoulder. 'Let's go and sort them out.'

'It's only round the corner,' said Percy when they got into the street. 'They does it just to get me upset. Reckons I'll 'ave one of them 'eart attacks then they can have the bike for good.'

They went into the cowering street. 'End house,' said Percy, his voice dropping to a whisper. 'I'm *afraid,* Dangerous,' he said timorously. 'I'm scared of them.'

'Go down to your house,' Davies told him calmly. 'I'll bring the bike down in a minute.' He looked at the man's twitching face. 'Now, you're sure they've got it? You haven't just lost it?'

'They got it, all right,' said the man emphatically. 'I seed them take it. I got digging to do on the 'llotment.'

'Right, push off home then. I'm just about ready for the Angel Brothers.'

He was too. Inside he felt like a kettle, boiling and confined. He went to the door and banged on it fiercely. It opened at once. Both brothers, in their late teens with a string of convictions behind them, came to the door at once. They more than filled the frame. 'Don't bang the fucking thing down,' complained one. He saw who it was. 'Oh, it's you,' he said.

'It's 'im,' his brother confirmed grimly. 'What you want then?'

'Percy's bike,' said Davies. He stepped forward and put one finger of each hand up their respective nostrils. 'Get it now.'

The youths, looking frightened, made honking noises and backed into the tight hallway. Davies put his foot in the door. 'Get it,' he repeated. He patted his overcoat breast. 'I am an armed officer and I'm going to shoot you bastards if you don't get that bike.'

He could see that they thought he had gone mad. Both began to back away. '*One* of you,' he ordered getting hold of the shirt collar of the nearest. 'You stay with me.'

The brother who was free backed into the dimness of the hall. The other rolled his eyes at Davies. 'You ain't supposed to come around shooting people,' he grunted. 'You ain't allowed.'

'*I* am,' Davies told him. 'I'm licensed to kill, I am.'

The first youth reappeared in the passage. He wheeled the bicycle towards Davies. 'We found it,' he said.

'Before it was lost,' Davies growled at him. 'All right lads, wheel it down the road to Percy's house and give it to him. Tell him you found it. He'll be very grateful.' He took each pair of eyes in turn. 'Both of you.'

They glanced at each other and each nodded. Docile as choir boys they wheeled the bicycle between them along the pavement to the house at the other end of the terrace. 'You knock,' said Davies pointing to the brother nearest the door. 'Nicely.' Grimacing the youth did so. Percy's frightened face appeared.

'Hello, Percy,' said Davies blithely. 'These two nice lads found your bike. They've brought it back to you.'

A great smile filled the man's tatty face. 'Fanks,' he said taking the bicycle indoors. He looked gratefully at Davies. 'Fanks,' he repeated. He closed the door.

'Now you two run off home and watch children's telly,' said Davies to the youths. He touched them each on the shoulder. 'One thing you ought to know is that Percy is an SPP – a Specially Protected Person. He was in MI5 during the war. If he gets hurt then there's big trouble. So leave him alone. Now piss off.'

'Christ,' said Davies morosely. 'I thought he was going to go straight through his ceiling. He went bloody berserk. You'd think I'd let a murderer get off the hook instead of getting one on it.'

Jemma patted his hand on the table in the Babe In Arms.

Mod nodded deeply. 'And the top dog will take all the credit,' forecast Jemma.

'You can bet on that,' said Davies. He sighed. He was so upset Mod had to buy the drinks. 'I told him that I wanted to check it out first so that I wouldn't be wasting his valuable time.' He glared at both faces. '*And* because *I* wanted to do it,' he said doggedly. 'God, I'm the one who turned it up.'

'He was not the least grateful,' said Mod in his studied way. 'Not a man who is sure of his position. I knew a librarian like that once.'

Jemma silenced him with a glance. 'Not a grateful man at all,' agreed Davies. 'Shouting about me wasting valuable time. Russian Mike would be a million miles away by now. In South America somewhere. All that crap. Was I for the high jump if he slipped through the net! Christ, they didn't even *have* a bloody suspect – and now I'm being accused of perverting the course of justice.'

'Well, it wasn't South America,' observed Jemma looking again at the *Evening Standard*. The headline said: 'Wormwood Scrubs body: Man detained'. Her eyes went down the item. 'South Harrow,' she said. 'And Detective Superintendent Harvey making a nice guarded, self-congratulatory, puffed-up statement. I bet you'll never get a mention.'

'That's a racing certainty,' said Davies.

'Speaking of which,' put in Mod in his diversionary manner, 'the horse you had me bet on the other day at that betting shop ...'

'It won,' nodded Davies. 'I saw. Evens.'

'There were expenses, of course,' warned Mod. 'I had to go back to the shop to collect my winnings. Five pounds sixty. And you know how much bus fares are these days.'

'But they're not a fiver from here to Marylebone,' argued Davies. 'What about the rest?'

'I used it to buy these drinks,' pointed out Mod.

Davies said grimly: 'Well, they can have their glory. Take all the bloody credit when the villain goes back to the Scrubs for life. I'm going down to Bournemouth at the end of the week.'

Jemma eyed him. 'At least', he said, 'that's my own case. My own murder.'

Fourteen

By now it was April. 'April airs are abroad,' quoted Mrs Dulciman. She held onto Davies' arm as they strolled along the promenade.

'Certainly are,' agreed Davies sniffing the salt breeze. The sunshine was thin but there were already people in deck-chairs, sheltered by wind breaks, on the sands. More were sitting on the seats along the beach railings. Mrs Dulciman suggested that they should sit there too. They found a bench and sat observing the sea. An unspeaking old couple were already on the beach taking in the same bland scene. 'Would you mind leaving us alone,' Mrs Dulciman asked them precisely. 'We have private things to talk about.'

Davies was astonished and even more so when the couple nodded understandingly and moved away. 'Very subservient, some people,' said Mrs Dulciman with satisfaction. 'It depends entirely on their upbringing.'

They sat in silence. 'The season does not really begin before Whitsun. Then the grockles come,' said Mrs Dulciman eventually. She half turned to Davies and squeezed his arm. 'What have you found out, Mr Davies?'

'A few things,' he said. 'If I didn't keep ending up in hospital I'd be almost there by now.'

'Really. How clever of you. Do you know what happened to him?'

'I will soon,' he replied. He regarded her seriously. 'Mrs Dulciman, I have something to tell you. It may come as an unpleasant surprise.'

'Oh,' she said mildly. 'And what is that?'

He said bluntly: 'I'm afraid Mr Dulciman was engaged in the pornography racket.'

She burst out laughing. A man passing by with his dog turned sharply at the laugh. 'It's all right,' she said waving him away.

'Pornography,' repeated Davies lowering his tone. 'You *do* know what I mean?'

'Know what you mean? My dear boy, fifty years ago I was one of the best pornographic models in the business.'

All Davies could say was: 'You?'

'Me,' she confirmed. 'That's how I met Dulciman first. I was not aware that he had taken it up again when we came down here. But then, he never told me much.'

She turned to him smiling sweetly. 'I do believe you are shocked, Mr Davies.'

He rubbed his chin. 'Well, it was a bit of a surprise.'

'My mother was famous for it,' she said almost gushing. 'Before the First World War. And during, of course. That's when she made her money. Then there was an unfortunate accident. In Paris. They used to use those magnesium flashes that exploded so that you could take the picture. Somebody's hairs caught fire. Most unfortunate.'

Davies stared out to sea. He had thought that he was past being astonished at anything. From the corner of his view a pink figure progressed down to the shore. In was Nola Cloudsley-Clive swinging her tennis racquet. The gulls began to bay in anticipation. She threw up a piece of bread and struck it with the racquet.

'Old idiot,' said Mrs Dulciman with scarcely subdued bitterness. 'Look at her, done up like a flaming flamingo. What a way to serve out your life.'

She appeared unconscious of the pun. Davies said: 'She's serving the gulls now.'

'Dulciman knew her, of course. You've found that much out?' It was a question as though to test him.

'Er ... yes,' he nodded still watching the scene on the beach. 'She lent him some money, I believe.'

'She and goodness knows how many others. And "lent" is scarcely the word. They *gave* him the money – gladly. He was that sort of man. He didn't ooze charm, he poured it out. By the bucket. When he had his own teeth he was even more devastating.' The reference served to remind her. 'Did you ever come to any conclusions as to who might have sent his teeth through the post, by the way?'

'Not really,' he lied. 'If I knew that I might be well on the way to solving the whole caboodle.'

'In that case', she said almost hugging herself, 'I must tell you.'

'You know?' he asked managing to appear astonished.

'I certainly should do. It was me! I sent the teeth to myself!'

'Why would you do that?' he asked looking as if everything was becoming too complex for him.

'To encourage *you* to take the case, of course, silly,' she enthused. 'A kind of bait.'

'Well, well. Who would have thought it,' he said shaking his head. 'Just to give me the come-on. Well, it certainly worked. You're a devious woman, Mrs Dulciman.'

She giggled with pleasure. 'I'm so pleased to hear you say it. Sometimes it is difficult to acquire new skills when you have become less than young, or more than young, whichever it should be. Deviousness *is* a skill, I think.'

'Oh, I agree,' he said. 'You certainly had me fooled.'

'Those teeth were sitting around for five years. I kept them in the first place in case he came back and needed them. But then I had this bright idea. And, as I say, it worked.'

Davies nodded. 'Here I am working on the case. Amazing.' His tone changed. 'How come he left his teeth behind when he went out for the last time? Were they a spare set?'

'Reserve teeth,' she acknowledged. 'When he went out to the Moonlighters Club that final evening he was wearing his best set. Perhaps he had an assignation.'

'His business, the pornography business, was run with Pengelly.'

Now she was surprised. 'Was it now? That's most interesting. I thought Pengelly had to make a living at something. He was no good as a detective.'

'Apparently they knew each other in London, when Pengelly was called something else, and they set up the studio and the models and everything then. But things went wrong. Some of the London gangsters began to lean on them, I suspect, and that is when your husband decided to quit and come to live down here.'

She nodded thoughtfully: 'I always thought we decamped a trifle hurriedly,' she said.

'Then, at some time, Pengelly contacted him and suggested that they should start up again in a quieter way, out of London, and that's what happened. They used young people from this area, most of them out of work, for the models. But once again it became too successful. Dulciman had borrowed the money to start the whole thing up from people like Mrs Cloudsley-Clive out there ...' He squinted into the lowering sun at the tall angular woman still swinging the tennis racquet, '... with no intention of repaying it. But, once more, the London gang or gangs got to hear of it and they began to put the squeeze on again.' He looked at her sadly. 'I'm afraid, it is a possibility that Mr Dulciman's fate may well have been tied up with that situation.'

'Poor Dulciman,' she sighed but with no great feeling. 'That might have been nasty.' She returned the expression. 'You think he might be down somewhere helping to hold up the motorway?'

'It's a possibility.'

'Well, I hope he didn't suffer too much,' she said.

Father Ignatius O'Rourke was sitting in a deck-chair behind the Catholic Church reading *Woman's Own* when Davies found him.

'So many of my problems are with women,' he said. His expression altered. 'Not directly, you understand. I have kept to my vows if others haven't. But women are always coming to me for advice. The only way I can give it is to read the experts, the Agony Aunties, don't they call them, in journals such as this. They seem to have all the answers.' He was a small, wispy man, with a red-button nose. 'I would not like you to think I have taken up knitting,' he smiled.

Davies introduced himself. 'A private eye,' echoed the priest after the policeman had told his semi-lie. 'Now there's a thing. What is it, a murder?'

'It might be.'

The priest looked as if he were trying to think of a suitable recent case. He failed. 'Now who would that be?' he asked.

'At present it's merely a missing person,' replied Davies.

'Ah, one of those. They often come back dead, don't they?'

'Yes, they often do. This concerns a Mr Dulciman. He disappeared about five years ago.'

Father Ignatius looked puzzled. 'Not a missing person I know,' he confessed. 'But then I was not here five years ago.' He brightened. 'I have just had audience with the Holy Father, you know. In the Holy City.'

'I heard,' said Davies.

'Who told you?' asked the priest a trifle concerned.

'I had some inquiries made and you were away,' explained Davies. 'How was the Holy Father?'

'In good health by the look of it. He spoke to us only in German, unfortunately. I went with an ecumenical group from Salisbury and apparently through some mix-up they decided that we had come from Salzburg. I did not understand a single word he said. Nor did any of the others.'

'Life's like that,' said Davies. 'Full of misunderstandings.'

'And mysteries,' said the priest. 'Now what was your particular mystery?'

'It really concerned your predecessor.'

'Who now, I trust and hope, knows the answers to all mysteries.'

'Yes, I understand he has died.' Davies allowed a proper pause. 'But I believe he ran a Catholic youth club and the members were involved in the campaign to keep the local beaches tidy. They wore special caps and T-shirts.'

The priest appeared a little surprised but said: 'Oh, they did too. I was asked to carry on with the good work, but I declined. I have enough concern trying to cleanse souls without having the beaches to worry about.'

Davies nodded. 'I need to find one, just *one* will do, of the young people who took part in the campaign five years ago. One of them found a pair of shoes.'

'Ah, your clue,' said the priest with satisfaction. 'Did your man walk out to sea then?'

Davies glanced at him appreciatively. 'He may have done. Or he may have just wanted to give that impression. Or somebody else may have wanted to give that impression.'

'The malefactor,' agreed the priest with a small smile of satisfaction. He rose from his chair. 'Father Fergus did leave records,' he said. He folded his *Woman's Own* carefully. 'Come on, I'll show you. He was a great man for keeping files in order. Unfortunately, I am not.'

He led the way into the house, nodding his head rhythmically like a closely shorn donkey. 'Now fancy there being a murder,' he ruminated. 'And all that time ago.' He turned sympathetically at the door. 'The trail, if that is the word, must be a touch cold.'

Davies nodded. 'I'm trying to breathe some life into it,' he agreed.

'But then after a while, a few years even, I expect people tell you things they would not mention in the first instance. They don't think there is any harm in saying them then.'

'Exactly,' said Davies. 'That is one of the great plusses. Not that what people remember is always correct, far from it, but it's given them time to come to opinions. They don't think it's so important to hide embarrassing things.'

'Their perspectives have changed,' agreed the priest. He led the way into a dim and extravagantly unkempt study. Books were piled on the floor, in one instance to replace the missing leg of a chair. There were piles of newspapers and pamphlets, half a dozen plastic coffee beakers, a pile of grubby towels on the desk, and in a corner a slide projector throwing a bright picture of a large white bird with a vivid yellow neck onto the screen.

Father Ignatius tutted. 'Forgot to turn it off,' he said, now doing so. 'I burned my last living to the ground, although that is a secret we must share. It was officially unexplained.'

'You're interested in birds,' said Davies looking at the now dark screen.

'The derivation of words and phrases,' corrected the priest. 'I am writing an illustrated book, for young people, showing how some of the things we say came to be.' He turned on the projector. 'This is a solan goose, otherwise known as a gannet. You know that to be a gannet is a phrase for being greedy.' Once more he flicked the switch. A snarling wolf appeared. 'And another phrase is to be a glutton. This is a glutton, the Scandinavian wolf.'

People's private, sometimes secret, interests, sometimes passions, never ceased to intrigue Davies. The priest shut off the projector again and blew on it as if in an attempt to cool it. 'Now,' he said in a businesslike way. 'Father Fergus' files. They are in here.'

He led the way once more from the room and into an adjoining smaller room which was as ordered as his own had been in disarray. 'My housekeeper, whom I inherited with this house, keeps these filing cabinets dusted. I even found her polishing them one day.' He winked at Davies. 'I think she has a suspicion that he may come back some time.'

He turned on the light. It beamed powerfully over the cabinets. 'He put that in,' said Father Ignatius. 'It's like the

Light of God, isn't it.' He began sniffing along the labels on the outside of the cabinets. He tutted. 'Look at that will you,' he said without enabling Davies to do so. 'He kept lists of everything. From who was born to who was wedded to who died and who scrubbed the vestry floor. Amazing.' He glanced sideways at Davies. 'But this day it all may be justified.'

He sniffed along the files. 'There it is. Easy. Youth Club. It's divided into years. Five years ago you say, Mr Davies. Here we are.'

The small man tugged violently at the metal drawer. Davies leaned to assist him but it was already opening. The priest stepped aside in invitation. 'See if you can spot it,' he suggested. 'This light is too much for me. I'll never get used to Heaven.' He went towards the door. 'I'm going to ask Mrs Finnister to make some coffee. Would you like a cup?'

Davies thanked him and said he would. His hand went into the cabinet and he lifted out a file. He checked the year. Nineteen eighty-eight. That was it. He put it on a small table which took up most of the rest of the space in the room. There was a wooden chair and he took this away from the table intending to sit to study the file. But it was not necessary. Almost the first document that he took from the folder was the one he sought. It was headed: 'Youth Club volunteer beach party' and was a list of a dozen names. He could feel himself smiling gratefully as he looked down at them.

He took the list and then went through the rest of the file. There were letters and memos and further lists headed 'Duty Rosters'. He picked out the list for 16 September, the date that Dulciman's shoes had been found. There were a dozen names on it. He checked them with the original document. They were all included.

Davies returned to the priest's study. Father Ignatius was sitting behind the desk which had been all but concealed by other objects, some of which he had now pushed to one side. He had taken some vestments from the back of a chair and he now invited Davies to sit down. Two mugs of coffee were standing on the desk. 'It's instant,' he said half apologetically. 'Mrs Finnister made proper coffee for Father Fergus. His general food was a good deal better too.' He leaned forward confidingly. 'An inherited housekeeper is like a woman married twice. Always making comparisons, usually unfavourable.' He looked at the two pieces of paper in Davies' hand. 'You found something. That was quick indeed.'

'Father Fergus' filing system,' said Davies.

'Ah, yes,' shrugged the small man. 'I suppose that orderliness has its concealed virtues. Like cleanliness.'

Davies began reading down the names. 'Andrews, Arthurson, Ferris, Gannet, Milford, Mulligan, Ling ...' The priest began to nod at them. 'All these families are still here,' he said. 'Although I'm not too sure about the Milfords. They have stopped coming to church. They may have moved away.' He looked at Davies brightly. 'Can I help you to contact them?' he suggested.

'Now that would be a great help.'

'I think coming from me the inquiry would be less startling than from a detective, don't you think?'

Davies agreed. The priest studied the names on the list. 'Of course, this was five years ago, and these young people will be nineteen, twenty, even older by now.'

'There are plenty of holes in it,' conceded Davies. 'After this time they may not be able to recall anything. Although finding a pair of floating shoes is not an everyday occurrence.'

Father Ignatius rubbed his small, cherry nose. 'Did this person realise, at any time, that the floating footwear might be connected with a murder?'

'You would have made a good CID man,' smiled Davies. 'It's possible they did not. As far as they were concerned they found the shoes and took them up to the hotel and that was that. End of story. The porter at the hotel took the shoes but did not take the name of the young person and I don't know whether the police traced him, or even tried to trace him. He simply found the shoes.'

'But why take them to the hotel?' asked the priest.

Davies eyed him with appreciation. 'Exactly. Why didn't he just leave them floating? What's a pair of waterlogged shoes? Perhaps he was astute enough to realise that they ought to be reported, that somebody might have drowned. A pair, not one. So he headed for the nearest place where an adult might take over – the hotel.'

Father Ignatius studied the list again. 'What questions do you want me to ask?' he glanced up. 'If I can contact these people, that is,' he warned. 'They ought to be out working now, or studying somewhere. But these days, you never know.'

'Let's hope we're lucky,' said Davies. 'If not I'll call them later. This evening.'

'Maybe we'll be lucky,' echoed the priest. 'Now, the questions ...'

'Right,' said Davies. 'Well, first of all ask if the person can remember a pair of shoes being found on that occasion, 16 September five years ago, and who found them. It's just the sort of thing that might stick in someone's mind.'

Without asking anything further the priest discovered the telephone below the pile of soiled roller towels screwed up on the desk. He uncovered the telephone directory from the same area and handed it to Davies. 'You read the numbers,' he suggested. 'The print gets smaller every day for me.' He handed Davies the list.

Davies said: 'We'll try the less common names. Arthurson. That will do for a start.' He looked through the directory. 'Only two entries.'

'It will be the one in Holdenhurst Road,' said the priest. 'The father died.'

Davies read the number and watched Father Ignatius dial with exaggerated care. The call was answered quickly.

'Hello, is that Mrs Arthurson? It is. Good. This is Father Ignatius from the church ... No, there's no trouble.' He turned his eyes up to Davies and rolled them. 'No, no. I wanted to have a word with young Brian. Is he there? Oh, good ...' He covered the mouthpiece and whispered to Davies. 'They think because it's a priest that it's bad news.' He returned to the phone. 'Hello young Brian. What are you doing these days? Not much. Well, I expect something will turn up. I want to ask you an odd question, but it's important to see if you can remember. You know the beach patrols that Father Fergus used to organise, picking up the litter and suchlike ... ? Right, that's it. Can you cast your mind back some way, five years, 1988, 16 September. Someone, one of the members of the youth club, found a pair of shoes floating in the sea ... Do you recall that? You don't. Think hard. No, you don't. Well, thank you Brian. Hope your life improves soon.'

Shrugging, he put the telephone down. 'He doesn't remember,' he said. 'But knowing the confusion in his family I'm not surprised. His sister had a baby and was supposed to have it christened. Everybody turned up and they forgot to bring the baby, can you believe.' He sighed. 'What's the next name?'

'Ferris,' said Davies. 'Ferris, Ling, Gannet ...'

'It's Garret ... Father Fergus' handwriting. But it looks like Gannet, doesn't it, the solan goose. Sometimes these things are signs. Anyway I know where they live. They come to church regularly and they're a clever enough family. Although in that case the lad will be out at work or at his studies, I imagine.' Davies found the entry in the directory and told him the number. He dialled it.

'Is that young Andrew Garret?' asked the priest. 'It is. Fine. This is Father Ignatius ... No, no trouble. I just wondered if you could remember something from some time ago ...'

Davies watched the priest's face as he recited the questions. At once his expression lightened. 'You do? Who was it? Ah, yes, I know them. The Howells, right, Old Christchurch Road. Yes I do. Thank you Andrew. Hope you're better soon and back to work.'

Slowly he put the phone down and turned smiling towards Davies in the same movement. 'You heard that,' he said.

Davies was already searching for the number. He gave it to Father Ignatius. 'What question this time?' he inquired.

'Ask him if he remembers picking up the shoes.' He thought about it. 'Then I think I'd like to meet him. Perhaps you could come too, Father.'

'I will,' said the priest rubbing his small hands together. 'I'm enjoying this.'

With pedantic care he dialled the number. 'Now, hello there, Mrs Howells. How are you? No, there's no trouble. It was young Peter I wanted. No, nothing to worry about. Ah, good for him. I see. Well perhaps I could call about then. Right. Thank you. Oh … yes, God be with you also.'

He replaced the telephone. 'He's got work,' he said to Davies with a touch of triumph. 'The lad that is, not God. He comes home about four.' He studied rather than looked at the wall clock. The hands were large but it was an hour slow. 'I can't put it right, I daren't touch it,' he forestalled Davies. 'Father Fergus put it there. As you already know he was a thorough man and when he put it on the wall, that is where he meant it to stay. Only God could shift that clock.'

'But it's only slow,' pointed out Davies. 'You could move the hands.'

The priest looked a trifle annoyed as if he wished he had thought of that. 'I'll wait until summertime,' he decided. 'My hours are too full to keep altering clocks.' He looked at his watch held by a strap like a dog collar on his wrist. 'This has stopped. Last week,' he said.

'It's three thirty,' said Davies looking at his watch.

'We could have our cup of coffee and make our way down there,' the priest said. 'We must continue with our investigation.' His small face wrinkled. 'In the meantime perhaps you could tell me the details. I would like to know *exactly* what it is we are investigating.'

Mrs Howells had put on a new dress for their visit. There was still a label hanging from the back. When her son came home from work he silently went to the sideboard drawer, took out a pair of scissors and cut off the label. 'Look at that,' exclaimed Mrs Howells, 'and I've been wearing this dress like that for ages.'

She brought them tea. Peter Howells was a tall, thin youth with sandy hair and a haunted expression. 'Nice to see you've got a job,' said Father Ignatius. 'So many haven't.'

'I did training,' said Peter tiredly. 'Also I did retraining. You know. Carpentry, plumbing, interior decorating, roofing.'

'You're well qualified,' put in Davies. They had not told the boy why they were there and he had not asked.

'I've got a job in Perkins,' he said.

'The pork pie manufacturers,' beamed the priest as if the youth had said the Stock Exchange. 'And how is it?'

'All right,' shrugged Peter. 'If you like killing pigs.'

The priest glanced uncomfortably at Davies. 'Yes ... well ... they have to ... well.'

'He thought it was a job in the Dispatch Department,' said Mrs Howells putting the teacups on the table.

Her son regarded them bleakly. 'Like sending off the pork pies. Dispatching, that's what I thought it meant. But it turned out to be killing them and gutting them afterwards. I can't stand it any longer. I quite like pigs.'

'With all that training you should get another job,' encouraged Davies.

'I'm overqualified,' muttered Peter. 'The only thing I can get is in the chicken processing place. You only slaughter hens there. I might as well join the army. At least you only have to kill something now and again.'

Sympathetically his mother poured the tea. 'His dad was an undertaker, you remember, Father.'

'So he was,' agreed Father Ignatius who had forgotten.

'At least the people were already dead,' said the youth. He seemed suddenly to realise that they had come especially to see him. 'What was it about?' he asked.

'A murder,' said Father Ignatius tactlessly.

Davies put his hand across his eyes. 'A possible murder,' he corrected.

The boy looked alarmed. 'Why me?' he asked. 'What did you want me for?'

'He's a detective,' said the priest.

Davies got in before Father Ignatius could say anything else. 'It's about those shoes you found on the beach five years ago.'

Peter looked puzzled but then his face cleared. 'Oh right,' he said firmly. 'I found them in the water. But it was ages ago.'

'Five years,' repeated Davies. 'I am a private investigator and I am trying to clear up the disappearance of a Mr Vernon Dulciman. They were his shoes.'

For the first time the young man looked interested. 'Were they? Well, what about that then. Did he end up in the sea then?'

'He may have done,' put in the priest, patently feeling the matter was drifting away from him. 'Or he may have been done away with.'

The youth laughed nervously. His mother stood with her fingers to her mouth. 'But all I saw was his shoes,' he said. 'I didn't even know whose they were until now. Nobody told me. That was the last I heard of it.'

Davies blew out his cheeks. 'You didn't leave your name,' he said. 'It did not seem that important at the time, I know.'

'Not to me,' said Peter. 'And nobody asked for my name. I just took them up to the chap in the hotel.'

'They were floating in the shallows were they?' Davies asked him. 'Floating about?'

The young man frowned. 'That's right. I didn't actually see them first, now I remember. There was a woman there and she pointed them out to me and when I got them she told me to go up to the hotel with them because they might be important. I was only fourteen and I used to do what my elders told me. So I did.'

Davies was staring at him. 'This woman … What was she like?'

'Not very old. I've seen her in the disco and around Bournemouth. Not very old but quite fat. She just said to take them to the hotel.'

'Mildred,' breathed Davies to himself.

'She's gone,' said Bertie spreading his hands.

'Gone? Where?' asked Davies. The porter had been standing on the steps outside the hotel when Davies arrived. Now he looked up and down the street as though seeking an answer.

'Goodness knows, Mr Davies, I don't. Nor anybody else here. She just up and went. No notice, no anything. Everybody was put out. We're just starting to get busy.'

'That's not like Mildred, is it,' said Davies. They walked into the lobby. A new, confused-looking girl was behind the reception desk.

'Not one bit,' said Bertie. He paused. Sometimes Davies had watched people do this, a stiffening of the face, an expression of surrender, when they were about to say something they thought they might later regret. Bertie took a step closer. 'I've got to tell you something, sir,' he whispered. 'In private.'

'Where?' said Davies. Bertie indicated with his hand and they went down the stairs to his quarters. Davies could feel his excitement gathering; things were starting to happen. Bertie unlocked his room and Davies followed him in. The porter sat heavily on the armchair and indicated the couch to his visitor. Davies chose to sit on the arm. 'What was it, Bertie?' he asked.

'I've been tossing up whether to tell you. But I have a sense of loyalty, you know. If somebody does me a favour, and I say I'll do something for them, I try to do it. And if they say it's secret then I try not to tell anybody. But I think I've got to let you into it.'

'What's the secret? Tell me.'

'It's Mr Dulciman.'

'Yes.'

'I've got some stuff of his.'

'What sort of stuff?'

'I don't know. It's in a suitcase.' He nodded across the room to where, as Davies had seen on his first visit, suitcases and boxes were lined against the wall. 'One of them. The big brown one.'

'He asked you to look after it.'

'Right. Well he did *me* a favour once. Like I told you I didn't care for him, nobody did, horrible man, but he did me this one favour and I kept the case for him in return. I was in trouble with the bookies. You know me, Mr Davies, a hot shot at backing favourites to lose. Three hundred pounds I was down. Owing. And that was a lot of money for me. And it was five or six years ago.'

'So he helped you out.'

'Gave me the lot,' said Bertie shaking his head. 'I couldn't believe it, sir. I must have said something, like half joking, like I do, about being in bother with my betting, and the next day he asked me quietly if I needed any help. I just could not believe what I was hearing. But I said I was in trouble, and how much, and he gave me the money. Just like that. He said it was a loan and I could pay him back when I had it, when I had a big win. In a funny way I thought he was, well ... lining me up ... in case he needed help at some time.'

Bertie shook his head. 'That was not long before he disappeared,' he related. 'So I had no chance. But he asked me to look after that suitcase for him.' He nodded towards the wall. 'And naturally I did. And he said it was highly confidential, that I was never to mention it to *anybody*. And naturally again I said that I would not. That's why I've taken so long to tell you. I like you and I know what you're trying to do for Mrs Dulciman but I've always kept my word up to now and I gave Mr Dulciman my word.'

'I understand, Bertie,' said Davies adding quickly: 'Have

you got a key for it?' He looked towards the suitcase the porter had indicated. The porter looked shocked. 'Oh, no, I just put the case there, where it is, and more or less forgot about it. It's just where it was. Mr Dulciman had the key I suppose.'

'And he never came back, as far as you know, to open it again?'

'Never, I would have known. I keep my door locked.'

The two men, as though in a rehearsed movement, turned and regarded the suitcase. It stood at the end of a row of dusty pieces of luggage, long locked by the look of them, lined like abandoned rail wagons in a shunting yard. 'Let's take a look in it,' grunted Davies. 'It might answer a lot of questions.'

Bertie became anxious. 'Yes, of course, we must,' he said, his voice low. 'But, like I said, sir, there's no key. He took it with him.'

Davies was already moving towards the luggage. 'We might need a chisel,' he said. He stood looking down at the sturdy suitcase, large and brown. It had two wide straps around its girth and three tarnished brass locks.

'A chisel,' echoed Bertie, the nervousness squeaking in his voice. 'Yes ... well I can get a chisel.' He remained where he stood, still by the couch. 'Easily. But ... it will be like breaking and entering, won't it, Mr Davies?'

'Something like that,' returned Davies casually, and still looking at the case. He tested the locks, then looked up and saw Bertie's expression. 'Don't worry, Bertie,' he said. 'Dulciman's not coming back for it.' He grinned grimly. 'For all we know we might even find him inside there.'

Bertie shuddered. 'Don't say that,' he pleaded. 'I couldn't ...' He achieved a nervous smile. 'But I would have smelt him wouldn't I.' It seemed to decide him. 'I'll get the chisel.'

While he was gone from the room Davies tried to move the suitcase. He did so with difficulty. It was full of something. He wiped the dust from around the locks as if to make opening them easier. Then on the far side of the case, nearest the wall, he saw the remnant of a label. He pulled the case further into the room. The label was torn off but not sufficiently to make the words 'The Rock Hotel, Gibraltar' unreadable. Below this was the edge of some large and flamboyant handwriting but he could not make out the words. Bertie came back with the chisel and a hammer. 'Thought we might have to give it a whack, sir,' he said. He had gathered his courage.

'I'll do it,' said Davies. 'Then you won't get any blame if it goes wrong. You don't even have to say you were here.' He held out his hands for the tools.

'Oh, I don't mind,' said Bertie with his new confidence. 'After all, it's been in my room long enough. Five years and he gave me three hundred. That's hardly thirty bob a week, is it.'

'Not enough to lose on a horse,' agreed Davies. 'Here, let's get it into some space.' Bertie moved the couch back and Davies tugged the case into a clear area. There were two more labels, each one with the words 'The Rock Hotel, Gibraltar' with 'Mr and Mrs Vernon Dulciman' in faded handwriting. 'Here goes,' he said, the chisel in one hand and the hammer in the other. 'Mr Dulciman here we come.'

Bertie's alarm reappeared for a moment and he took a pace back. 'Here we come,' he repeated in a low voice, 'Mr Dulciman.'

Davies put the chisel under the first lock and gave it a sharp blow with the hammer. It shuddered. He repeated the blow. 'They made real suitcases in those days,' said Bertie in the tone of an expert. 'None of your plastic rubbish.'

Another swift strike with the hammer, and another, and the lock gave in, flying away from its fixings. Davies then went to the second side lock and gave that the same treatment. It came away quite easily on the third blow.

He hit the middle lock three hard times with the chisel. It gaped on the third blow and he struck at it again triumphantly with the hammer to finish it off but only succeeded in hitting his own thumb. He howled with pain and thrust his thumb in his mouth, taking it out to put it between his thighs and then to remove it and rub it with his other hand. 'Did that hurt, sir?' inquired Bertie, concern wrapping around his face.

'Oh, nothing,' responded Davies through clenched teeth. 'Just smashed my thumb.'

Bertie said: 'I'll get the First Aid box.' He turned as though anxious to be away from the scene.

'Forget it,' called Davies after him. 'It's not that bad. It just hurts when you bash yourself with a hammer.' He swung a vengeful blow at the middle lock, completely severing it from the case. It flew away and hit the wall before dropping to the floor.

'It really must have hurt,' said Bertie as if trying to find an excuse for the violence.

There were still the two thick straps holding the case. Davies stood, still rubbing his thumb, and together the two men studied the case. 'Perhaps it's just old clothes,' Bertie suggested.

'Three hundred quid is a lot for old clothes,' muttered Davies. He bent and opened the first strap buckle. Bertie made as if to undo the second but Davies waved him aside. 'My responsibility,' he reminded.

The second buckle was tough and tight. Davies tugged at it and then parted the strap from the brass. The case sagged open. 'It's full of papers,' said Bertie peering from above. 'I wonder what they are.'

'We'll soon see,' said Davies turning the suitcase onto its back. He grunted with the effort. With almost the same movement, he opened the lid. It was packed with large brown envelopes. The flaps were only tucked inside and he picked one up and opened it. He turned it to an angle and out slid a large picture of a young girl sitting on a lavatory. 'It's not the minutes of the parish council,' said Davies.

'Oh, my God,' exclaimed Bertie. 'I've never seen anything like that before.'

'I hope you haven't,' returned Davies. He looked at the next photograph. The whole batch were of the same subject, the pretty young blonde astride a toilet pan, taken from various angles including underneath.

'It's pornography,' said the shocked Bertie.

'That's what it's called,' said Davies glancing sideways at him.

'I've never seen anything like it,' said Bertie in the voice of a man pulling himself together. 'Open one of the others.'

Davies did. He blinked at the photographs. Three men and one girl. 'I don't think you ought to see that one,' he said sliding it back into the envelope.

He selected another. Two naked girls, one tied to a post, the other with a cane. 'Sadism, that is,' said Bertie informatively.

Davies held up another picture. 'And that's sodomy,' he said. Another: 'And that's fellatio ... and that's cunnilingus.'

'Don't they have some funny names,' said Bertie. He looked at Davies. 'Mr Dulciman collected pornography,' he suggested.

'Dealt in it,' corrected Davies. There were some thicker envelopes to one side, yellow, with string around them. He picked one up and took the string away. 'Magazines,' he said emptying the contents. Half a dozen fell out in lurid colours. One was called *Big Fat Girls* and on the cover posing indecently, her huge breasts thrust out, her legs astride, was Mildred.

'Hello, is that Pengelly?'

'It is. What do you want, Davies?'

'To eliminate you from my inquiries.'

'Oh Christ. Now what?'

'I'm almost there, Pengelly.'

'Good for bloody you. It's nearly eleven at night you know.'

'Sorry. I expect you're in bed with a nice cup of cocoa and Enid Blyton.'

'What do you want?'

'I've turned up a lot of your stock-in-trade. Yours and Dulciman's. Very naughty.'

'So? Get off the phone and have a good time.'

'Stop putting ideas into my head. No, there was just one

question, Pengelly. This consignment, nasty as it is, doesn't seem to me to be the stuff that murders are made of.'

'So, what's the point?'

'Why did the London operators move in on you?'

'Oh, I get it. You still think they may have done for Dulciman?'

'It's a possibility. He may have been in, got in, much deeper than you believe. When you split from him he may have got into murkier waters. But I can't see anyone knocking him off for naughty nudes.'

Patiently Pengelly said: 'It was the economics of it, Davies. Pornography is like any other business. Costs. Down here it was relatively cheap. These kids, as I told you, thought that they were on a bonanza for fifty quid. And they were fresh looking, not the worn-out shaggers you get in London. Amateurs turned professional. The studio costs were low, everything was half price compared to London and you got a nicer sort of participant. Get it?'

'And that's why the London elements became interested, started to put the touch on you? And that's why you got out, because they were moving in?'

'Like I told you, that was it.'

'All right. Thanks.'

'Don't mention it, Davies. Just don't bother me again.'

'Unless I find out you *done* it,' said Davies smiling down the phone.

She called at eleven thirty. Bertie, who was clearing up and locking up, did not recognise her disguised voice and put her through to Davies' room. He was lying in bed watching the moon through the window. 'Dangerous,' she whispered. 'I've got to see you.'

He sat up quickly in bed. 'I want to see you too. Where are you?'

'Not now. Tomorrow. I might as well get a little romance out of this while I get a chance.'

'Where?'

'On the hilltop. You know, in the army area where we went.'

'I was afraid you might say that. You've been drinking.'

'Cider, that's all. Oh, Dangerous, it was so lovely before. This will be the last time. I'll tell you what happened. I'll be waiting for you up there.'

His heart was sad. 'You silly girl,' was all he could say. 'What time?'

'Nine o'clock. The sun will be on the hilltop then. You can get a bus at eight from outside the hotel.'

'All right, Mildred. I'll see you there. Leave off the cider.'

'I'll see you too. Darling Dangerous.'

Fifteen

He slept little that night; when he eventually did a parade of people passed through his gritty dreams, Pengelly combing Kitty's hair, Nola Cloudsley-Clive swinging a squawking seagull around her gaunt blonde head, Bertie dancing with a naked girl, Mildred weeping, Jemma laughing wildly, and through them all the face of Vernon Dulciman baring his false teeth at his wife who merely blinked. The only absentee was Mod. During one of his half-awake moments Davies wondered if this was because Mod himself slept soundly and was therefore unavailable to intrude into anyone's nightmares.

Sticky-eyed he caught the eight o'clock bus outside the hotel. Bertie watched him go through the lace curtains of the lounge. The morning was mild but grey, the sea sullen and with no wind. He sat on the top deck of the bus watching the empty beaches move by, then into the empty suburbs and out into the empty countryside. At the hamlet with the pub and the telephone box, he got off and, after cautiously looking about him, took the narrow path up which he had followed Mildred. There were spring leaves on the hedgerows and they showered overnight water on him as he passed. He reached the stile with the skull-and-crossbones warning and tentatively climbed it. From beyond that he could see the whole horizon and at once he spotted her. She was standing on the top of the ridge waiting for him. As she had said she would. Heavy in body and in spirit, he began to climb the slope. Why did it have to be her?

Mildred stood poised theatrically as he gained the last steep and grassy incline. 'It's much harder this time of the year,' she called with blatant cheerfulness. 'The grass is longer and wet.'

'Don't I know it,' he shouted back. 'My socks are soaking.'

She laughed in her sharp, jolly way and then stopped and silently watched him as he stumbled up the final few yards. At the summit she held out her hands and pulled him heftily up the last hump. 'Hello, Dangerous,' she said melodramatically. 'Have you come to get me?'

He was attempting to regain his breath. 'Why, what have you done?' he puffed eventually. He studied her face, white and pudgy, black-ringed below her eyes. The eyes themselves looked sore. Her hair was caught behind her neck but straggles of it had come loose and were lying damply across her forehead. She was wearing her brown anorak and large jeans. 'God, it's hot getting up here,' said Davies.

He opened his coat and flapped it like wings. Set-faced she stepped towards him and put her arms about him. He hugged her and kissed her on her pallid cheek. 'What made you run away?' he asked.

'I knew it was all coming out,' she said. 'You were finding out.' She began to sniffle. 'I couldn't face it all. Then, when I came out here three days ago and began thinking, I thought at least I owed it to you to tell you what happened.'

He regarded her with astonishment. 'You've been out here all that time?'

She gave a grin of achievement. 'Three days. I've been living in the house down there.' She nodded to the abandoned hamlet below. A single chimney pot projected through the mist lolling about the roofs. 'The house that Alfie and I used to pretend was ours.' She could see his face was full of concern for her. She smiled tightly and said: 'It's very cosy. Come on down and I'll make you a cup of coffee.'

'I could do with a coffee,' he said. He tried to see the sea but today it was out of view. She put her big white hand into his and they descended the slope together. 'You shouldn't be out here, staying out here,' he said. 'It's very risky.'

She laughed, her laugh light as she lumbered alongside him. 'I know the exact times when they play war, the army,' she assured him breathlessly. 'I've got them written down. They always put them in the local paper so that people won't be frightened.'

They reached the level ground, the hill was between them and the way he had come into the zone. Her jeans and his trousers were wet to the knees. 'They don't use it for manoeuvres so much now anyway,' she said taking his hand again and moving towards the end house of a tumbledown terrace. 'Not since the cut-backs. It's quite safe if you know.'

The small village was tightly together. One house had been demolished and two more were without roofs. It was easy to imagine how it had been fifty years before when it had been lived in. The church still had its tower, although there was daylight showing through a hole in it. The stone houses dripped and the ground underfoot was muddy and strewn with small debris. She led him towards the door of the house she had indicated, pushing it open creakily and throwing out her arm. 'Welcome, Dangerous Davies,' she said.

He ducked below the askew lintel. Inside it was like a damp bunker. The windows were screened with opaque plastic which had torn in places, the ceiling sagged, the floor was covered with a pattern of mildewed mats. There was a scarred wooden table and a couple of uncertain-looking chairs, a cupboard with its door clinging to one hinge and a set of double bunks against the wall. Mildred swept her hand about. 'There. It's all right, isn't it.'

She saw his expression and turned quickly away from him. 'I'll put the kettle on,' she said in a low voice. In one corner on an enamel-topped table was a loaf of bread, a half-empty glass cider jar, something in a metal dish and a small primus stove. She lit this and picked up a black kettle from the floor.

'The water's all right,' she said over her shoulder. 'I get it from the stream.'

Testing one of the chairs tentatively first, Davies sat down on it. 'Mildred,' he said. 'What are you doing out here?'

'Don't worry, I'm going to tell you,' she said suddenly starting to sob. She turned towards him tears racing down her cheeks. 'Can't you wait a minute until I've made the coffee. You'll hear it all, Dangerous, don't worry.' She turned away and then back to him again in the next moment. 'While the kettle is boiling would you like to see where Mr Dulciman is buried?'

Davies thought he was going to fall off the chair. 'Buried?' he repeated stupidly. 'Dulciman? Out here?'

'Out here,' she repeated firmly. Like a busy housewife she wiped her hands on a ragged towel and said: 'Come on, I'll show you.'

Almost blithely she led him out through the low door and into the overgrown village street. 'This way,' she said, taking him eagerly by the arm. 'I thought you'd be surprised.'

Dumbstruck, Davies said: 'I am, a bit.' He hurried along with her.

'It seemed like a good place,' she enthused. 'Nobody out here and you don't even have to dig a hole. The place is full of craters. All he needed was a few spades of earth on him and then the army bulldozer came along a few days later and filled him in nicely.' He still could not believe this was happening. He kept looking at her sideways as they went; he licked his lips. She led him around the corner at the end of the sagging terrace. Beyond was a field indented with shallow depressions, most overgrown with grass. 'Now which hole was it?' Mildred asked herself. She brightened and moved forward resolutely, halting after twenty paces and pointing to a saucer of earth covered with grass and weeds. 'Mr Dulciman's down there,' she said. 'I'm almost sure that's where he is.'

*

He sat at the rough table, his head half buried in his hands, although he was still looking at her over them. She was pouring the coffee. 'Alfie and I brought him out here,' she said with a touch of bravado. 'We put him in Alfie's little car, he had a blue Metro, and drove out here in the dead of night.' She turned with the coffee mugs. Davies could hardly take his eyes from her. 'It was the most exciting thing I've ever done. Ever.' She was trying to stop herself talking madly, trying to suppress and slow her voice. 'We just left the car by the telephone box and wheeled him along the lane in a wheelbarrow, and up here. He was a dead weight – well, he was dead, wasn't he – but we managed. Alfie, although there was not much of him, was quite strong and I'm used to lifting things about. You have to in hotel work.'

'Can we go back a bit?' suggested Davies spacing his words with great care. 'I'd really like to know how Mr Dulciman became dead in the first place.'

She was sitting opposite him at the table now and she leaned over and slapped his wrist playfully. 'All in good time, Dangerous. I want to tell it *my* way.'

He regarded her over the coffee mug. 'You're enjoying this, aren't you,' he said.

She hunched her large shoulders. 'I am a bit, funnily enough. It's not often I get a man's undivided attention.' She leaned forward and began to cry again, great bulbous tears. She moved her coffee mug as though to catch them. 'Oh, he was such a hateful bastard, Dangerous. Hateful ... hateful ...'

As she said it there was a gunfire sound, sharp and startling, followed at once by an explosion that seemed very near. Earth fell on the roof of the house, dust and small pieces of debris showered from the ceiling and the stone walls shuddered. They stared at each other. 'I thought you said ...' began Davies.

Another explosion followed. This time nearer. Mildred put her trembling hands to her face. 'Oh God, why am I always getting things wrong!'

She jerked into movement and tugged him with her onto the bottom of the bunk beds. 'It's only mortars,' she said.

They rolled into a thick bodily ball, their heads together, their arms protecting each other. 'They don't use the big guns here now ... hardly ever.'

Another report and another explosion followed as though in answer. 'Oh Christ,' she snivelled. '*Now* what have I done?' The rickety house quaked. More of the ceiling fell down, a hail of plaster followed by a lump which fell across the table and hung there like a thick cloth. 'They never aim for the houses!' she shouted desperately.

'The one across the road is demolished,' he grunted, his head locked into her shoulder. The firing ceased and the dust settled. There were no sounds. 'We've got to make a run for it,' he urged.

'No! No!' She held onto his arm. 'Stay where we are! We could get into terrible trouble.'

Davies closed his eyes. He was sweating and the dust was sticking to the sweat. He could feel Mildred's large body vibrating. They both stiffened as a series of distant reports sounded and at once there came three successive and deafening explosions. The house reeled again and more of the ceiling came down. 'Grouping,' said Mildred knowledgeably.

'We've got to get out of here,' gritted Davies. 'This place is going to get a direct hit.'

'All right,' she said determinedly, although she still trembled. 'We'll hang on until they stop for a minute. Sometimes they have a Naafi break.' She began to sob again. 'I've caused all this trouble, Dangerous. I don't want you to get killed.'

'We won't get killed,' he answered more stoutly than he felt. Slates suddenly cascaded through the hole made by the missing plaster. But now the shelling paused. 'Come on!' he pulled her arm. 'Let's run!'

Mildred went first, bounding like an overgrown child, almost squeaking as she went. He followed her from the shelter of the door, trying to run doubled up, as they did in war films. They dodged between the broken houses. The air was swirling with smoke and dust. A fire had started somewhere across the roofs and was crackling through rafters. They ran wildly, breaking clear of the village and heading across the open ground around the base of the hill. There were freshly made craters ahead. 'This way,' she shouted. 'They won't use the same range twice.'

For once he thought she might know what she was talking about. His lungs ached, his legs wobbled, his breath tightened, sweat filled his shirt. But as if it might afford some protection, he kept his overcoat on. They crouched in the lee of the rising ground. Then the firing started again, to their left this time, the brown earth thrown up violently, their feet feeling the shudders.

'Let's give it another go,' she panted. 'We're nearly there.' Without waiting for his agreement she bounced off over the cratered ground around the base of the hill. Davies swore and followed her. Another shell landed close enough and they both slid feet first into a muddy crater. There was three feet of water at its base and together they tobogganed down the mud and into it. Brown and cold it enveloped both of them to the waists. 'Oh shit!' bellowed Mildred. 'Now look what's happened.'

'I know! I know!' bawled Davies. 'I'm in here too!' He never knew how they climbed out. Three times he slithered back. But with surprising agility Mildred was scrambling clear before him and holding down her wet hand to give him a final heave. Once out of the hole they made a last dash for the line of bordering trees and crouched in the ditch, shivering, trying to fill their lungs, wiping the mud from their eyes. Again the guns opened fire. They could see the explosions, like instant trees, around the stone village. The ground below them still shook but now they knew they were safe. The firing ceased.

Mildred looked at his wrecked exterior and said: 'I'm ever so sorry, Dangerous.'

They staggered towards the lane keeping to the hedge. Over the stile they climbed painfully and along the path until they reached the telephone box. 'We can't go on like this,' moaned Davies caked with wet and mud.

Mildred ran her fingers down the brown mud on her face. 'No, we can't,' she said meekly.

As though she had overheard, a woman appeared at a cottage door. She was wearing an overall and a bucket-shaped hat. 'You do look a sight, the pair of you,' she said without much emphasis. 'Come in and get dry.'

Mumbling thanks they hurried into the cottage. As soon as he was inside the door Davies saw that it was not the woman's home. The furniture was twee-country and there were two modern paintings and a bronze of a sealion. 'They're only here weekends,' said the woman who appeared to read thoughts. 'I come in an' clean after them. From London.' She studied their state. 'Been over on the MOD have you?' she said again without surprise. 'I could 'ear they was shooting over there.'

Briskly she pointed to a door. 'Go in there and get your stuff off,' she told them. 'There's a bathroom attached.' She looked oddly at Mildred. 'All right for both?' she asked.

'Fine,' Mildred assured her. 'We're getting married soon.'

Davies closed his eyes but he was too wracked to say anything. They went into a bedroom, nicely furnished with country wooden dressing-table and wardrobe and a large, well-stuffed bed. 'Oooh, isn't that nice, Dangerous,' said Mildred, astonishingly regaining her former mood. 'Wouldn't mind trying that out.'

The woman called through the door. 'There's some dressing-gowns in the bathroom. And you'll be wanting some clothes. They've got plenty.'

Davies, who thought nothing would ever again surprise him, shrugged. Mildred went into the bathroom and emerged with two towelling robes, one in pink and the other in deep blue. She tossed the pink one to Davies but then laughed and gave him the blue. 'For somebody who's buried a dead body in a battlefield you seem to have recovered remarkably,' he said tersely.

Mildred put her fat fingers to her full lips. 'Hush, Dangerous,' she warned. 'I bet she'll listen at the door.'

Wearily Davies began to take his clothes off. 'I'd always dreamed about doing this with you,' said Mildred pulling off her soaked and coated anorak.

With a heave she took off her sweater. Her great brassière bulged. 'He took pictures of me,' she said, her voice dropping in tone and volume. 'Dulciman.' Davies paused in pulling the shirt over his head.

'Use the shower,' the woman called through the door. 'There's plenty of water. They forget to turn off the immersion.'

'Thanks very much,' Davies called back.

'Yes, thanks,' called Mildred. Her sad eyes were held on Davies. 'He gave me a load of flattery and I fell for it,' she mumbled. 'I would, wouldn't I. He told me I had an exciting figure. That's the very word – *exciting*. Then he said I could be a model and he wanted to take some pictures of me, *art* photographs. I ended up stark naked and doing things I wouldn't have dreamed.' She was crying again now. She pulled him to her and rolled him against her bosom. 'I'm such a bloody fool, Dangerous. I wanted to be a model – me! Look at me for Christ's sake.'

'And he got you to do it,' he said calmly. 'Pose.'

'Right, he did.' Snivelling, she pulled herself away. 'I'll go and get showered,' she said, wiping her face. She looked about the bedroom. 'I hope all this is all right.'

'After all that's happened to us using somebody else's bedroom is nothing,' he said.

She made as if to go to the bathroom. 'Then he did *the* terrible thing. He used the pictures of me in a *dirty magazine*. On the *cover*! I was so ashamed. And the most terrible, terrible thing was the magazine was called ...' Her voice caught again and her face went into her hand. 'It was called: *Big Fat Girls*. Oh, Dangerous, oh, God. Can you imagine how I felt? I wanted to kill him right then, the bastard. Kill him and kill him and kill him.' She was crying copiously now. 'I was just waiting for the right moment.'

As she went towards the bathroom door there was a discreet knocking and the cleaning woman called: 'Don't be too long, will you. My old man comes home at twelve and he won't like you being in here. I don't care, but he does. I'll get you some clothes.'

Mildred quickly showered and emerged pink in her pink robe. She seemed almost coy now. 'We'd better get a move on, Dangerous,' she said. He walked past her into the bathroom. It was tiled and shining with an assortment of sponges and toiletries arrayed on an old-fashioned washstand. He used the lavatory and quickly got under the shower gratefully feeling the hot water washing away the caking mud. It stung into the scratches on his arms and face and he realised he was heavily bruised on the shoulder. His ribs ached ominously.

'I've got you some togs,' the woman called through the door. 'Come on out when you're ready.'

They went back into the main room. The woman had the air of doing this sort of thing all the time, succouring an unending stream of people in need. 'They've got so much stuff they don't know what they have got,' she said. She had produced two separate piles of clothing, one male, one female. 'Help yourself,' she invited. 'I'll get you a cup of tea.'

Mildred was picking up sweaters and skirts and ladies' trousers. 'Good stuff this,' she said to Davies who was examining an Arran sweater and a tracksuit with a Gucci label. He looked more closely at the clothes.

'Are you sure?' he called towards the kitchen.

'Help yourself,' she invited firmly. She was carrying two cups of tea. 'That will look nice on you,' she said to Davies nodding at the sweater. 'You don't have to worry. They're rich as biscuits, these two.'

They dressed from the selection and drank the tea. 'I'd offer you something stronger but I don't like taking their booze,' said their hostess. 'They'd notice that.' She nodded towards the window. 'It's a bugger getting caught over there isn't it,' she said. 'When they start their shelling. My hubby's been in it twice. He goes over to help keep the pheasants and partridges down. All unofficial, of course. But he's had to run, believe me.'

Davies said he would keep his shoes but the woman would not hear of it. 'That pair,' she said. 'Those Hush Puppies. See if they fit. He's about your size. He only wears them for knocking about.'

Reluctantly he put the shoes on. They fitted at a pinch. Mildred was standing proudly, completely fitted out, although the shoes were too small. 'Actually *she's* quite dainty,' said the woman. 'The stuff you've got on, dear, belongs to her mother, who's huge.'

'We must return this somehow,' said Davies.

The woman's face abruptly hardened. 'No question of that,' she said. 'I expect to be paid. I haven't done this out of the goodness of my heart.'

'Oh, no, of course not ... How ... ?'

'How about fifty quid?' she said. 'Then I'll ring for a taxi. You'll want a taxi, won't you.'

Wearing their new clothes, they sat dumbly together in the back of the taxi heading for Bournemouth. They could not talk about what had happened. The driver had ears like an elephant, although afterwards he apologised for not conversing because he was deaf.

They were greeted outside the hotel by Bertie, his face anxious, his sparse hair pale in the April noon. 'Ah, sir ...' he began as Davies climbed from the taxi. He saw Mildred and blinked.

'Like the new outfit, Bertie?' she asked with her desperate blitheness. He could not summon an answer. Too many things were going on. She hurried past him into the hotel.

Davies, who wanted to know a lot more from her, was about to follow when Bertie caught his arm.

'Sir, you'd better keep the taxi.' With a porter's gesture he halted the cab as it was about to drive away. 'It's Mrs Dulciman, sir. She's asking to see you.'

'Asking?' said Davies. He recognised the nuance: 'Oh no ...'

'She's been taken in, sir. They rang here for you because they say she's only got hours.' Bertie looked near to tears. 'It's urgent.'

'Oh, that's sad,' said Davies his head dropping. Too many things happened at once for him too. 'I'll go. Is it the same hospital as before?'

'Her usual one, sir.'

Davies peered into the lobby but Mildred was not there. Noting his look Bertie said: 'She'll be gone to her quarters. I'll see she don't vanish again. Not till you get back.'

Davies thanked him and climbed back into the taxi. Bertie gave the driver the hospital location, having to repeat it with a shout. The deaf cabbie apparently thought that he could contribute to the drama. 'My old uncle went last week,' he bawled over his shoulder.

'Where?' asked Davies. His mind was buzzing.

'Only God knows, sir,' responded the man loudly. 'Either up or down. The funeral was on Friday. The best thing that anybody could say about him was that he wasn't the worst one.'

'Oh, good. Yes. Well that's something.'

At the hospital the receptionist saw him approaching and sensing his urgency, put down the telephone. 'Mrs Dulciman,' he said. 'I've come to see her. It's urgent. My name is Davies.'

'Yes, Mr Davies,' said the young woman. 'They're waiting for you. You can go right up.'

She went to the lift with him and said: 'Third. They'll be relieved to see you.'

A doctor and a sister were waiting for him on the landing. 'She's not going to be with us long,' said the doctor with a practical sadness. 'She wants to speak to you urgently.'

Davies said: 'Isn't there any chance?'

The sister shook her head and the doctor said: 'Not this time.'

Going into the room Davies suddenly felt very strange in his odd, new clothes. Mrs Dulciman was lying in the quiet place, afternoon sunshine lying across her bed and lighting up a bowl of flowers. Her face was calm and waxy but lit with a smile when she saw him. 'Dangerous,' she breathed. 'You're here. I knew you would.'

She held out her slim hand and he held it. 'Don't exert yourself. Don't try to talk too much.'

Her smile was a shadow. 'Dear Dangerous,' she said. 'This is the one time I *must* talk. We must talk.'

The lie came as if by magic: 'I've discovered what happened to Mr Dulciman,' he told her. 'He ... he went to Gibraltar.'

She even flushed. Her neat mouth opened in amazement. Then she smiled, broadly now. 'I might have known it,' she said. 'Where we were happy. Once. We used to take our holidays there.'

'He left this country,' said Davies deliberately, 'and went to the Rock Hotel ...'

'Our old place,' she mused. 'I remember the flowers at this time of the year. So that's what the old fraud did.' She closed her thin eyes as if trying to picture the past. Then she said quite strongly: 'Is he still there?'

He swallowed and plunged on with the lie. 'He died there last year. He had moved from the hotel and had taken an apartment under a false name.'

'I bet he was with a woman?' It was a question.

'I don't know,' he answered carefully.

'He would not be by himself. Well, I'm glad.' She smiled towards him again. 'Someone once said that nothing matters very much and in the end nothing matters at all. I think that I am reaching the moment when nothing will. So I want to tell you ...' He had been standing but he quietly pulled up a chair and sat confidingly close to her. Her eyes were closed and with a rush of anxiety he tried to see if she were still breathing. She saved him the trouble: she opened her eyes. 'I thought I had killed him,' she whispered. 'I am so relieved I didn't. I'm grateful to you, Dangerous. So grateful.'

'You thought you had killed him?' repeated Davies slowly.

Mrs Dulciman gave a small, spectral laugh. 'I pushed him down the stairs, you see. The stairs outside our hotel suite. He was such a pig that night. Even more than normal.' She reached out again and her hold on his hand became a clutch. Slivers of wet were lying under her eyelashes. 'He was such a bastard, so abominable you know. But I did not want to be a murderer. That is why I asked you to investigate. I *had* to know what happened to him. I hope you'll forgive my lies but there never was a son – what did I call him, Gervais? – from a previous marriage and since there was not one he could not have abandoned his wife and family as I told you. It was all a fairy-tale. I was afraid you might find that out very early in your inquiries.'

Mentally Davies thought he should have done. He said: 'So you retained me really only to find out what had happened to him?'

'Yes, because, you see, he vanished.'

'He did?'

'I got up in the middle of the night after I had pushed him and he tumbled down, and I went to the bottom of the stairs in my dressing-gown and he wasn't to be seen. That's when I thought he might have got up and walked away, which would be typical, he was always lucky, and made his exit from our life. To the Rock Hotel, Gibraltar.' She tutted quite firmly.

'The last you saw he was lying at the foot of the stairs,' prompted Davies.

She shook her head weakly. He said: 'Don't distress yourself. You mustn't get upset.'

She smiled gratefully at him. 'I'm not going yet, Dangerous,' she said. 'I heard them say I've got hours.'

He patted her hand gently. 'You'll come through, you see.'

'I don't think so, not this time. But I did not *see* him at the foot of the stairs. I had given him a shove and went back into the room as quickly as I could. I was so angry. As I say, I did not go out there again for several hours. And then he had gone.'

'What made you push him?' asked Davies soberly. 'Then?'

'Anger, pure and simple. It was what they call the last straw. He came back that night and had been drinking and was so unpleasant, boorish, I cannot tell you. I was used to such behaviour but this time he was particularly nasty.' She began to cry softly again. Davies tried to comfort her. 'I'm not terribly sensitive, Dangerous ...'

Her voice dropped to a hardly discernible whisper. '... I was, as I have told you, a model for certain photographs years ago, so I'm not too sensitive, but he was so dreadful. He snatched the bracelet that he had bought me at Asprey's. He said he had to have the money. And when I tried to stop him he pushed me against the wall and ... and ... he called me *old*. He said "*old*" as an insult. "You are *old*," he said. "*Old, old*. Get out of my way!"'

Davies shook his head. She was crying fully now and he tried to comfort her. 'To say that to *me*, after all that time. *Old*. What a dreadful thing.' She snivelled and found a lace handkerchief. He put his hand out to help her. She gave him the handkerchief and he wiped her tears. She blew her own nose. 'He stormed out of the door,' she whispered, 'and shouted back at me again: "You're *old*!" Oh ... I simply could not restrain myself. I followed him onto the landing and pushed him from behind. As hard as I could. He went flying, head over heels, down the stairs. Bouncing and bumping. He did not utter a sound. And I went quietly back into the room and closed the door. I really thought I had done for him, murdered him. But he must have recovered and simply got up and walked away leaving me to worry and wonder for all these years. That would be typical of him.' She paused. 'I disposed of all his papers, or as many as I could find. I couldn't find his passport. I'm sorry I misled you, Dangerous. You are a wonderful man. But I had to find out. Now I know.'

She closed her eyes and once more he thought it was for the last time. He was half-way to the door, hurrying on tiptoe, to fetch the doctor, when she called from the bed. 'Dangerous ... my solicitors, Geary & Co., of Poole, have a sealed envelope in their hands. They will send it to you very shortly. Goodbye Dangerous Davies, and thank you.'

'Is she dead?' Mildred never resisted melodrama. She was sitting, still in her purloined clothes, in the reception area of the hospital, regarded suspiciously by the receptionist.

'No,' returned Davies. 'But it won't be long.'

Her face worked a little. There was whisky on her breath. 'Poor Mrs Dulciman,' she sighed. 'All her troubles will be over soon.' She stood up. 'I followed you but she wouldn't let me come up.' Mildred nodded at the receptionist who gave her a hard look before smiling at Davies. 'She fancies you, Dangerous,' said Mildred.

'Let's be on our way,' said Davies as patiently as he could. He took her elbow and led her out of the hospital. 'Leave the booze alone,' he said.

'I needed something after all that drama this morning,' she shrugged. 'It's a wonder you didn't.'

'There were things I had to do,' he said pointedly. They were walking along an avenue of heavy trees going towards the sea. The trees were light green with new leaves. 'Mrs Dulciman', he said in a level voice, 'told me that she pushed her husband down the stairs at the hotel.'

'That's right,' said Mildred in a tone that suggested he should have known that from the start. 'I saw her do it. Me and Alfie.'

There was a bench at the end of the avenue overlooking a clifftop green. To it was fixed a plaque: 'In Memory of John Wild. For rest and contemplation.' Davies took her arm and led her to the seat. They sat down facing the sea stretched like satin. 'You saw her do it?' he echoed.

'That's right. Naturally I've never told anybody. Alfie and

I swore never to. We heard this commotion when we were creeping from my room and we waited in the corridor. Then I peeped around and saw Mr Dulciman at the top of the stairs and Mrs Dulciman came from her door and stood there and just shoved him.' Mildred made a pushing motion with her hands. 'And he went tumbling off down the stairs.' She blew out her big cheeks. 'That's twice that's happened to me, Dangerous. I told you before, didn't I, about how I saw my mother give my old man a push in the same way. I've seen two murders the same and I'm still only twenty-five.'

He made no attempt to work out the logic of the remark. 'And then what happened?' he asked.

'Well, I'm a mad hatter as you know and Alfie, even though he wasn't that big for a soldier, he was *really* crazy. We both liked Mrs Dulciman and I hated, hated, with all my heart, that Mr Dulciman, for the reasons I told you. The nude photographs he took of me and that magazine. *Big Fat Girls.*' She almost spat out the title. 'The lousy swine.' She regarded Davies, her cheeks streaked and smudged like those of a child. 'I never told Alfie about the photographs, of course, because he would have killed Dulciman there and then. Remember Alfie was in the Medical Corps. He could have poisoned him.'

'So then you and Alfie decided to dispose of Dulciman's body?' Davies prompted.

'That's right. We felt it was the least we could do. We wanted to help the old lady and I was getting my own revenge as well. He was stone dead when he got to the bottom of the stairs and she had gone back into her room. Alfie knew right away. There was nobody about, those are the back stairs of course, and it was late. So we lugged him outside and put him in Alfie's Metro. It was a bit of a squeeze but we jammed him in somehow.' She giggled. 'It was a bit funny really. Alfie loved it. He liked a bit of a lark and he didn't give a damn what he did.'

'I can see that,' said Davies. 'And you took him out to the military area and dropped him into one of the shell craters.'

'Just like I told you. That wasn't easy but Alfie found a wheelbarrow in one of the gardens, it might have even been that house where we got these togs. There was nobody around so we wheeled Mr Dulciman up the lane, got him over the stile, and that was a job, we couldn't stop laughing. And, like I told you, we put him in the crater and shovelled a few spadefuls of earth over him. Enough to cover him. The army bulldozer regularly fills up those holes and that was what it did.' She looked thoughtful. 'What I could never understand was why Mrs Dulciman asked you to find out what happened? After all *she* pushed him.'

Davies said: 'She did not know whether she had killed him. All she knew was that she pushed him down the stairs. Then he vanished. I told her a few minutes ago that he survived and cleared off to Gibraltar, for ever.'

'Why Gibraltar?'

'That's where they used to go.'

'You knew that?'

'I saw a suitcase, an old one, with their names on the label, Mr and Mrs Vernon Dulciman. The Rock Hotel, Gibraltar. I knew they'd been there but I didn't know how many times. Anyway she will die thinking he escaped.'

'Brilliant,' she said. 'That's bloody brilliant. You are.'

She kissed him earnestly, her breath still laden with scotch. 'And now what happens?' she asked. She smiled raggedly at him. 'Are you going to arrest me, or hand me over to the police, or something?'

'Mildred, you've got to get away from here,' he said seriously. 'You've got to straighten your life out.'

'You're not going to *tell* on me?'

'No.'

She giggled hugely. 'I knew you wouldn't,' she said. 'I'm going to Greece for the summer. I've got enough saved and I might get a job out there. In a cantina or whatever they have, a taverna. Sun and wine and virile men.'

'That should keep you out of trouble,' he said doubtfully.

He rose from the bench and she held onto his arm while they walked along the cliff path towards the road again. 'What about the shoes?' he said. 'Dulciman's shoes found on the beach? I suppose you planted them, got that lad to take them up to Bertie, so that it might indicate that Dulciman had gone into the sea.'

'You're a good detective, Dangerous.'

'I keep trying.'

He plodded up the hill for the final time to say his farewells at the Moonlighters Club. To his surprise Phineas was propped up at the bar conversing with Pengelly. Pengelly was wagging his finger. Davies regarded the pair quizzically. 'Mrs Dulciman has died,' he announced.

'So none of it matters,' said Pengelly.

Davies remembered the old lady had said the same: not much matters and in the end nothing matters at all. He sighed. 'Not now.'

'I'll buy you a drink,' said Pengelly. 'You probably need one.'

Davies said he would have a scotch. He wondered what they were doing together. Pengelly provided the answer as he raised his glass. 'Here's to Eventide Enterprises,' he toasted.

'Eventide Enterprises,' echoed Phineas less convincingly.

'Eventide Enterprises,' repeated Davies. He looked from one to the other. 'Whatever they may be.' He put his glass down. 'What are they, by the way?'

'My new business,' Pengelly told him. 'Phineas here is going to be my chief executive.' Davies glanced at Phineas who shrugged. 'I came to thinking', continued Pengelly, 'that there's a mass of untapped talent, resources, and money in this town, all of it possessed by older people, retired people. My intention is to form an organisation, a network of organisations, to tap those resources.'

'Right up your street, tapping resources,' said Davies evenly.

'Give me a chance,' said Pengelly in an injured tone. 'I've converted my offices and we will be operating from there. We will have a share issue ...'

'I thought you might.'

'It has to be capitalised.'

'What will be the area of activity?'

'*Areas* of activities,' corrected Pengelly. 'They'll be widespread. Marketing, outings, all sorts of things.'

'Marketing and outings,' ruminated Davies.

'Holidays,' said Phineas not to be left behind. 'Holidays for the elderly.'

'Not putting them on coaches and whizzing them around Europe so they can stare out of the windows,' put in Pengelly quickly as though to keep Phineas quiet. 'Old people can still have fun. Participation. They want to achieve something – apart from old age. I want to stir up feelings of adventure in seventy-plus year olds.'

'Bungee jumping,' suggested Davies.

'You're being negative,' muttered Pengelly. 'My aim is to mobilise the potential of the elderly, physical, emotional and financial, and give everyone something to work for, something they can look forward to.' His face straightened dramatically. 'Apart from death.'

'We've already sounded out people,' said Phineas. 'Mrs Cloudsley-Clive for one. The energy that woman wastes hitting bread to seagulls.'

'The seagulls would disagree,' said Davies.

On cue Nola Cloudsley-Clive appeared in the doorway. She advanced and greeted Davies before turning to Pengelly. 'One of our first endeavours will be to renovate the ladies' room for these premises,' she affirmed. 'I've been locked in for ten minutes.'

Davies told her that Mrs Dulciman had died that morning. She stood, oddly, in silence, her head bowed, for an exact minute. Then looked up and smiled. 'There,' she breathed with a sort of relief. She glanced at Davies again. 'Mr Pengelly has told you of our plans, I take it?' she enthused. 'At last there will be some purpose in life, apart from feeding gulls and ducks.'

Davies watched helplessly while Pengelly treated her to a fond smile and said to Davies: 'We thought we would call the Eventide Enterprises travel section "Golden Years Holidays".'

'These, after all,' said Phineas ponderously, 'are the golden years.'

Mrs Cloudsley-Clive fixed him with a look. 'Bugger the golden years,' she said.

The Babe In Arms was crowded for a lunchtime. Detective Superintendent Harvey and other senior officers had come from the magistrates court where they had seen the man known as Russian Mike committed for trial charged with the murder of Julie Willis, aged sixteen. Davies watched them ordering scotches at the far end of the bar. Harvey spotted him and beckoned him over. 'I won't be a minute,' Davies said to Mod. 'I'd just like to hear this.'

Harvey put a well-fed arm about Davies. 'Well, Russian Mike is on his way,' he affirmed. 'The bastard. He won't do that again.'

'I should hope not,' said Davies, searching for something to say. Harvey bought him a scotch and he stood silently in the group while they congratulated themselves. The Detective Superintendent leaned chummily towards Davies and whispered, 'It's a big feather in my cap, of course, Davies, nicking him. But I think everybody deserves some credit.'

'So do I,' said Davies. He excused himself and went back to Mod. The policemen eventually left with laughter and much back-slapping. He waved to them as they went out. '*You* gave them the clue,' muttered Mod. 'Lot of credit you get.'

Davies drank reflectively. 'But I solved the case I *wanted* to solve,' he said.

'When do you think you'll be getting your fee?' asked Mod carefully.

'I had a call yesterday from Mrs Dulciman's solicitors. They wanted to check my address.'

'My giro didn't arrive this morning,' grumbled Mod.

Minnie Banks said: 'My *Teachers World* didn't come today.'

Mrs Fulljames put the tureen on the table. 'They promised to send me the shrub catalogue. Promised it right away. I thought some new shrubs might cheer up the garden. But for some reason ...'

Sick at heart Davies rose slowly from the table. Astonished they watched him walk like a robot into the kitchen. He stood staring from the window. 'Did *anybody* get any post this morning?' he asked without turning.

'There wasn't any,' said Mrs Fulljames. 'There was nothing on the mat.'

From his position at the kitchen window Davies could see the low glow of the garden bonfire. 'Elvis ...' he muttered. 'That Elvis ...'

'Whatever ... ?' exclaimed Mrs Fulljames as he wrenched open the door from the kitchen to the garden.

'He's gone mad,' said Doris with satisfaction. 'I always knew he would.'

Davies plunged into the garden. The fire was low, glowering. Little more than ashes. Elvis was lurking in the evening shadows by the fence. The other residents of Bali Hi grouped by the kitchen door. 'Whatever's going on?' called Mrs Fulljames.

'Son,' said Davies as calmly as he could to the youth, 'what have you been putting on this fire?'

He knew a guilty look when he saw one. 'Bits and pieces,' mumbled Elvis. 'You can't get stuff see ... you 'ave to find it ...'

Grimly Davies advanced on him. 'Letters?' he demanded. 'Did you put this morning's letters on there?'

Elvis backed away. 'No ... no ... I didn't.'

The party from the house was slowly advancing down the

garden, keeping together as though for mutual protection. Davies turned and strode to the fire. He kicked at the ashes. '*I'm sorry!*' wailed Elvis from the fence. 'They was just lying on the mat. The door was open. I didn't think they was anybody's!'

It was getting dark. Davies, with Jemma's arm about him, went slowly into the yard, Kitty's food dish sagging disconsolately in his hand. 'I still can't believe it,' he mumbled. 'Five thousand quid up in sodding smoke.'

Jemma said without much hope: 'Maybe it was delayed. It may come tomorrow.'

'I got the man at home,' he repeated firmly. 'He said Mrs Dulciman's sealed envelope had been addressed and sent off yesterday morning. Express.'

'And there's nothing they can do? Nothing to replace it?'

Miserably he told her again. 'The solicitors didn't even know what was in the envelope. It was sealed up with my name on it. They won't hand out five thousand quid on my word. I could kill that dumbhead Elvis.'

'And the cheque stub is no help?'

'The man went from his home back to his office. He has Mrs Dulciman's chequebook. She hardly ever filled in the stub. And she did not in this case.'

He stumbled towards the garage. Kitty, hearing his approach began to howl. Jemma turned Davies towards her and, with the dog's bowl jammed between them they hugged each other, he using one arm. He lifted his head and surveyed the bleak enclosing walls, the early glimmering street lamp, the broken cobbles.

'Dangerous Davies of the Yard,' he muttered.

Jemma began to laugh and he looked into her face and began to laugh too. They stood laughing wildly and holding each other while Kitty howled for his dinner.